MW01104233

Destined to Lead: Redemption
Copyright © 2015 Laura Thornton

ISBN-10:
1506185398

ISBN-13:
978-1506185392

Cover Art Copyright © 2015 Laura Thornton

Destined to Lead:
Redemption

Table of Contents

To the one who redeemed me,
My God, Lord, King, Saviour and Friend,
Jesus Christ

Pronunciation guide

Word – Pronunciation	Object
Admirai – ad-meer-rai	Largest Moon
Aika – I-ka	Flower/Herb
Aimaia – I-MAY-a	Wheat-like Plant
Ainee – I-knee	Name/Largest Island
Anfa – ann-fa	Creature
Animo – an-knee-MO	Tribe
Aria – R-E-a	Island
Beifin – bay-fin	Name
Belo – bay-low	Name
Blakeslee – blakes-LE	Creature
Chirpl – chirp-ill	Creature
Coballen – CO-baal-en	Name
Dani – dan-E	Name
Dereen – de-REEN	Name
Dorat – door-at	Name
Fea – fee	Creature
Emera – E-mare-a	Name
Gakkar – guh-car	Name
Galinda – ga-lin-da	Name
Gaorun – ga-O-run	Name
Heka – heh-ka	Name
Iota – I-O-ta	Island
Inbar – in-bar	Name
Jivo – GEE-VO	Name
Kajiya – ka-GEE-yah	Name
Karei – ka-RAY	Name
Kip – kip	Name
Kivolta – key-VOLT-a	Creature
Koiyan – koi-yan	Yellow Sun
Lera – leer-a	Name

Magik – magic	Position
Midyan – mid-yan	Blue Sun
Mirabile – meer-a-bill	Moon behind Nimparte
Mirabilia – meer-a-bill-E-a	Tribe
Mirabilian – meer-a-bill-E-en	Tribal Possessive
Mysterium – miss-tear-E-um	Planet
Napel – na-pell	Name
Narev – na-rev	Name
Narine – na-REEN	Cave Name
Nijiru – knee-GEE-RU	Name
Nimparte – nim-par-ti	Smallest Moon
Onta – ont-ah	Name
Onti – ont-E	Creature
Orn – oar-n	Name
Ovis – O-viss	Island
Palinda – pa-lin-da	Tribe
Palindian – pa-lin-DE-en	Tribal Possessive
Pato – pa-TO	Name
Pavoki – pa-VO-key	Creature
Proten – pro-ten	Name
Resurge – re-surge	Name
Ringic – ring-ick	Herb
Ronin – ron-in	Name
Rotari – row-tar-E	Name
Rosa – rose-a	Name
Royalin – roy-a-lin	Tribe
Royaliste – royal-ist	Island Cluster
Ruina – roo-in-a	Name
Sai – s-I	Name
Sarin – czar-in	Name
Sarka – zar-ka	Name
Servic – sir-vick	Herb
Sharack – sha-rack	Name
Spiede – speed	Creature

Triekestria – TRI-kes-tree-a	Name
Taic – tak	Creature
Tiu – tea-U	Name
Turten – tur-ten	Name
Volens – VO-lens	Moon
Volmari – vole-mar-E	Island
Volta – volt-a	Name
Voi – voy	Name
Zaylene – ZAY-lean	Island

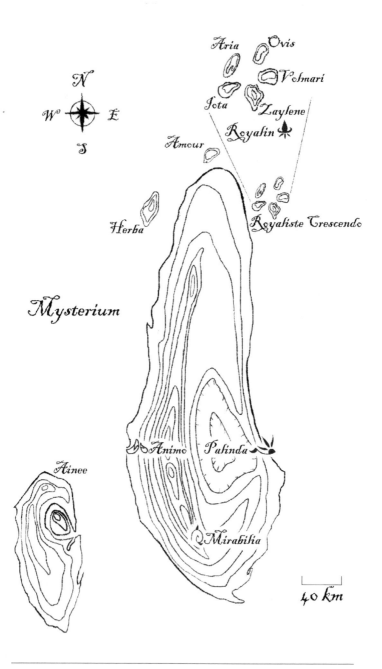

Preface: Damaged and Healed

Kajiya comes from a race of feline-like humanoids called feas, and is marked as a magik, destined to be the next leader of her tribe. But, after an encounter with a spiede results in her right to lead being revoked, she snaps, and ends up banished from her own tribe. She finds compassion in her brother, Resurge, and two best friends, Gaorun and Ainee. Together with Gaorun's pet onti, Onta, they set out on a quest to regain Kajiya's honour.

They soon discover that they are being chased by an army ordered by Turten, the fea responsible for Kajiya's banishment, to kill her. They manage to escape to the island of Ainee unseen, and find it home to Rotari, a four-hundred year old stone creature created by magic. Rotari then shares with the group her tale of woe, and proposes to train Kajiya in magic. Kajiya accepts the offer, under the condition that Rotari teach Ainee healing magic as well. While training, Kajiya discovers that she cannot use water magic, and not even Rotari's tutelage is able to help. Changing tactics, Rotari orders Kajiya to kill an innocent animal for the sake of learning, but Kajiya refuses. Rotari loses control, and Kajiya and Ainee scarcely escape the blakeslee's wrath. They leave for the mainland immediately and decide to head for the mountain tribe of Animo.

After arriving in disguise to a less-than-warm-welcome, Kajiya decides to explore the city. She learns that one of the guards who met her at the gate, Sarin, is not only a mute—but a fea who had been captured by the spiedes! Then, when Kajiya finds herself face to face with a spiede once again, she discovers that Animo has been facing a large threat from the subterranean creatures. A rally is held to get volunteers to help the resident warriors take down the spiedes. Disgusted by the lack of willingness of the feas of Animo, Kajiya volunteers thoughtlessly, and ends up leading the charge, using her magic to light the way. However, the battle turns to a slaughter, favouring the spiedes, and Kajiya and Sarin are caught by the spiede king, who keeps them as pets. They manage to befriend the king's other captive pet, a taic whom they name Rosa, and escape thanks to the return of Kajiya's water magic, but not before learning that the spiedes are using Turten, plotting to take over the surface world!

Once back in Animo, Kajiya enlists Ainee to help her cast one last spell, and finally discovers Turten's plan; to pass a law that will turn all the woman of the four tribes into nothing more than slaves.

Enraged, Kajiya vows to protect the feas of all tribes from both the spiedes and Turten.

Prologue: Words from the Heart

Her heart pounded in her ears. She could feel the unnaturally cold air cut through her thin fur and turned her head to see her pursuers. The giant creatures were gaining. She could see the lightning-quick movements of their spindly legs; sense the gaze of their enormous eyes; feel the grip of their mandibles closing on her. Her movements were slow, and the air seemed to thicken. They were upon her.

Kajiya's red eyes snapped open, and she found herself gripping the sheets very tightly, digging her claws into her palm. She commanded her hand to loosen before she hurt herself, but her body wouldn't respond. She felt paralyzed, but she knew better. She knew what it was like to *actually* be paralyzed.

With a grunt, and some visible effort, she managed to sit upright and swing her clawed feet over the side of the bed. Kajiya sighed, then flipped the green blankets off to the side and ran her fingers through her ice-blue hair before burying her muzzle in her hands. She let her head fall as she rested her elbows on her knees, and her long bangs surrounded her vision.

"It was just a dream," she whispered to herself, conscious of the other fea sleeping on the next bed over.

She knew it was more than that; this was no ordinary nightmare.

With her right hand, she grabbed her left shoulder, where a strange spiral marking cut across her deep blue fur. Her eyes opened slowly, and she stood, tail tip twitching.

A pale ambient light streamed into the room

from the cracks in the curtains as Kajiya padded over to a small desk. There was just enough light to see the obstacles in the room, but not enough to read or write by. Kajiya put her hands on her hips, and her tail flicked sharply.

Summoning the icy magic to her veins, Kajiya gathered it in a single fingertip before allowing it to take the form of a flame no bigger than a candle. As she sat down in the crude wooden chair, the blue fea reached over and ignited the real candle that sat on the desk. Waving her hand to extinguish the magic flame, the gentle light of the candle spilt into the world, revealing a large stack of paper with charcoal sticks sitting beside it. Immediately, Kajiya picked up the largest stick with her claws and set one end down on the paper.

And it stayed there for quite some time. Her mind was drawing a complete blank. Eventually, she just gave a sigh, and collapsed back into the chair, tossing the stick onto the paper as she did so.

Who was she to give an elegy? She sucked her cheek nervously; sure, she had been with the warriors of Animo as they battled the spiedes—she shuddered at the memory of the giant creatures from her dream. It hadn't been far from reality. Only Kajiya, a brown fea named Sarin, and a taic had escaped. She looked off to the side; sure, she was also a magik, destined to be the next leader of her tribe—but this wasn't even her tribe! Yet…

She sat back up, then took the charcoal in hand and wiped the black dust off the page; the feas who had sacrificed their lives to help stop the spiede invasion deserved *something*. Kajiya could only hope that she could write something worthy of their bravery.

She shuddered as a scream rang out in her mind, a memory, unbidden. Her fur fluffed out, and she stiffened until the imagined sound had passed. A long breath escaped her lips, and she put the charcoal stick to the page again, until the page was littered with hastily scribbled words and many scratches where she had decided that the words weren't good enough.

Finally, she set the stick down, forcing it out of her cold, cramped hand, and picked up the paper with a smile. She had *something* at last.

> *A thousand years will come and go.*
> *But still the legend of these great heroes will never fade*
> *The spiedes came at them high and low*
> *Until at last, the point was made*
> *Fur flew*
> *But to no avail*
> *They knew*
> *That despite their travails*
> *The end had come*
> *And as the wind blows*
> *Through the mountains high*
> *Let them not be forgotten*
> *But let us now together show*
> *Our respect, for those who die.*

There was a stirring in the bed behind her, and Kajiya leapt to her feet.

"Morning," a groggy voice came.

"Morning, Ainee. I finished," Kajiya said, her voice full of enthusiasm.

Ainee pushed her blue hair out of her eyes and away from her purple fur. She let out a tired sigh and sat all the way up.

"Let's see it."

Kajiya drew back the curtains, allowing more sunlight into the room, then passed the paper to Ainee.

Ainee's pink eyes went back and forth as she followed the disjointed words. Her expression betrayed nothing to Kajiya. Finally, Ainee stood up and went over to the window where Kajiya was waiting and held out the paper.

"It's okay."

Kajiya drew back at once, anger rising up in her, but she subdued it. Now was not the time for pride. She wanted this poem to be the best it could be.

"What do you mean?" she asked, a slight hiss finding its way into her voice without permission.

Ainee shook her head. "The rhyme scheme seems cheesy, and really cheapens it. There's no real sense that you were there at all, no sense of what it was like for them. People are grieving, Kajiya! It needs to be more respectful. Besides," she added, "it's just not you. It's too poetic."

The blue fea's fur began to rise and Kajiya opened her mouth to defend herself, only to close it again, suddenly aware of falling back into old habits. She changed her tactic.

"What do you think I should do?" she asked quietly. "The funeral's the day after tomorrow—I've been trying to come up with something like this for nearly a week now!" Kajiya hissed, finding her voice rising with each word.

Ainee placed one hand on Kajiya's shoulder and shook her head again. "I can't say I know Kajiya. But, I'm sure if you just write what's on your heart to say, it'll be perfect."

Kajiya let her hands fall to her sides. "I don't know what I want to say," her voice was full of tears.

Ainee's grip on Kajiya's shoulder tightened as she pushed the poem into Kajiya's hand. "Then maybe you should go look up some elegies in the library. I'm sure you could at least get a sense of what to aim for from that."

            *   *   *

By now the yellow sun, Koiyan, was just above the horizon and the cobblestone streets had begun to bustle with feas of every colour and size. Kajiya walked carefully, attempting not to bump into too many other feas. Despite the passage of time, Ainee's watchful eyes and healing hands, Kajiya's body still ached. Each step brought a small prick of pain to the soles of her feet.

She began to consider Ainee's suggestion, but let out a small snort instead. She bridled as she remembered the librarian's previous reception of her—she had been all but physically kicked out. Sure, back then she had kept her identity as a magik a secret, but Kajiya couldn't bring herself to visit a place with someone who could be so rude. Realizing that her feet lay on the path towards the library, she changed direction, spinning on her heels. As she lowered her snout, a familiar face stood out in the crowd. A smile broke out on Kajiya's snout as she raised a hand in greeting.

She walked up to the brown fea, her smile fading as she noticed that he was wearing nearly as many bandages as her in addition to the thick grey head-wrap that covered all but his eyes and ears. And what she could see of his green eyes seemed to grow concerned. He brought his fists together, then drew them back apart, opening his hands as he did so.

A corner of Kajiya's mouth leapt back up at the gesture, and she wagged her head ever so slightly.

After spending so much time with the mute, trapped together by the spiedes, she found it strange that he didn't use the magic she had taught him to communicate. At the same time, she understood his reasons; he was a warrior, and to warriors, magic was a last resort in life or death situations, as Kajiya's brother was keen to point out. Kajiya let out a small laugh at the thought of her brother, and then shook her head more solemnly for Sarin.

Despite the fact that Sai, the general of the Animo warriors, had allowed Sarin the use of magic for communication, Sarin was a warrior at heart. Kajiya knew that he wouldn't speak unless it was both important and necessary. While she missed hearing his dark sultry voice in her head, Kajiya had wanted to make more of an effort to understand his strange hand signs, and had learned that this particular motion meant 'trouble.' She could only hope that it was a question, like she had surmised.

Sarin took one hand and made a talking motion.

Kajiya glanced off to the side before releasing a large sigh, and then placed her hands on her hips. "I think I'd better."

Sarin nodded, then, with a sharp jerk of his head signalled for her to follow him. Kajiya padded after him obediently, but stopped abruptly as he sat down at a food cart. She raised an eyebrow, but Sarin merely patted the seat beside him, plunking down three golden coins on the counter. The attendant swept them off with a smile, and set to his grill.

Kajiya slid onto the stool. "Avian meat for me please."

Sarin gave her an inquiring stare.

"Rosa," Kajiya said defensively, referring to the taic who helped them escape the spiedes. "I don't want to eat taic meat—at least not until I'm far enough away from Rosa that she would never know," she added, blushing as her mouth watered at the memory of the warm meat that seemed to melt in her mouth.

Kajiya had only had taic meat once, but it was an experience she looked forward to one day repeating—unlike her experience with the spiedes.

The shopkeeper slapped two slabs of meat on the grill, and Sarin leaned back, nodding skeptically. He rested one arm on the counter, then pointed to her, and repeated the motion for trouble.

"It's this whole eulogy thing," Kajiya admitted, looking at her hands as they rested on her lap.

Sarin leaned closer as she continued, and Kajiya cast him a fleeting glance, hunching her shoulders.

"I just don't know what to do!" the words were coming faster than Kajiya could speak them. "I-I mean, I'm not qualified for this! I'm just some foolish magik and I-I have no idea what I'm doing," she said, staring intently into her lap.

Sarin tapped the wood beside her, then, as soon as Kajiya's eyes rose, he made as if he were flicking the pages of a book, then pointed back the way they had come.

Kajiya shook her head, and her ears sank. "Ainee already suggested the library for research. But…"

Sarin leaned back in towards her pressingly,

and Kajiya shied away from the intensity of his gaze, more than grateful for the sudden intrusion of the shopkeeper as he placed their food in front of them.

"'Ere ya go. One avian special, an' one regular taic."

"Thank you," Kajiya said, looking away before starting towards the meat.

Before she could even touch it with her claws, Sarin grabbed her, firmly, but not harshly.

Kajiya looked back up at him, and let her shoulders fall. This was a battle she could not win.

"But the librarian threw me out before... Before this whole spiede thing," she said.

Sarin released his grip, and turned back to his own food, thinking for a moment before standing abruptly, startling Kajiya. He held his palms towards her, and then rushed off into the crowd. Kajiya blinked, she recognized his motion for 'wait,' but where on Mysterium was he going? After a moment, Kajiya turned back to the slab of avian meat awaiting her, but found that she had lost her appetite in spite of the way her mouth watered.

I should eat, she reminded herself, starting to pick up the small piece of meat between two claws. She paused, noticing for the first time the knife that sat on the table. She picked it up, smiling to herself.

"Fancy."

There was a fork on the other side of the plate, so Kajiya lifted it, and speared the meat with all the grace of a panicked anfa. After so many weeks of eating with her hands, Kajiya found herself out of practice—not that she had used utensils very often before.

She was just rediscovering the joy of cutting

the sweet dark meat to reveal a small puff of steam in the middle when Sarin reappeared. His breathing was slightly laboured, and he held out a book with a triumphant look in his eyes.

Kajiya froze, fork halfway to her mouth. She quickly stuck it in and held onto the fork with her teeth, reaching out to take the book with her now-free hand.

She studied the green cover for a moment as she set down the knife, then removed the fork from her mouth and chewed. It was a book of poetry and speeches.

"Where'd you get this?" She raised an eyebrow, looking at him from the corner of her eye.

He tapped his chest with a fist, then made a triangle with his hands.

"Your home?" Kajiya clarified.

He nodded, then made a series of gestures that Kajiya didn't recognize, first pointing to himself, then cupping one hand over the other and finally seeming to pluck something out of the air.

Kajiya stared blankly for a moment. "What?"

Sarin's face fell, and he breathed out heavily. He moved a flat hand from left to right, then tapped his head. Kajiya smiled sheepishly; she did recognize that one. Never mind.

"Thank you anyway," she said.

He beamed under his cloak.

She opened the book, forgoing the knife and skewering the rest of the meat with the fork, so that she could just bite chunks off. She scanned the table of contents—and found to her surprise that there was a section on the elegy *and* a section on the eulogy. She paused for a moment. Elegy. Eulogy? There was a difference? She flipped to the beginning of the elegy section.

The elegy is a poem written in response to the passing of a significant fea or group of feas. While the form of each elegy is unique to the fea that writes it, most do follow a general pattern.

Kajiya's brow furrowed, she never did like being told what to do. However, it wasn't exactly like she was getting anywhere on her own. She kept reading.

First, there is the lament, or grief stage. Here the author expresses their sorrow at the fea(s) passing, and their impact on their lives.

Kajiya took a bite of her meat, and moved her head from side to side as she thought. It would probably be good to start with something like that. The feas of Animo would certainly be able to relate.

This then transitions into words of praise for those who passed, and finally, the poem ends with words of condolence for those similarly affected.

Kajiya leaned back. The pattern certainly *did* make sense. But what would it look like to write something like that? She ripped a large chunk of avian off of her fork and looked down at the book to find an example on the page.

A vein of ice flows
Over the river
Where he fell

Like a leaf ripped out of the sky
A tree uprooted
And coals growing dim
He fell

He was the doll from my childhood
Clutched and cried upon
The pages of my diary
Where all my secrets were kept
But more treasured still

But these coals cannot burn all the pages
Of his life
The fresh ground where he was
Makes room for new bushes to grow
The leaf lands
To cover the doll's face

And we all break the ice.

Kajiya drew a breath sharply; there was no way she could write something like that! But... The book was right, it was powerful. She looked back at the prose, then the poem again. Everything seemed to fit. She nodded to herself, and passed the book back to Sarin as she tore off the last piece of meat on the fork.

She swallowed.

"I think I know what I have to do."

        *   *   **

"Well?" Ainee looked over Kajiya's shoulder as the blue fea put down the charcoal.

Kajiya picked up the paper; her hand hurt from writing so fast.

"I just finished," she said, holding the page beside her head.

The page was snatched out of Kajiya's hand, and she twisted in the chair so that she could watch Ainee's face as she read. After a moment, Kajiya began to speak.

"I know it's a little short, but it's only the first draft," she said explanatively.

Ainee held the page back out to Kajiya. "It's good."

Kajiya's jaw gaped.

Ainee rolled her eyes. "It's not perfect; still a little rough around the edges, and I'm sure you can improve it, but it's better. Much, much better. This will get to straight to their hearts for sure."

Kajiya's jaw closed in a gentle smile.

Chapter 1: Announcements

A dark grey cloud floated lazily over the stone village, skimming the tops of chimneys before rising to join the rest of its brethren in covering the entire sky. Below them was a sea of colour and black. A quiet murmur rose up from the crowd; a murmur filled with suppressed sobs and sniffles. Before the crowd was a large stage, and a deep red male fea in a black tunic and black pants stood at a wooden podium. Behind him sat a variety of feas, and one in particular fiddled with the paper in her bright blue hands. The front half of her hair had been tied back, and her eyes darted about as her shoulders rose.

Kajiya took a deep breath; it was almost time.

The red fea began to speak, and his voice carried far over the crowd, helped by a strange cone that amplified his words.

"Thank you, Sai, for those powerful words. And now, as our time together is coming to a close," he turned to Kajiya, signalling with a flick of his tail for her to stand, "the future magik of Mirabilia, Kajiya, has a few words to say."

The blue fea stood at once, smoothing out her black taic-fur dress as she did so. The material felt strange to her, and the long slit up the left side left her leg feeling unusually exposed. Her ears fell down to the side of her head as she walked up to the podium. She gave a small nod to the head of ceremonies as he stepped back. She set the crumpled paper down and spent a moment smoothing it out.

Kajiya took a deep breath and forced her fur to lie flat, relaxing her shoulders. She opened her mouth.

"We all lost something when the spiedes attacked," she began to read. "A father. A friend. A loved one," she said, looking up as she spoke. "I worked with these feas personally, and I can attest to their bravery. Their perseverance. Their strength. They were the finest warriors I've ever seen," she paused, "and will probably ever see."

A lump formed in her throat as the crowd's murmuring grew. She glanced away for a moment, then looked back over the multitude, raising her head.

"But this is not the end."

Her words seemed to startle the crowd, and she felt all eyes turn to her. Her fur prickled, but she did not stop.

"They gave their lives so that we would not have to fear," she said, trying to pick out individual feas in the crowd to speak to. "So that we could sleep at night. They gave their lives to protect us. A thousand years could pass, but their names would still remain in our hearts, and our memories."

Suddenly a scream rang out in Kajiya's mind and she stiffened slightly. How long was that sound going to haunt her?! She looked down at the page, trying her best to ignore the memory.

"They would not want us to spend our lives grieving, and waste the freedom they've given us," she continued. "Instead, let us honour their memories, by fighting even harder to make sure that their deaths will not be in vain. By standing for what is right, no matter the consequence. And by loving one another, while we have the chance."

A few of the black-clad feas started to stand straighter, showing their tear-flattened muzzles as they looked at her. Kajiya felt her heart skip a beat. She had finished the speech she had prepared, but it was clear that they expected her to keep going.

Help.

She took a deep breath. "So let us go out today, and live the life that they died for, and not waste a second more."

Kajiya gulped, suddenly finding her own eyes watering. This time however, while hugs and whispered words of comfort spread throughout the crowd, she saw a few nods of approval and agreement. She breathed out. Now, she was free to leave.

Kajiya stepped back from the podium, and the red fea stepped forward once more. She was reluctant to take her seat, and instead stood awkwardly off to the side as the head of ceremonies began to speak, but the sound of her own heart pounding, and the emotion of the day drowned out his words, until she noticed that the band had begun to play again, and the mourners were trickling back to whence they had come.

She felt a clap on her shoulder, and turned to face a magenta fea with angular red stripes, the general of the Animo warriors. The ones whose service she had just ended.

"That was well said, Kajiya," he said, his voice solemn.

Kajiya tried to smile. "Thanks, Sai. I hope I did them justice."

He let out a weak smile as well. "I think they would have liked it."

"Kajiya!" a voice called out.

Kajiya turned to see Ainee bounding up the stairs, wearing a similar dress to hers, black and sleeveless. The only difference was that where Kajiya's dress rose up her neck, the purple fea's dress was a V-neck that went to just below her collarbone.

"Ainee," Kajiya said as two others came up on the stage.

Both were male, and wore matching black pants, and dark tunics. One was a midnight green fea with navy-blue stripes, and other was an azure fea just slightly darker than Kajiya. An orange onti with a black bow on her head stood on the green fea's shoulder.

"See," Ainee said, drawing Kajiya's attention as she put her hands on her hips and raised an eyebrow. "I told you that as long as you spoke from your heart you'd be fine."

Kajiya shrugged sheepishly. "I know."

The other blue fea stepped forward, holding out an arm. "That was really powerful, Kajiya. I couldn't be prouder of my little sister."

Kajiya blushed at her brother's praise. "Thanks, Resurge."

The green fea nodded in agreement. "So, what now?"

Ainee rolled her pink eyes. "Now, Gaorun, we have to plan what to do next."

Gaorun grinned, and scratched the onti on his shoulder under her chin. He cast Sai a fleeting glance and turned to Kajiya. "So, should we…"

Kajiya followed his gaze and shook her head. "Not today."

Sai raised an eyebrow. "Is there something I should know?" he asked, rising to his full height.

Kajiya shrunk back a bit. "Well, yes. We're getting ready to leave. We're not exactly sure what we're going to do though—there's something we need to meet about. Not just you though," she said, attempting to anticipate Sai's words as he opened his mouth to speak. "But the whole Assembly."

Sai nodded. "I'll summon them tomorrow. Today is a day to grieve."

Kajiya nodded. "I agree." She cast a fleeting glance back at her friends. "What we have to share is not exactly easy news either."

Sai's lips pursed, and his tail flicked, but eventually he dipped his head. "I'll see you at noon tomorrow then."

"Noon then," Kajiya confirmed.

With that, Sai turned to an orange fea with kind purple eyes who was waiting for him on the other side of the stage.

Kajiya blinked and stepped forward hastily. "And don't forget to thank your wife for lending us these clothes. I don't know what we would have done without her."

Sai partially turned back to her. "I'm sure Galinda will be pleased to hear that."

Gaorun unclipped the bow from the onti's fur and held it out. "And you might want to tell her to wash this before she wears it again. Onta kept trying to get it off by rolling on the street. Sorry about that," he said, allowing his head to sink into his shoulders before he gave the onti a short glare.

Onta raised her snout and snorted.

Sai let out a small laugh. "I'm sure it'll be fine, but thank you anyway."

"Sai," Galinda's voice floated over to them, and her thick tail swished from side to side in time with the slow beat of the music. "We should be going, dear," she said, taking his arm. "There's quite a line-up waiting to see you."

Sai let out a sigh. "Well, I guess I must be off."

Kajiya gave a small bow. "Of course," she turned to Galinda. "Thank you for the dresses, when should we return them?"

Galinda's purple gaze floated over to her. "Oh, just run them over to the house anytime. You're always welcome."

Kajiya blushed a little. "Thank you."

Galinda raised a hand as she and her husband started off.

Kajiya turned back to her friends, reaching up and letting her hair down as she did so.

"So," she began, "shall we go back to the hotel?"

Kajiya jumped down from the stage without waiting for a response, and flicked her tail, causing her bell to ring out into air just as the band finished the music. The town square was nearly empty, with only a few discarded tissues littering the cut stone streets.

"Slow down there, Kajiya," Resurge said, a hint of jocularity to his voice. "My bones are still a little sore."

Kajiya flinched as she saw the white bandages that stuck out from under her brother's tunic. He had been injured fighting off a spiede that had come into the village and attacked her. Kajiya gave a small shudder at the memory of the spiedes, the creatures whose eyes were as big as her face, with four long spindly legs that had killed so many only a week ago. The creature whose venom had once paralyzed her.

She gave a small jump as a hand fell on her shoulder, and looked to see Gaorun standing in front of her.

"You were zoning out again," he said, a touch

of concern to his voice.

Kajiya's ear fell beside her head. "Sorry."

Ainee clambered down from the stage. "You sure you're okay? First the nightmares, and then…"

Kajiya held her hand up. "I'll be fine. Don't worry about it, okay?" Her voice turned serious. "Besides, we have more important matters to attend to."

Gaorun released her shoulder as Resurge joined them and the group started down the street.

"Yeah," Resurge said, "Turten."

Gaorun turned to the dark blue fea. "Was it wise to wait so long to tell them about this?"

"It's not like we really had a choice," Ainee said before Kajiya could open her mouth to reply. "Between the shock of losing so many to the spiedes, and planning this whole service, I don't think they would have had the time to give Turten's plot proper consideration."

"Besides, what's done is done," Kajiya added with a matter-of-fact tone. "And we were in no shape to go off yet. I mean, Ainee just finished healing my wounds, and Resurge's bones are still bruised."

Resurge shrugged. "But they should be fine by tomorrow, right?" he confirmed, looking at Ainee.

Ainee's face softened. "I hope so. Those ribs took way too long to heal."

Kajiya glanced over to her friend, nodding in agreement. The spiedes had done an irrevocable amount of damage, to everyone.

Still, Kajiya bit her lip as she walked up the steps to the hotel. She wanted to get to Royalin, and put a stop to Turten's plot as soon as possible.

"I'm just worried," she thought aloud as she

opened the door to the lobby, "about Palinda. Turten said that they had delayed the Grand Assembly—but we don't know why or how." She turned back to the others as they started down the thin hall to their rooms. "What if they arrived already? What if we're too late?"

"We're not too late," Resurge's thick voice shattered the silence in the wake of Kajiya's words. "Look, if you need to, cast another spell with Ainee and check on him. But with something like this, we're better off taking our time to do it right. If we rush too much, Turten might be able to gain the upper hand."

Her brother's words made sense. A sigh left Kajiya's lips as she leaned up against the cool flat stone wall of the hall. She gave a single nod.

"Let's do it."

The door to Ainee's and Kajiya's room banged as they burst in. The girls sat down in the bed immediately and locked hands. Kajiya could tell from the look on Ainee's face that the purple fea was just as worried about Palinda's arrival as she was. Kajiya tightened her grip as the boys sat down.

Ice began to fill Kajiya's veins, and the magic grew in strength. It was much more powerful than it had been the last time they had cast this spell. As the magic began to flow between her and her friend, Kajiya began to suspect that both of them would be able to see and hear Turten.

"Sight," she whispered, partially to help her focus on the spell rather than her fears, and partially to let Ainee know which of the two spells she would take.

Ainee's hands tightened in response, and Kajiya felt Ainee's spell numb her ears.

Like before, everything was blurry to Kajiya

except for Turten. He was sitting down at a table with some other feas. It looked like it was a meeting of magiks and the Assembly heads. They were eating and making very idle chatter. At the moment, Turten was sharing the story of how he had lost his tail. If she could have, Kajiya would have rolled her eyes—she had heard that story more times than she could count.

"It was because of my self-sacrificing service, saving that poor woman from that ferocious taic," he was saying, "that caused me to lose my tail. You can't understand what it's like, to be unable to walk straight. I was forced to retire from being a warrior, my life and livelihood…"

Kajiya turned her attention elsewhere; she knew how the story ended. After revealing his heroic acts to the Assembly, Turten was offered the position of an assembly member, and after only a few short years, worked his way to become the youngest Assembly head in history. Not that Kajiya particularly cared about his exploits. After all, he was planning to enslave half of their species! She mentally snorted, and turned her mind's eye to the other feas. While she wasn't able to make out the features of most of them, her heart leapt for joy as she spotted her father at the table. Kajiya longed to reach out and touch him, but the spell couldn't quite do that, and she forced herself to look at the other feas before her concentration broke. After a moment, she noticed two empty spots at the end of the table. Kajiya moved her sight over to the empty chairs, and then back to the whole table.

Relief flooded over her. There were only six feas at the table—and no plates set out at the last two spots. The feas from Palinda still hadn't arrived. The world was safe. For now at least.

*   *   *

The dark red-brown wood of the door felt cool under Kajiya's hand. She breathed in slowly, then released the air. She turned to the others, who all gave her encouraging looks.

Animo's assembly hall was like Mirabilia's in that there were three sections. There was a hall for the assembly members to meet before the Assembly was called to order, a hall for those seeking an audience to wait, and of course, the main hall itself. But it was here that the similarities ended. In Mirabilia, the assembly hall had been raised on a platform high above the jungle, and was a circle with two rectangular wings coming off of each side. Animo's assembly hall, however, sat on the corner of the street, with the main section on the corner. Down one street was the waiting area, and down the intersecting street was the gathering hall.

Kajiya was standing on the rough stone steps that led up to two large wooden doors with black metal handles. They towered over her head by at least a tail-length. These doors were the entrance to the main hall from outside. The walls surrounding them were a dark grey stone similar to the steps, except that it was perfectly flat, whereas the steps were slightly rough.

Kajiya turned back to the door, her heart heavy. Now was a time of grieving, and while life went on, Animo's Assembly had refused to see anyone until they had sorted things out for themselves. Kajiya had no clue how Sai had managed to call them together to see her.

She pushed the grand doors open; all that mattered now, was seeing that they understood exactly what she was asking.

Kajiya could hear the others' footsteps behind her as she padded into the centre of the square. This would be the second time that she would appear before an Assembly. She took careful note of the rows of feas that faced her. A raised section of the stands acted as a desk for them, and she could see that they all had parchment and a writing utensil. She looked up at the spot where the Assembly head should have been, in the centre, facing her directly, but the seat was empty. Kajiya bit the inside of her cheek; of course the Assembly head was gone. Both he and Animo's magik, Beifin, had been summoned by Turten to a Grand Assembly—although every now and again, it was referred to as a 'Major' Assembly. Kajiya took a better look around the stands, a lot of the highest seats, those reserved for the most wise and fair of the Assembly, were empty. They must have gone with Beifin to the Grand Assembly.

A tail brushed against Kajiya's, and she glanced over to see Resurge giving her a small nod. Kajiya looked around; she had reached the centre of the hall without even realizing it. She took a deep breath.

"Feas of Animo," she began, doing her best to project her trembling voice. "We have gathered you all here today, to discuss a very real threat."

"The spiedes, we know!" a voice called out from the left.

"If that's all, then you need to know that we are going to deal with this threat!" another voice called from behind Kajiya on the right.

"We respect your authority," a voice said from the front, and Kajiya was able to catch a glimpse of the fea who spoke; his fur was turning grey with age, "but it would be best if you allowed us to work through this on our own." He stood and turned, making it clear he was about to leave. "We appreciate your concern."

"I'm not talking about the spiedes," Kajiya said before he could take a step.

A quiet murmur broke out among the Assembly's members, and the greying fea sat back down.

"Then," he said, "what are you talking about?"

A small prickle ran through Kajiya's fur. It seemed strange to her to have to speak about this so freely.

"You are all aware of the circumstances of my—" she faltered, "my banishment from Mirabilia?" Her ears pinned themselves to her skull as her shoulders rose.

The voice from the left replied, "No, actually. By the time word reached us, we had only heard that you had been both banished and reinstated. The reasons behind these actions were unimportant."

Kajiya's ears perked in surprise.

"We never actually did find out why, did we?" a voice from the right said.

All of a sudden, a chorus broke out from the feas present, each turning to his neighbours and inquiring, but all stopped as the elderly fea stood.

He stroked his chin, which Kajiya noticed had unusually long fur springing from it. "Perhaps it is time that we did find out. Please, elaborate."

Before Kajiya could reply, Resurge's voice broke the eager silence. "Perhaps it would be best for someone else to describe the initial reason behind not her banishment, but why her birthright as a magik was revoked."

Kajiya blinked, then nodded. It would be more impartial if it came from someone who wasn't her. She turned to Gaorun.

The green fea nodded, and Kajiya stepped over so that he could take the centre of the hall, crossing her arms as she did so.

The elderly fea raised an eyebrow, then sat down again.

"I was there that night. Kajiya," he paused, then turned to her with a slightly apologetic smile, "was a very different woman than the one you see before you now."

Kajiya stiffened a little with surprise. She blinked, then thought back. If she were to do it over, knowing what she did now, would she go into that cave, or would she have *listened* to Gaorun's warnings?

Her friend's voice continued, unfaltering, "She awoke me in the middle of the night, and had devised a plan so that she could see inside the Narine, a cave on the side of the mountain closest to Mirabilia."

The feas of Animo straightened up at once, eyes wide, and Gaorun paused, Kajiya guessed so that the murmurs could die from the crowd before he continued. Small snippets of the many conversations reached her ears.

"She wanted to see *inside* a cave?"

"…didn't she know about the spiedes?"

"Crazy…"

"…insane."

Kajiya drew her crossed arms closer.

"Back then," Gaorun's voice silenced the last few murmurs, "we believed the spiedes to be nothing more than legends. Although I had inklings that the tales we had been told were more than just the product of some fea's over-active imagination, Kajiya was stubborn, and would not hear me." He smiled back at her. "In Mirabilia, there are no caves, and no spiede attacks," he said, and Kajiya guessed that he was attempting to answer their questions before they even got the chance to ask them. "As such, I don't believe either of us truly understood the danger we were putting ourselves in. Now, Kajiya's plan was this; she had noticed that at Midyan's setting, light would reach into the cave. So, all that was to be done was to wait for that time, go in, take a look around and get out. I was to wait at the entrance of the cave while she explored. We tied a vine between us so that she could not get lost, and well…" He let out a sheepish laugh and scratched the back of his head. "I'm not exactly sure what happened in there, but I *believe* that was the first time that Kajiya saw a spiede." Gaorun turned to Kajiya, and she nodded affirmative.

The entire Assembly rose to its feet almost simultaneously, wide eyed.

"What?"

"She *saw* a spiede on her *own* and lived?!"

"How did you get away?"

"That's not possible!"

The elderly fea reached up to the Assembly head's seat and banged the wooden hammer, signalling for silence. It took three or four bangs, but eventually all eyes turned to him, and he set the gavel on his own desk.

"Perhaps, since your companion is unsure of what happened, you'd best recount it to us yourself, Kajiya."

Kajiya nodded and took Gaorun's spot,

uncrossing her arms. "Everything is just as he has said, except, while I was still in the cave, Koiyan rose, and Midyan set completely. I was left in the dark."

None of the feas sat down, but a few leaned forward to hear her better. Kajiya took a deep breath and began to gesticulate.

"I thought I heard something behind me," she said, "so I lit a fire with magic, and, well, yeah, it was a spiede. It was probably an adolescent, now that I think about it. Anyway," she said, shaking her head slowly to get back on track, "my fire blinded it, and I ran."

Kajiya stiffened slightly as she heard a sickening crunch in her memory. She'd best tell them about that.

"There were some weird spear-like rocks on the ceiling of the cave," she continued before the murmurs could break out again, "and the spiede, scared, I guess, by its sudden blindness, hit the floor and managed to make them fall. I didn't look back, but I heard those rocks crunch as they killed the spiede."

"Stalactites."

"She survived without any training."

"She would have won a test of courage."

Kajiya's ears perked at the last comment. A test of courage? Her red eyes flashed to Resurge. She could vaguely remember him telling her that what she had done was a test of a warrior's courage in the other tribes.

Resurge stepped forward, and Kajiya moved to the side for him. The murmurs grew dim on their own.

"While in Animo, what my sister did is indeed a test of courage," the dark blue fea looked in the vicinity of the voice who had mentioned it, "in

Mirabilia, that test has been outlawed," a strange moment of recognition entered his voice, and Kajiya looked at him confusedly. "It was outlawed by Turten."

The red irises of Kajiya's eyes were fully visible as she understood her brother's pause. She turned to Ainee, who looked as shocked as she was, then to Gaorun, who was nodding darkly. If Turten had been the one to outlaw that test—could it be that he was already in league with the spiedes, and didn't want anyone to find out? Kajiya's mind raced. What if—what if the spiede she had met that night… was a messenger between the spiede king and Turten? Kajiya didn't even bother trying to hide her tail as it puffed out completely.

Resurge glanced over to his sister, then turned back to the elderly fea who seemed to be taking the place of the Assembly head. "It was for this that Kajiya's right to lead was revoked."

There was no quiet murmur this time; only an outraged cry that rose up from all present.

Kajiya looked up and around in shock; none of them could accept this as a valid reason to revoke her right to lead. She let her mouth gape just a bit. Then, was it true? She had been denied her right to lead unjustly?

She stopped as anger at Turten started to flare in her chest. There was more to this story, and she let a small wave of guilt wash her anger away.

Kajiya stepped back into the centre of the hall, and flicked her tail harshly, causing the bell to ring out clearly. Then, as icy magic entered her blood, Kajiya caught the sound in her mind, and amplified it with magic, so that each and every fea could hear it as clearly as she could.

"I'm afraid our tale is not one of justice undone," she said, eyes narrow. "While Turten did indeed deny me my birthright unjustly—I'm afraid that, my banishment *was* just."

The feas of Animo looked around in confusion, and one by one, began to sit back down.

"Continue," the elderly fea said.

Kajiya was about to speak when Ainee put her hand on Kajiya's shoulder. "I've got this."

Blinking, Kajiya let Ainee take her place. Some of the feas bristled; Kajiya knew it was because a woman, an *ordinary* woman was speaking to them, but she was grateful for Ainee's intrusion. She never wanted to relive that day ever again.

"I'm afraid I did not see this event first hand," Ainee began, her voice taking on the sternness only a healer could use, "but I was informed of it directly afterwards by Magik Proten, who did."

The bristling feas sat up straighter, and those who weren't leaned forward. The purple fea had captured their attention.

"Upon learning of her right to lead being revoked, Kajiya grew angry. She went in directly to Turten, who then taunted her in such a way that none of us realized it until Gaorun," she said, pointing to the green fea, "realized that we were being chased. Oh, sorry. I'm getting ahead of myself. Anyway," she added, bridling for a fraction of a second, "Kajiya became truly *mad* and attacked the Assembly."

A fierce heat infiltrated Kajiya's cheeks, and she looked at her feet. She could feel every eye and every gaze turn to her.

"However," Ainee said quickly, "she came to

her senses before she could actually hurt anyone, but the damage was done. The motion to banish her came without opposition."

A profound silence settled over the hall. No one dared to move. Kajiya wasn't sure she could. Finally, she let out a sigh and stepped forward again.

"I overreacted. Horrendously so," she admitted, and tears threatened to break her voice. "And I can't express, my regret. My repentance." Her eyes fell for a moment, then she looked back up at the Assembly. "But my banishment is not why I'm here. Not why I called you here, it is unimportant. But in order for you to understand why I am here, you needed to know everything. *Including,* that after we four," she gestured to her friends, "set out from Mirabilia to regain my honour—Gaorun discovered that our Assembly, which often hires warriors to enforce rulings, had instructed them to find, and kill me."

Shock cascaded throughout the Animo Assembly.

Kajiya continued, "We now believe that the whole Mirabilian Assembly was *not* involved, but only one fea. Turten. We managed to outrun the warriors, and escape to the island of Ainee, where we rested and waited. Then we travelled here."

Kajiya paused for a moment internally; should she have told them about Rotari? No, her training and the blakeslee's betrayal had nothing to do with Turten. They didn't need to know about it.

The greying fea's voice broke into her thoughts. "And so, when the warriors were unable to find you, they reported you dead to their superiors and your father?"

Kajiya nodded. "We believe so."

"So, what then is the urgent trouble that you have summoned us here to hear?" he asked, spreading his arms wide.

"I was getting to that." Kajiya struggled to keep her voice calm. "When I was captured by the spiedes with Sarin, I heard the leader of the spiedes, their 'king,' if you will, and one of his messengers talking. They were talking about a recent shipment of fea slaves."

Nearly all the feas bristled at her words, but Kajiya tried her best to ignore them as she continued.

"While they were talking, I managed to overhear that not only had Turten sent these 'slaves,' but also that he was working with the spiedes."

Howls of anger erupted. Even the banging gavel could not quiet them.

Silence!

Kajiya jumped as the voice resounded inside her head, and she turned back to the entrance. Standing in the corner where she had not noticed them before were Sarin, Sai and Rosa. Sarin bowed to her, and Kajiya bowed back.

The rest of the Assembly had hushed as well, looking rather startled. Kajiya had no doubt it was the first time that many of them had heard Sarin's voice.

It rang out in Kajiya's head once more. *Kajiya is right. I awoke her because I knew of Turten's name. But I did not realize the gravity of what the spiede king was saying.* The brown fea stepped forward, Sai and Rosa falling in step with him.

And I believe there is more that Kajiya has to say. He gave her an encouraging nod.

Kajiya smiled back and turned to the Assembly once more. "I believe that Turten contacted the spiede king to help him rule over the tribes, but the spiede king plans on betraying him, and taking over the entire surface world."

The Assembly bristled, but each of them had a wary eye on Sarin, and didn't dare speak a word, lest he call out to their minds with magic once more.

"With this in mind," Kajiya said, "I cast a spell with my friend, Ainee's help," she gave the purple fea a quick nod, which Ainee returned in kind, "and discovered two things. Firstly, that Turten is already at the Royalin tribe, but Palinda has presented a delay, so he cannot reveal the purpose of the Grand Assembly he has called. And I also discovered what that purpose is. He wishes to pass a law that will turn all the woman of all *four* tribes, and all of what they see as the 'lower class,' into nothing more than slaves."

Again, all the feas present turned to one another, bewildered.

Kajiya took the opportunity to continue, "As such, and as a future magik myself, I intend to stop him by travelling to Royalin and exposing his dealings with the spiedes." She took a breath. "Now, I understand that you cannot spare any warriors to accompany me and my friends as we attempt this journey, and now, more than ever, the spiedes threaten, but if you could be so kind as to supply us for this journey, and prepare your borders against attack from Turten as well…"

Kajiya's chest rose and fell dramatically. She became slowly aware that her insides had been chilled, and the icy magic had come unbidden, not only that, but in a strength she had never felt before. Try as she might to let it melt, it kept coming in fresh waves, until she felt like she was going to freeze. As it was, she was already wearing her half-tunic, which unfortunately exposed her to the cold mountain air.

Despite the ice's abundance, there was something different about it. Kajiya pursed her lips; when it had come before she caused the cave-in that had sealed the spiedes off from Animo, it hadn't been so abundant, but it had been… more purposeful. That ice had a quiet strength that felt completely different from the ice that ran through her veins now. Kajiya's brow furrowed. What was the difference?

Just as it finally started to thaw, the elderly fea rose. "Thank you, Kajiya," his voice rang out clearly. "You have given us much to think about. Sai, Sarin, you two may stay and help us deliberate."

Sai and Sarin nodded in unison.

Rosa's ears flattened sadly.

"Thank you, Belo," Sai said, bowing low to the greying fea.

"As for the rest of you," Belo continued, "it would be best if you were to wait outside. We will send for you when we have reached a verdict. And please, take the, um," he paused, eyeing Rosa, "royal steed with you."

Kajiya and the rest of the group copied Sai's bow.

Come on, Rosa, Kajiya said with magic, shivering as the iciness numbed her throat.

The taic padded forward with them, out the door and back into the street. Had it not been for the solemnness that hung over Kajiya like a chirpl's shadow, she would have thrown herself into Rosa's long fur the second the door closed behind them. Instead, she satisfied herself with a hand in the taic's white fur, and sat down on top of the steps. The others took their seats below her. Kajiya hazarded a glance around. The street was deserted.

Immediately, Gaorun turned to her. "Sure," he said with a jocular eye roll, "they can bring in a giant taic, but I can't bring Onta."

Resurge shot the green fea a quick glare. "It wouldn't have been appropriate."

Gaorun stiffened. "I'm just trying to lighten the mood, sheesh."

Kajiya traced the contours of the stone step with a claw as she sat. Rosa settled down behind her, and Kajiya took the opportunity to rest on the taic's wonderfully warm stomach. Something seemed strange to her. Not one thing in particular, but something that she couldn't quite put her finger on.

"Kajiya?" Ainee's voice betrayed her concern.

Kajiya blinked, and turned to her.

"You weren't zoning out again, were you?" Ainee started to rise to her feet.

Kajiya shook her head hastily. "No, just thinking, that's all."

"About what?" Ainee asked, settling back into her seat.

Kajiya leaned back into Rosa's fur, and tossed a few locks over her stomach as a type of blanket.

"Nothing important," she mewed.

That was a lie. Kajiya's ear flicked with the thought—truthfully, she was sure that it *was* important. She just didn't know what 'it' was, or why it was important. Surely it couldn't be that important if she couldn't figure it out?

She blinked, a snippet of memory coming to her. Help. During her eulogy she had asked for help. She sat up straighter. The next words she had said were exactly what the crowd had wanted—no, needed to hear. How had she known what to say? And back in that cave with spiedes surrounding her—what had made her think she could use water magic?

Something touched her neck, and Kajiya jumped, feeling ice spike her insides as she turned, wide-eyed to see Rosa's face. Kajiya's fur was completely puffed out, and she brought her shoulders all the way to her ears as the taic's deep brown eyes stared curiously into hers. Kajiya's chest felt small, like she couldn't breathe.

Ainee was at her side at once. "Kajiya! Kajiya!"

The words barely seemed to reach the blue fea, and a deep fog surrounded her mind.

Kajiya!

Like light in the darkness, Ainee's silent cry sliced through the fog, and Kajiya turned to her, slowly at first. She shook her head and shuddered.

"*What happened?*" Ainee demanded, placing her hand to Kajiya's forehead.

Kajiya shook her head again. "I-I don't know. I just—I just…" She looked away. "I'll be fine. I just need a moment."

Ainee leaned back, her pink eyes betraying her concern. Kajiya couldn't look. She didn't want them to worry about her. There were far more important things at hand. She would be fine. She had to be.

An apologetic nudge came from Rosa, and she placed her head in Kajiya's lap, ears flat. Kajiya looked down at her, and let a small smile surface on her face. She placed her hand on the taic's head, scratching behind her ears, as she often did with Onta.

Don't worry about it, she said silently, *okay?*

Rosa breathed out heavily, but looked up at Kajiya with a hint of a smile in her face.

Resurge stepped up the steps. "Are you sure you're okay?"

Kajiya nodded. "Yes, I'll be *fine*. I can't live my life afraid of every sudden movement."

Resurge stepped back down reluctantly. "If you say so."

Kajiya nodded, standing. "We have to focus on what's most important right now."

"Stopping Turten, right?" Gaorun said as he got to his feet.

A determined glint entered Kajiya's eyes. "Of course."

The door behind them creaked, and they all turned around as Sai poked his head out.

"They're ready for you."

Kajiya cast the others a fierce glance, and they all returned her gaze in turn. Her fists clenched, and she stepped up over Rosa's girth as Sai opened the door fully.

Head up, she told herself as she stepped back into the room.

It took her eyes a moment to adjust to the dim light of the hall. Despite it being overcast outside, the ambient lighting had been far brighter than the torches that lit the assembly hall. Again, Kajiya found her feet leading her to the centre of the room.

Belo was standing with Sarin below him. As Kajiya watched, Sai walked over to take his place beside Sarin. Belo had his hands behind his back, and once all of the feas had stopped moving, he began to speak.

"Magik Kajiya," he began.

Kajiya's fur tingled at his address. She had never been called 'Magik Kajiya' before.

A sadness entered Belo's pale yellow eyes. "I'm afraid you were correct in your assumption that we are unable to supply you with warriors to protect you during your journey. You understand that we must put the immediate safety of our people before even credible threats."

Kajiya dipped her head, and Belo returned the gesture.

"However," he continued, a corner of his mouth rising, "the Assembly of Animo would be *honoured* to help you in any way we can. Your assistance in the attack on the spiedes was invaluable, and you managed to save one of our own as well. More than that," he paused, "you acted with no regard for yourself, but out of goodwill towards our tribe. We can only return the favour. What supplies will you need?"

Chapter 2: On the Road Again

Kajiya shifted the load on her back. It had been a long time since she had had to wear the dull green pack, and now, laden with furs and other supplies, it threatened to pull her to the ground. She moved her shoulders around again, hoping to get it to settle, but it would not. Eventually, she sighed and shrugged it off, letting it drop to the ground.

A little ways away, Ainee and the others were also trying on their packs, getting accustomed to the heavy weights. More than just Kajiya's tail had been waving about, trying to get their owners balanced. Had they even had this much stuff when they originally set out from Mirabilia? Try as she might, Kajiya couldn't remember, but she didn't think so.

A hand clasped Kajiya's shoulder, and she gave a small jump, before turning around to see Sarin. His eyes smiled at her. Kajiya smiled back in spite of her pounding heart.

"Thank you for helping us get all this ready, Sarin," Kajiya said.

He waved a hand nonchalantly.

"I mean it," Kajiya insisted. "I don't know how we would have gotten all this done without you!" She paused. "You sure you don't want to come?"

Sarin's eyes darkened. He shook his head and gestured to the large wall beside them. Kajiya followed his gaze and let out a sigh. The wall was almost four times her height and rose straight out of the mountain. Behind it and the giant stone doors, was Animo. She dipped her head in understanding; Sarin couldn't leave his people when they were so vulnerable. As much as Kajiya wanted her friend to join them on their journey, she couldn't argue with him. Instead, she held out her hand.

"I'm going to miss you."

Sarin nodded, and took Kajiya's hand.

Gaorun bounded over to the pair, Onta hanging on for dear life aboard his pack. "Are you ready, Kajiya? It's almost time. Sai should be here any moment!"

Kajiya released Sarin's grip, and twisted to look at Gaorun. "I think so. I was just about to grab the rest of my stuff. How are they doing?" she asked, indicating Resurge and Ainee with her head.

Gaorun turned and almost sent Onta flying off of the top of his pack in the process.

"They look like they're doing fine to me," he said.

Kajiya let out a small giggle and reached up for Onta before Gaorun could turn again. The orange puff-ball gratefully nuzzled her face before wrapping herself around Kajiya's neck.

The sound of footsteps caught Kajiya's ears, and she looked over her shoulder to see Sai approaching, with Rosa at his side.

"It's good to see that you're all ready," Sai said, rolling a piece of paper that he held in his hands.

"What's that?" Kajiya inquired, tail curling curiously as Resurge and Ainee joined them.

"This," Sai said, hitting the rolled up paper against his open palm, "is a note for Beifin when you reach him, detailing everything that you told us, the attack, and the Assembly's ruling. Now, do you have everything you need?"

Kajiya looked around, but everyone was

already straining under the weights of their packs. Even Resurge. A grin broke out over her face.

"I think we're good. Gaorun?" Kajiya reached up and plucked Onta off of her shoulders, then set her on the ground.

The onti gave a huffy snort and leapt up onto Rosa's back, much to Kajiya's surprise. Fortunately, the taic treated Onta as nothing more than a small insect hitching a ride. She gave the onti a short sniff, then thumped down on the ground.

Kajiya breathed a sigh of relief as Gaorun finally replied.

"I should hope we do!" He smiled. "We've *only* got enough food for a month! And I've got more nets than I could hope to trap with."

Ainee gave Sai a small bow. "You must thank your healers for me—they were kind enough to replenish my herbs, and even taught me a few new techniques."

Sai nodded as he held out the paper. "Of course."

Kajiya took the paper gingerly and passed it behind her to Resurge.

Sarin seemed to notice something, and moved away, but before Kajiya could see what he was going to do, Sai began to speak again.

"So, you know where you're going, right? I don't remember getting you a map." A hint of concern came into his green eyes.

Resurge stepped forward, taking another piece of paper from one of the side pockets of his pack, replacing it with the paper for Beifin.

"We should be fine, but perhaps before we go, you could advise our route? I'm afraid we're not quite as familiar with the mountains as you are," he said, unfurling the map they had used on the rest of their journey.

Resurge passed the map to Sai and took his pack off, making sure that it sat on the ground nicely before he turned back to the general. Kajiya joined him and the others gathered around.

"Which way were you thinking of taking?" Sai looked at Resurge.

Kajiya cut in before her brother could answer. "I was thinking that we would do our best to take the direct route," she said, tracing a straight line from Animo to Royalin with her fore-claw.

Resurge nodded in agreement. "We can't waste time."

Sai shook his head. "I'm afraid if you went that way, you'd spend half your time running from taics. There are quite a few colonies in that section of the mountains—your best bet would be to get to flat ground as soon as possible, and *then* take the direct route by cutting through Palinda's territory."

Kajiya blinked, and bit her lip. She had hoped to get to Royalin as fast as possible; after all, she didn't know how long Palinda was going to delay the Grand Assembly. As it was, Kajiya knew they couldn't be far away from Royalin now... Unless... Kajiya backed away from the others for a moment, allowing Resurge and Gaorun to talk paths and routes with Sai unheeded.

She put a crooked finger to her lips, and rested her elbow on her other arm. The Palinda tribe was nomadic; what if the messenger from Royalin, the one who should have delivered news about the Grand Assembly had been delayed—or even just unable to find them? It wouldn't be the first time.

Kajiya smiled as she remembered a story; a few generations back, Royalin's magik had been about to pass down his title to the new magik, and as always, there was to be a large ceremony in Royalin, where all the tribes' leaders would attend to give the new magik their blessings. However, for this particular magik, the messenger, after alerting Animo and Mirabilia, had spent the next eight weeks searching Palinda's territory to find them!

Kajiya nodded to herself; surely that was the case. Even so, each second they spent standing around was another second that the messenger could find Palinda. Another second that they could be one step closer to helping Turten realize his goal.

Something yellow descended on Kajiya from above, bringing her out of her thoughts. She smiled, and turned around to Sarin, taking her shoulder-bag from him as she did so.

"Thanks, Sarin—I wouldn't want to leave without this."

I didn't think you would, he responded.

Kajiya's face grew conflicted. "Sarin, why don't you always use magic?"

The smile faded from the brown fea's eyes. *It's still unfamiliar to me. And as a warrior, I don't want to use it unless I have to.*

"So why are you using it now?" Kajiya asked quietly.

He blinked. *Because I don't know when I will see you again, and I don't want you to misunderstand my signs.*

Kajiya smiled weakly, and readjusted the bag around her shoulders. "Thank you."

Suddenly, an idea struck her, and she opened up the shoulder bag, and started to rummage around. It took her a moment, but eventually Kajiya found what she was looking for; she pulled out a red and gold book.

"Here," she said, holding it out, "since you were kind enough to lend me that book of poetry, here's one of my favorite books. It's about these weird creatures called 'humans'—they can't use magic or anything, so they made things to do magic for them. It's really interesting. I finished it a couple days ago."

Sarin blinked, and took the book from her hand. He put his spear into the crook of his elbow, and opened the cover and started to flip through the pages.

Thank you, I'll be sure to return it to you when I get the chance. Who knows, if I like it, I may have to expand my personal library.

"You have your own library?" Kajiya asked with a gasp.

Sarin blinked in surprise, and it seemed to Kajiya that he thought that she should already know this. Then he blinked again and his shoulders rose in a laughing motion.

Right—I forgot. I told you about it, but I don't think you understood me.

Kajiya grinned sheepishly. "I guess not."

"Kajiya!" Ainee's voice carried over the brown rocks of the mountain; while Kajiya and Sarin had been talking, the others had left, and were a good thirty tail-lengths ahead. "We're ready! It's time to go."

Kajiya looked over her shoulder, and her tail flicked, sending a pure note into the air from her bell. "I'll be there in a minute!" She turned back to Sarin. "I guess this is goodbye then."

He nodded. *I guess so. Would you like me to help you with your other pack?*

Kajiya nodded gratefully, then with a moment of gleefulness, she put her hands to her chest, making a fist with her right, and covering it completely with her left. Then she flipped both of her hands out in front of her chest, opening her right hand as she did so, as if she were offering him something. And she was. Gratitude.

The shock of seeing his own sign for 'thank you' was evident in Sarin's eyes, but the shock quickly gave way to an unspeakable joy, and he merely turned around and grabbed Kajiya's backpack from where she had left it. He held it up, and Kajiya carefully put her arms through the straps. Sarin let go slowly, and Kajiya's bell sounded a cacophony as she regained her balance.

Kajiya turned to face Sarin one last time, and gave him a small nod. She didn't know what else to say.

I will read the book, his voice infiltrated her mind once more, *and we'll talk all about it later.*

Kajiya smiled. *I'll look forward to it.*

Before the goodbye could become any more lengthy than it already was, Kajiya turned and ran for the others, giving Sai and Rosa one last wave. By this time, Kajiya suspected that her friends had already said all of their goodbyes as well, and as soon as she joined them, they set off.

The terrain was difficult, as many of the red-brown rocks were loose and slid out from under their feet as they walked. This, coupled with the added weight of their packs, kept the group silent with concentration for a long time. Slowly, the village of Animo became smaller and smaller, until at last, when Kajiya looked up, it was only a small speck in the distance. She could barely even tell it wasn't just some large boulder that rested on the mountainside. She sighed, then turned her eyes and attention to the landscape below.

There was a small swath of forest at the very base of the mountain, still a good three or four hours away from what Kajiya could tell. There were blue and purple trees in abundance, and Kajiya couldn't help but compare them to the island of Ainee, where green-leafed trees had predominated.

It's amazing what a few days' journey can do to a landscape, she thought to herself.

Beyond the treeline though, was something completely unfamiliar to Kajiya; a field. Not a clearing full of green grass, but a field, filled to the brim with a strange white-yellow plant. From her current height, Kajiya couldn't tell what the plant actually was, or what it looked like—if it was a plant at all. For all she knew, it could have been some sort of pattern in the dirt. But, she had often heard of traders from Palinda carrying strange yellow mats made of an exceedingly long grass with them. Kajiya had always assumed that the grass had just dried out, but now, looking down on Palinda's territory from above, she wasn't so sure.

Realizing that she *was* looking down on Palinda's territory, Kajiya gave a start. Were they that close already? She peered down below without breaking her stride. Perhaps if she looked hard enough she could see where the tribe was! Then they could meet up and she could warn them—Kajiya shook her head. It was impossible to tell what things were from her vantage point, and even if she had wanted to cast a sight spell to see what Palinda was like, she knew that in order for a seeing spell to work, one had to be able to picture what they wanted to see. Or at least, she had to. Kajiya paused mentally; Rotari had said she had been watching the mainland for years. Had she actually been able to travel around the entire continent in her short life, and was thus able to watch anywhere, or had her four-hundred years of practice just increased her abilities? Kajiya laughed at herself. The answer was obviously the second option.

Just then, a movement from below caught Kajiya's eye; Onta's tail was high as she scouted out the easiest path for her fea companions to follow.

"Gaorun," Kajiya called out.

"Yeah," he responded, keeping his eyes on his feet.

"I've been meaning to ask this for a while," Kajiya began as she noticed that the group had come to a very steep decline, and cast her eyes down to her own feet. "How did you teach Onta to scout ahead like that?"

"Oh, I just threw a piece of anfa meat on difficult trails, and gave her more if she kept her tail up. She figured it out pretty quickly. Onti are really smart animals."

Kajiya laughed as her bell chimed. "You make it sound so easy!"

Gaorun joined her laugh. "If only it was! Getting her to keep her tail up was the easy part—teaching her to scout ahead without incentive was *exceedingly* difficult. Took me almost a month!"

"Why did you teach her to scout ahead?" Resurge wondered as he staggered down the boulders.

"Sometimes anfa like to go places where there are lots of really gnarly roots and vines; it can get very difficult to track them without getting hurt. Unless, of course," he said with a touch of pride in his voice, "you have a great onti like Onta to help find the way!"

The mountain seemed to echo Gaorun's joy as the group found their way down the path that Onta had scouted out.

Suddenly, Kajiya felt the rocks beneath her feet give way. Panic flared in her chest as her stomach rose. With a small screech, she fell onto her rear, and was forced by her pack to remain in a sitting position as she started to skid down the mountain's face. Her tail roared in pain, and she could feel the rocks and dirt threatening to tear her pants. Her eyes watered; not only could that be even more painful, but embarrassing. Kajiya couldn't let it happen!

The icy magic came to her with nothing more than a thought, and she quickly strengthened the anfa hide before it could become damaged. Kajiya could vaguely recognize the calls of the others as they tried to run to her, and feel the faint tug of magic as either Gaorun or Ainee—Kajiya couldn't tell which—tried to slow her descent.

Her heart fluttered as she looked ahead. She was headed for a cliff. A little past the cliff was the beginning of the swath of forest she had spotted earlier. A crazy idea came into Kajiya's mind, and no sooner had the thought fully formed, than she found herself airborne. She happened to glance down, and wished she hadn't. She had at least seven seconds of airtime before she would hit the ground. It was truly now or never.

Ice welled from the core of her being, and

Kajiya could only hope she wasn't too out of practice. She felt everything around her, the air and how it moved, the packs she carried on her back and even her own fur. Slower than she would have liked, Kajiya used the magic to slow everything to a stand-still. Her body hung in the air, and Kajiya breathed a short sigh of relief. She hadn't forgotten how to fly after all. She pushed with the magic and, not trusting her strength, flew for the nearest tree, which was only three tail-lengths away as opposed to forty to reach the ground, or twelve to get back to the cliff.

She landed on a branch, but didn't release the magic until she stood next to the trunk, where the branch would be most likely to hold her added weight. As soon as the ice left her system, Kajiya collapsed on the trunk, and became aware of her friends calling out to her. She turned weakly to them, not as tired as she expected to be, but still exhausted.

"Just stay there!" Resurge was saying, hands cupped around his mouth as he stood at the edge of the cliff. "We'll be right over!"

Kajiya nodded weakly as her friends then turned and ran for the safe way down. Even Onta seemed to understand their panic. Kajiya crept closer to the trunk, and settled down to wait. Her heart was still racing, and she realized abruptly that the entire incident had probably only taken a maximum of ten seconds, in spite of how long it had seemed to her. She dug her claws into the bark of the tree. Time passed without Kajiya really being aware of it, and before she knew it, Gaorun's hand appeared on the branch below her, with Resurge just a few branches lower. The green fea held out his free hand with a small smile.

"Give me your pack," he instructed.

Kajiya complied with some difficulty, and was able to get the huge backpack down to him. It felt like it was going to rip off her arm as she held it by one strap, but Gaorun seemed to take it with ease as he passed it down to Resurge.

Gaorun held out his hand again as Resurge started back down the tree. Kajiya nodded and took off her yellow shoulder-bag. She gave it a quick look over; it was dusty, and a little scuffed up at the bottom, but not overly damaged. She handed it to Gaorun, who promptly put it over his own shoulder.

"Alright," he said once he had finished adjusting it, "now you. Take this branch here. That's right, and now this one."

Together, the two feas worked their way down the tree, until they reached the bottom. Kajiya held onto the last branch, which was still a good two-and-a-half tail lengths off the ground, and stretched out her arms completely while feeling the dirt with her tail before dropping down.

She let out a loud breath, and stumbled up against the tree, then slid down into a sitting position.

"I think we should stop here for the night," Resurge said, eyeing both the sky and Kajiya. "We can start out again in the morning. I think we made some good progress today."

"Well, we're off the mountain at least," Ainee said as she kneeled beside Kajiya. "How are you feeling? Not too tired?"

Kajiya shook her head. "Not from the magic at least."

Ainee smiled. "Of course."

Gaorun looked up at the sheer cliff, and placed a hand to his chin. "You know," he began, a thoughtful tone to his voice, "this kinda reminds me of the first time you tried to fly."

Kajiya stiffened at once. "I thought you promised never to talk about that!" she hissed, face turning red with the memory.

It had happened a few years ago, not long after a troupe of feas who liked to put on plays came to Mirabilia. During their performance one of the feas had flown with magic—more like an extended jump, but it had set Kajiya's mind a-working nonetheless. Soon, she had convinced Gaorun to join her as she tried to fly for the first time.

Kajiya had chosen a place she thought ideal for her first flight. The weather was perfect as well; not too warm, not too cold and not too windy. She had pestered her magic mentor about flight until he had explained the basics to her, and as she stood on top of the cliff, her imagination soared with the sheer thrill of flight.

The cliff she had chosen was small, only about five tail-lengths from the ground, but still large enough for her to jump and get some good hang time as she figured it out. She had no doubt that she would get it on the first try. Below, a little river ran through the forest, and there was a small glade on the other side. Kajiya thought the glade was a perfect landing spot. All she needed, was Gaorun.

She had turned, and found with joy that the trapper-in-training had managed to get away from his lessons early. With him, as always, was the small onti that he had rescued from a chirpl. Kajiya smiled at him.

He smiled back, then looked over the cliff. "If you actually pull this off, it'll be so cool!" he said.

Kajiya nodded. "I know, right!?"

Gaorun looked back over the cliff. "But if you don't—you know you're dead, right?"

Kajiya had rolled her eyes, then bridled as she put her hands on her hips. "That's why you're here, silly!"

"To make sure you don't die?"

"Of course!"

"Are you ready then?"

Kajiya narrowed her eyes and leaned towards her green friend. "Are you?"

Gaorun leaned back a bit and put his hands up defensively. "Totally!" There was a hint of a quiver to his voice.

Kajiya ignored him, and turned back to the cliff.

"Stand real close to that edge there, right beside where I'm going to jump." She pointed to a small tuft of grass on the very brink of the cliff.

Gaorun nodded, then padded over to where she had pointed. "Here?"

"A little to the left—my left! Perfect! Alrighty then, here I come!" Kajiya cried, running towards the cliff at full tilt as ice began to crystalize in her veins.

Gaorun must have known something was wrong from the moment she passed him, because he reached out and grabbed her tail without even waiting for her to realize that she didn't have enough magic to complete the spell.

Kajiya had let out a small gasp as her tail dislocated, and she slammed back into the cliff face. All she could do was whimper as she heard Gaorun hiss something to Onta.

She guessed it was an order to find her father,

*for, after what seemed to be an eternity, just as
Gaorun's grip was starting to fail completely, she felt
her body being lifted by the wind. Never before had
Kajiya been so glad to get in trouble! Fortunately, her
recklessness had convinced her father that she needed
to be taught how to* properly *learn such dangerous
spells, and her mentor spent the next few weeks
teaching her how to fly.*

Gaorun turned to her, and the motion brought
Kajiya back to the present.

"Oh, did I?" he asked innocently.

Kajiya's face burned. "Yes, you did, *Gao.*"

Now Gaorun's orange eyes lit with fire. "I
thought I told *you* not to call me that!"

Kajiya raised her snout. "Gao, Gao, Gao!" she
sang.

Gaorun took a step towards her. "Why I—"

"That's enough!" Ainee hissed, holding a hand
to each of them. "We're all tired, but that's no excuse
to be at each other's throats!"

Kajiya blinked, and the heat faded from her
face. As usual, Ainee was right. Not that Kajiya was
going to admit that. She just stayed silent, her red eyes
looking at the dirt beside her. What should she say?
What *could* she say?

Resurge's thick voice cut the air. "I think we'd
best start setting up camp. Something tells me that the
sooner we sleep, the better."

Kajiya couldn't have agreed more.

*   *   *

The morning air brought a crisp scent to
Kajiya's nose, and she rose from the covers groggily.
A few blinks left her eyes, and she put a hand to her
head as her sore tush reminded her of the previous

day's little adventure. She sighed, and stood up as she exited the tent.

Resurge had found a small clearing under the cover of the jungle where they had set up camp. Kajiya smiled at the tree-tops. It felt good to be back in the forest. She hadn't realized how strange it had been to be able to see the sky so clearly. She paused; then again, it had usually been quite overcast in Animo, so she hadn't been able to see past the clouds most of the time anyway. She walked over to the base of the cliff where the trees didn't obscure her view; there were no clouds today.

"Oof!" Kajiya grunted as she walked into something.

"Oof!"

Someone.

Kajiya put a hand to her head as she opened her eyes; there, rubbing his blue hair, was Gaorun. Kajiya blushed at once and looked at the ground as she remembered the previous day's spat.

"Sorry," she mewed quietly.

He blinked, then turned to her. "It's okay. Doesn't hurt too much."

Kajiya looked back up at him at once. "N-no, for yesterday too."

Gaorun blinked, then shook his head. "It's fine. We were all a little on edge."

"Even so—" Kajiya protested.

Gaorun placed a finger to his lips. "Please. Don't spoil this for me."

Kajiya tilted her head to the side.

"Spoil what?"

Gaorun smiled, then gestured to the sky. "The early-morning silence."

Kajiya closed her mouth, and tuned out the sound of their breathing. Gaorun was right. The silence was deafening. She looked around. Everything was still. And beautiful. Absolutely beautiful.

After a long pause she turned back to him, but this time she kept her voice soft. "I really am sorry. There's no excuse for how I acted yesterday."

Gaorun's ear flicked, but he didn't respond. Kajiya let her face fall, and she twiddled her thumbs.

"You're forgiven." The words seemed to come from nowhere.

Kajiya's ears perked as she looked back up; Gaorun was giving her a mischievous smile.

"Think you can forgive me?" he said. "I'm afraid I forgot how embarrassed you were by that whole thing. I thought maybe you had gotten over it by now, but I guess…"

Kajiya shook her head. "It's fine. Just, don't bring it up unless you have to, okay? I had almost forgotten about it."

A corner of Gaorun's mouth moved upwards, and he scratched the base of his jaw. "Sorry."

Kajiya rammed him with her shoulder gently. "Don't worry about it."

He turned back to the forest, and let out a contented breath. Kajiya followed his gaze to the treetops, which were starting to sway with the wind. The sun hadn't completely risen yet, and the sunlight was instead falling upon the treetops as a skipping stone over water. Kajiya placed her weight on Gaorun's shoulder, her feet still sore from walking down the mountain with her overweight pack.

"Have you ever thought that maybe there's something more out there?" Kajiya suddenly blurted.

Her face flushed—why on Mysterium had she said that? Kajiya's insides turned to mush; what was it Rotari had said about there being a force greater than magic? The words she said, the magic that had come when the spiedes attacked and Sarin and Rosa were in danger, what had given those things to her?

Gaorun turned to her and smiled. "Yeah. A lot actually."

Kajiya blinked. "Why?"

Gaorun shrugged. "Dunno really. But, well, I guess it's kinda like a story."

"A story?"

Gaorun nodded. "Someone had to write it, right? Or, something I guess."

Kajiya turned back to the forest and sighed. "I guess."

Gaorun moved, and Kajiya almost fell over. The bell on her tail rang out in protest as she balanced herself.

"Well, I'm gonna head back to camp. My stomach tells me it's breakfast time, and Onta's probably yapping her little head off to try and find me," he said, shooting her a giant grin as he headed back into the forest.

Kajiya giggled at the idea of Onta running around, and waking everyone up, but she made no move to join him. Onta's yaps were both loud and high-pitched—she wanted to be able to hear the rest of the day.

Another sigh left her lips, and Kajiya walked back over to the base of the cliff and sat down to think. So Gaorun thought there was something else out there. Rotari knew there was. Or at the very least, believed there was. Kajiya closed her eyes; what *had* stopped the spiedes from killing her? Why was it that she should be fortunate enough to befriend the *one* fea who knew how to survive in that darkness? And whatever it was that orchestrated that—why would it care to help her say what she needed to say at a eulogy? And why give her magic? Questions, questions, questions, and with nary an answer to spare; Kajiya's head began to hurt. Eventually, she forced herself to stand again, head pounding. She needed a thinking break.

By this time, the entire forest was shrouded in sunlight, and thin beams streamed through the canopy. Kajiya put her hand in one, wondering what it would be like to catch one. Alas, as always, the light did nothing but change the colour of her fur a few shades. A corner of her mouth tugged upwards, and she continued on. The scent of taic meat rose through the air. Kajiya's mouth began to water, and she cast a furtive look around. As she suspected, Rosa was nowhere in sight—she was free!

Kajiya almost jumped for joy as she sprinted back to the campsite. She had only had taic meat once, and the prospect of having some variety in her diet came as wondrous notion.

Kajiya skidded in the dirt as she came around a tree at full velocity.

"And look who finally decided to show up," Ainee's voice cut through the crisp air smoothly, and she cast a sly smile Kajiya's direction. "You got hungry?"

Kajiya laughed. "You could say that—that smells delicious."

Resurge raised an eyebrow as his tail flicked from where he stood over the fire, holding a pan. "I thought you didn't like taic meat."

"I was just trying to be courteous to Rosa." Kajiya's shoulders rose as she walked forward, tail flicking.

Gaorun walked out into the clearing from his tent. Resurge stiffened visibly, and shot a wary glance to Kajiya. Kajiya ignored him; he probably expected her to still be mad with Gaorun. Instead, she walked over to the fire, and snatched a piece of meat from the pan. She tossed it from hand to hand as she realized just how hot it was.

"Ooh ooh ooh!" she hissed, blowing on it to try and cool it down.

Ainee looked over with a deadpan stare. "Serves ya right."

"Oh shut up," Kajiya hissed with a smile.

A quick movement caught Kajiya's eye, and she turned her head; Gaorun held a piece of meat between his claws. He grinned at her. Kajiya grinned back. Resurge looked at the two of them, then visibly relaxed with a small shrug. He shook the pan a little, and then walked over to Ainee.

"I suppose you'll be wanting some as well?"

"Why, thank you, Resurge," Ainee said with a small curtsey and coy smile.

Kajiya took a small bite out of the slab of meat, blinking in confusion as the meat came off in strings. Was taic meat always like this? Kajiya thought back to one piece she had in Animo before she had met Rosa—she hadn't really eaten that piece so much as consumed it in one bite. She pulled the meat away from her snout and slurped up the strings that hung out of her mouth. Either way, it was still absolutely delicious!

"So," she said as she joined Gaorun by the fire, "when do you think they'll figure it out?"

Gaorun gave a small shrug as he chewed, then swallowed. "Well, I think Ainee's starting to pick up on it. She's laying it on pretty thick."

Kajiya nodded. "They both are."

"Weirdos." Gaorun popped the rest of his breakfast into his mouth, and turned around to start packing up with Onta on his heels.

"Totally." Kajiya took another bite, ripping off some more of the meat fibres as she turned to join him.

* * *

Kajiya breathed out, wiping the sweat from her forehead. After spending so long nearly freezing her tail off in the mountains, the sensation and idea of *heat* was completely foreign to her. But here she was, sweating her way through the jungle. Koiyan's yellow light filtered through the trees, but Kajiya felt almost as if the thick canopy didn't even exist. It had never gotten this hot in Mirabilia! At least, not that she could tell. Perhaps the juxtaposition of Animo's mountains straight into the jungle was playing tricks with her mind, making her think it was hotter than it actually was. Perhaps not.

"You coming?" Resurge's voice rang out from far up ahead.

"I'll be right there, don't wait for me!" Kajiya called out, readjusting the bag on her back for the umpteenth time since setting out that morning. By now, Koiyan was high in the sky, and it was almost noon.

Kajiya broke into a heavy jog to catch up with the others; Resurge was checking the map. She breathed out as she reached them, and in spite of her words, she was secretly glad for the chance to take a break and lean up against a tree.

"…and if that's the ridge where we camped out," Resurge was saying, "then we should be somewhere in this vicinity."

Gaorun, who was looking over the dark blue fea's shoulder, nodded in agreement. "Then we should be really close to Palinda's territory."

Kajiya looked over to the right, where they would be travelling. She blinked. The scene didn't look very green. She squinted, yes… yes! There, in between the far trees, were stalks of tall white-yellow grass that Kajiya couldn't recognize!

"I see it!" she burst, pointing. "That white grass—those are Palinda's fields right?"

Everyone turned to see what she was talking about.

Gaorun squinted. "I think it's called aimaia, but yeah, that's it."

Kajiya let out an excited squeal. "Well, what are you waiting around for? Let's get going!"

Resurge grabbed Kajiya's shoulder as she attempted to start for the forest's edge. "Slow down there, Kajiya. We don't know what's out there. There might be some wild pavoki or kivolta. We'd best take this slow."

Kajiya folded her arms and grumbled unintelligibly under her voice; she hated it when her brother had a valid point. Which was almost always. Nevertheless, Kajiya managed to keep up with the rest of them as they walked the last few legs through the forest. She even managed to stay at the front, and keep a slightly-faster than normal pace, in hopes of speeding them up. However, everyone kept to their pace from before, leaving Kajiya rather impatient. She could barely restrain her excitement at finally reaching Palinda's prairie land.

The first step out of the moist jungle and onto the dry baked earth filled her with joy. She pushed the aimaia stalks over to the side, admiring the way that brittle grass could grow out of the ground so straight, despite the small breezes that swayed them. Kajiya snapped the top off of one with her fingers, and cradled its kernels in her hands. They looked like little beads. She stuffed them into her yellow shoulder bag—if she ever felt like making something, they would make for an interesting accessory. She probably never would, but at the very least, the kernels made a nice souvenir.

Then, as the others finally escaped the depths of the forest, Kajiya looked up, and was dumbstruck. The four feas stood at the edge of the field in awe; it seemed to go on forever. The field dipped in a gentle valley, and the sun above was clear in a cloudless sky. The sheer vastness took Kajiya's breath away. Kajiya couldn't even see the forest on the other side. Assuming there was a forest on the other side.

Onta let out a happy yap, and dove headfirst into the fronds of the aimaia. Kajiya lost sight of the orange quadruped at once, and only the twitching stalks betrayed her presence in the grass.

Kajiya smiled as the creature yapped every now and again, more than content just to stand back and watch her frolic now that they had reached the grasslands, but Resurge plowed ahead.

"We need to keep moving," he said simply. "Turten won't wait forever."

Kajiya's eyes fell; yes, she knew their mission

was important, but—she shook her head. Resurge was right, and that was that. Her grip tightened on the straps of her pack, and she steeled herself for the journey ahead. They still had a long way to go.

Her feet hit the ground in rhythm as the others began to pad after her and Resurge. Gaorun gave a low whistle, and Onta returned to him, looking up expectantly. He held out his hand, and the onti jumped up onto his shoulders.

Kajiya soon found herself growing to dislike the aimaia stalks. Any stalk that had been previously broken lay on the ground, seemingly just waiting to poke an unsuspecting foot. While Kajiya's feet had toughened considerably in the mountains, the short stabbing pains that came with each footstep were enough to make her bite her own cheek to keep from crying out. How the others were putting up with it so silently, she would never know.

Every now and again, they would come to large flat patches, where the aimaia had been downtrodden, or even seemingly eaten. Kajiya looked around when they reached the third large patch of flattened grass. Surely anfa couldn't have caused this much damage? Kajiya knew that there weren't too many anfa living out in the prairie, and she wasn't particularly sure she would recognize one if she saw it. She remembered once going to the market in Mirabilia, where some traders from Palinda were making exchanges. The anfa pelts there had confused her greatly—while the anfa from Mirabilia were a light brown-tan colour, with white spots on their backs and sloping stripes on their necks and legs to help them blend into the trees, the anfa pelts the Palinda traders had offered were almost a light gold-brown in colour, with strange white vertical striations. They were perfect, Kajiya now realized, to blend in with the aimaia.

But even so, as they stopped to examine one of the bare expanses, Kajiya realized that the area was far too wide for anfa to have flattened the grass. Anfa were notorious for their small hooves, and, as she looked at the ground, Kajiya spotted a wide cloven hoof print. Clearly, whatever had caused this was not an anfa.

Kajiya put a hand to her mouth in thought; could it have been the work of pavoki? Kajiya hadn't heard much of the plains-creatures, except that they were quite a bit bigger than taics.

"We should keep going," Resurge's voice broke through Kajiya's thoughts. "I want to at least reach that cluster of trees over there before nightfall," he said, pointing to a clump of green and blue on the left in the distance.

Kajiya nodded reluctantly, and was bending down to pick up her pack when a strange sound came to her ears. She stood at once, ears flicking every which direction as she tried to pinpoint the sound's source. Around her, she could see the rest of the group doing the same thing. Kajiya widened her stance the way that Sarin had taught her. Perhaps she would actually get to use some of the fighting skills he had imparted to her. Her hands stiffened, and she made sure her claws were bare.

Ice began to course through her veins, and again Kajiya was caught off guard by its fickleness. While she was still at full power, it was nowhere as powerful as it had been when she had stood in front of the Animo Assembly. It really did have a mind of its own. Or, at least, something did.

Kajiya brought her attention back to the crisis at hand. The strange sound, a weird combination of yap and growl, with the occasional arf thrown in, was getting louder, and still seemed to come from everywhere. Suddenly, Kajiya realized that whatever the creatures that were approaching were, there was a whole pack of them.

Her red eyes darted back and forth as she tried to spot the creatures above the grass, but there were no signs of them. Then an idea struck her, and she turned her attention to the grass itself. Sure enough, the white stalks were rustling in a pattern that no wind could create naturally. Kajiya readied herself. They were upon her.

Chapter 3: Talk and Action

The creatures jumped out from the grass without hesitation, and Kajiya caught a glimpse of one as she smacked it down to the ground, magic giving her hit more force than her tired body should have been able to muster.

The creature was a quadruped like Onta, but had a very long snout with a low thin jawline. Its two large ears curved towards the middle of its head, and seemed to be fixed in place. They didn't even move when it growled at her.

Kajiya stiffened, and stared back into its golden eyes, letting out a snarl of her own as she did so.

The creature's fur was tanned and golden, and it almost blended into the dirt where it stood. There were thick black stripes running down its body vertically from the spine to the stomach. Each pair of stripes met at the stomach, and tapered to a point.

The creature lunged for Kajiya again, and a second appeared out of nowhere. The two were almost identical, but the stripes were slightly different. The second had a few horizontal stripes just above its paws. The toes of its paws were a darker colour, and the colour continued up the back of the paw, fading the higher it got until it disappeared altogether.

Thick black claws clinked against a rock, and Kajiya looked at them with fear for a moment, then realized that the claws would have been dulled from the dry dirt of the plains. Kajiya took a step back—straight into Gaorun. She gasped, and looked behind her; everyone had been gathered together by the pack.

Even Onta was hissing from where she stood on Gaorun's head. Kajiya looked around, there had to be at least eight of the creatures! They were cornered.

There was nothing left to do but fight. Resurge swung his broadsword in one hand, and Gaorun bared his claws. Even Ainee had created a small fireball with which to defend herself. Kajiya flicked her tail, and her crystalline bell rang out clearly in the air.

She was just about to signal for the group to go on the offensive, when a loud whoop filled the air. Even the creatures turned to look. Another creature— no, two—shot out of the aimaia, but this time, they attacked their own kind! Kajiya blinked in surprise, and looked up. There, following the creatures out of the tall grass, were feas! They had light-coloured pelts, and carried light-blue bludgeoning sticks. They hooted and hollered, and the creatures started to back off. The feas flicked their long-furred tails, creating a small whooshing sound, and the creatures retreated further. They hit their sticks against the ground, and moved aggressively towards the creatures while their companion creatures darted forward and bit the attacking ones, barking the whole time.

Kajiya blinked, then narrowed her eyes and added her own voice to theirs. The ones closest to her shot her an inquiring glance, but they didn't object. Kajiya thrashed her tail, and her bell willingly gave a cacophony with which to drive the creatures back. She clapped her hands, and Gaorun joined her. Resurge and Ainee fell in suit, and soon, the creatures had backed all the way to the grass, tails between their legs. Finally, the creatures gave one last snarl, turned, and ran.

Kajiya couldn't help but breathe a sigh of relief

as the grass trails they left behind fell still. She leaned back, putting one hand to her chest.

"Thank you," she said, not surprised to find her voice a little hoarse as the light-coloured feas turned to her.

The main fea, an exceedingly pale cream fea with yellow stripes turned to her, only to stop dead. He raised a trembling hand to point at Kajiya's left shoulder.

"M-Magik!" he cried out in shock.

Kajiya stiffened, then looked at her shoulder; right. She had totally forgotten—according to the report that Turten gave the other tribes—she was dead. And that meant that there should be no female magiks.

The band of feas fell to their knees, and Kajiya took a step back.

"We are so sorry we could not come to your aid sooner!" the pale cream fea blurted, his long yellow locks falling over his face in what appeared to be shame.

His companions all nodded in order.

Kajiya held her hands up uneasily. "I-it's fine. You still saved our lives."

They didn't move, and Kajiya pivoted to the others, who all shrugged in turn. She turned back to the light-coloured feas, and hoped a more casual question would get them back to her feet. It always felt wrong to be bowed to.

"What were those things anyway?" She eyed the two that had remained, the two that had fought alongside them.

The cream fea lifted his head. "Kivolta. They've been getting bold lately." He glanced at the two that Kajiya was eyeing. "You don't need to fear them though—we've completely domesticated 'em."

Onta leapt down from Gaorun's head, and stared at one of the kivoltas in the face. She looked slightly frightened. It looked like it didn't really care, but was slightly intrigued by the vibrant creature.

"They're hunting aids, right?" Gaorun said, stepping after Onta cautiously.

The cream fea nodded. "Yes, the one your onti is looking at is Kip, and the other is Volta. They're mates."

Kajiya nodded as Kip lowered his snout as to look at Onta better with his crystalline blue eyes. The onti stiffened, then slowly backed towards Gaorun, lowering her tail. Gaorun swept her off her feet, and brought her back to his shoulder. Onta looked rather relieved, and nuzzled him, scurrying from shoulder to shoulder. The cream fea stood, and the others followed suit, allowing Kajiya to breathe just a little easier.

"It's a hunting aid too, no?" the cream fea asked casually, holding out his hand so that the onti might become familiar with his scent.

Gaorun nodded, crossing his arms with a smug smirk. "*She's* a good one too."

"*Ahem.*" Ainee raised an eyebrow as she held a fist to her mouth. "Sorry to interrupt, but who are you again?"

The cream fea jumped a little. "Did we not introduce ourselves?" He bowed to Kajiya again, and her shoulders rose uncomfortably as he spoke. "I am Coballen, and these are my hunters," he said as he rose began to point. "Pato," he pointed to a tan fea with red stripes, "Napel," a pastel purple fea with blue stripes, "Jivo," a light-and-dark green fea, "and finally," he pointed to the last one, a grey fea with grey-green stripes, "Tiu."

Kajiya nodded to each one in turn. There was no way she was going to remember all their names. She just knew it.

Coballen turned back to her. "Now, dear magik, if perhaps you would be so kind as to enlighten us as to your identity?" he paused. "You couldn't be Kajiya of Mirabilia, could you? We received word that she had been killed." He turned back to the others, and they all nodded in agreement.

Kajiya let a small laugh. "Well, you heard wrong."

All attention turned back to her, and Kajiya took a step back from the intensity of their stares.

Fortunately, Resurge stepped up to take the reins of the conversation. "We have been travelling for quite some time," he began, his voice unwavering, "and it is getting late. Perhaps you would be willing to show us where a good campsite would be?"

The hunters smirked, and the green one, Jivo, brushed his knuckles against his tan vest. "Oh, we can do much better than that. Come! Palinda will be glad to host a magik."

Kajiya's heart skipped a beat. "Pa-Palinda's near here?!" she cried out as the pale feas turned and started towards a seemingly random point in the aimaia.

Gaorun stepped forward, seeming equally excited. "How far?"

Kajiya grabbed her pack, and ran up the front of the group as Ainee and Resurge fell in step. Her heart soared. Palinda! Yet another tribe that she would finally get to see. She couldn't help but wonder what sorts of places the feas of Palinda lived in. All she really knew about them was that they were nomadic, never living in the same place twice.

Coballen turned to them with a smile. "Not far at all. We're just on our way back from an expedition."

Gaorun's expression hardened as he parted the aimaia. "How long?"

"Three days," the grey one, Tiu, chipped in without missing a beat.

Gaorun's expression turned to that of relief, and Kajiya quietly raised an eyebrow.

What is it? she asked with magic.

He glanced her way, then turned back to the Palindian feas. "Is Jiblin still with the tribe?"

Coballen blinked, then shrugged, turning back to the rest of his troupe. "Far as I know, why?"

Kajiya's eyes widened. Jiblin was Palinda's magik. And if he was still with the tribe—then Royalin's messenger hadn't found them yet. And that meant that there was a chance she could speak to him *before* Turten got to him! Make him realize the danger Turten was putting all of them in. The Assembly wouldn't start without him—and she could go with him! Prove Turten's lies and have him… Kajiya blinked, a sudden unease coming over her. Just what *was* she going to do with Turten once she had exposed him? Was his punishment even her decision? No, that would probably go to her father.

Resurge's voice brought Kajiya out of her thoughts. "We need to speak with him, that's all."

Coballen nodded, his long-furred tail swishing from side to side. Kajiya watched the movement for a moment. The cream fea's fur was remarkably fine, and in spite of the heat, he seemed to be perfectly at ease.

Kajiya wiped the sweat from her brow; she still loved the cool shadows of the jungle. She cast her thoughts back to Animo; the feas there had two layers of fur to protect them from the cold air. *Maybe we're just really good at adapting,* she thought to herself.

The two feas at the front, the purple one and the green one, stopped and started to move a bunch of aimaia stalks that had been laid over top of something.

"Sorry," Coballen said, "we can't really come back to the tribe empty-handed after three days of hunting."

The tan fea's voice seemed to come from nowhere. "No evidence of scavenging, Coballen!"

"Great! Good work, Pato. Think you can carry it all?"

Pato raised his head above the displaced grass. "That 'you' better have been plural." His ears were pinned to the back of his skull as his eyes narrowed.

Coballen laughed. "Of course, of course! Tiu, Napel! Help the poor guy out!"

The grey fea and the purple fea smirked, and leapt into action. Pretty soon, the creature's body was completely uncovered, and Kajiya had to stare. It was unlike anything she had ever seen before.

It had short bulky legs, each with a cloven hoof. The creature's fur was a dark dusty brown, with a darker stripe following its spine and sternum. Its face was long, but flat, and there was a pale grey blaze that went all the way to its chin fur. It had two small anfa-like horns on the top of its head, and directly underneath were two ears that would stick out horizontal to the ground if it were standing. A thick mane of fur came from its face to its shoulder. The rest of its fur was very light and sparse. Its tail was long-furred as well, and reminded Kajiya of the Palindian's tails.

She twisted her head to see it better, to see what it might have looked like standing. From what she could tell, the creature's shoulder came up higher than its head by at least half a tail-length. If it were to stand beside her, she would probably be able to *just* see over it. It was massive! She could only imagine how much it weighed.

"What is that?" she wondered aloud.

"That," Coballen said as the green fea jumped in to help his companions move the creature onto a sled they had hid nearby, "is a pavoki."

A breath left Kajiya's lips, and if she knew how to whistle, she would have. However, Gaorun did it for her.

"Must be a lot of meat on those things."

Coballen nodded, resting his fists on his hips. "Best meat in all of Mysterium too. Anfa's nice, but you ain't had nothing till you've tasted pavoki. Of course, we can't eat all of 'em. They're great traveling animals too."

Kajiya's ears perked, and she turned to the cream fea as the others finally managed to get the pavoki on the sled. "Travelling animal?"

Coballen laughed. "Of course! You foreigners, you wouldn't understand. But let me ask you, how do you think we get our wagons and tribe across this here plain?"

Kajiya's shoulders rose. "By walking?" she guessed.

Coballen nearly split with laughter. "Of course not! We've got ourselves a herd of pavoki that we keep all to ourselves. We've trained 'em to pull our wagons, and every now and again, we even ride them. It's quite fun actually."

Kajiya laughed, drawing back. "And they don't get creeped out by the fact that you eat others of their species?"

Coballen shook his head. "Nah, they ain't that smart. They're great for food and for work, but if you need brains, then," he reached down and gave Kip a pat on the head, "a kivolta's the animal to have. They're smarter than some feas I know." He gave Kip a large mussing, and the creature leaned into it. "Why, just the other day, we were goin' along all right, when this anfa, frightened as heck, came running at us, bucking 'n chargin'. I thought we were going ta be killed for sure."

Kajiya's eyes narrowed; she wasn't exactly sure, but it sounded to her as if Coballen was slipping into the same accent that some of the people in Animo had had. Why would he try to hide it? Or was he just trying to act formal for her in the beginning? Sarin had told her when she asked about it, that in Animo those feas who worked for a living, and were considered by some to be 'the lower class,' were usually the ones with the accent. Simply, they were too lazy to pronounce everything, and often fell into habits such as cutting off the last sound in a word. Those who then became warriors, and thus had to rely on precise communication, often had to take lessons to relearn the 'proper' way to say things. Because of this, most of the feas who spoke without the accent considered themselves to be 'high class,' and every now and again, when an official visited, many 'low class' feas would attempt to drop the accent in order to impress them.

Kajiya thought it was all a bunch of taic-feathers. Did it really matter if they spoke with an accent or not? She liked the way it sounded, but didn't think she'd ever be able to force her voice to follow its strange idiosyncrasies. While Kajiya did understand why feas who naturally spoke that way had to change their voice in order to become a warrior, she highly suspected that if there were more of the so-called 'lower class' than the 'high class' in the Animo warriors, Sai would be more than happy to make it the other way around, and change it so that everyone had to learn the accent. Personally, Kajiya thought it would be much more effective for them all to learn Sarin's language of hand signs. Surprise was always a good thing to have in battle, and the brown fea's silent communication was perfect for this. Unfortunately, it was probably easier to add a sound back in than it was to learn an entirely new language.

"Next thing I know," Coballen's voice shattered Kajiya's thoughts, "there goes Kip! Barkin' and growlin' up a storm! I was sure he was gonna get trampled—but he runs right past that poor anfa, and scares off the pack that was chasin' 'er! We managed to net the anfa pretty," he pointed to lump of fur that was being tied down next to the pavoki carcass, "and I'll be darned if that weren't the same pack that attacked you, now that I think about it. Well, they won't be comin' back anytime soon!" he laughed.

Napel turned to them from where he was finishing tying the final knot on the sled. "We're ready!"

Coballen nodded, and walked over to where the rest of them were. He placed his bludgeoning stick in the sled with the other four, and grabbed the rope that came from the sled's handles. Now that she was looking more closely, Kajiya could see that it had been raised up on two points, and would go smoothly over the ground, but leave a very distinct path in the aimaia to be followed. She looked out over the tall grass uneasily. What if they were being followed? She shook her head, no one who meant her harm even knew she was alive. Her gut darkened; no, the spiede king knew she was alive. But... She lifted her eyes up, where the yellow sun beat down and the sky burned blue. He could not follow her here.

Kajiya looked back down; if she was unable to stop the spiedes, then Palinda would be the safest tribe to stay in.

The rope on the sled pulled taut, and Kajiya looked up. Each of the pale feas had a piece of the rope in hand, and there was one kivolta holding the end of each rope.

"Let us help you!" Kajiya blurted.

Resurge was already moving towards the line with fewer feas, and Gaorun was headed towards the other. Kajiya bolted over to the line with Resurge before Coballen could protest.

"No, Magik, we've got this. You don't need ta—" he said, eyes wide.

A gentle laugh came from Ainee as she grabbed Gaorun's line. "You clearly don't know Kajiya." She sent the vibrant blue fea a kind glance and small smile. "Once she's set her mind to something, there's no stopping her."

Kajiya grinned. "That's funny, I could say the same about you," she retorted.

Ainee pulled harder. "Yeah?"

Kajiya dug her feet into the ground,

summoning the ice to her veins once more. "Yeah!"

The cart started to move, faster and faster. Soon, they were flying over the field, and a column of smoke became visible on the horizon ahead.

"That must be where camp is tonight!" Tiu's voice was breathless, but joyful, as he pointed it out.

Kajiya's back was burning from the combined weight of the pack and pulling the giant sled, but she put out an extra spurt of energy nonetheless. They were almost there! She could taste victory in her mouth. Turten's plan would be revealed to someone who could actually *do* something about it—tonight!

Chapter 4: Bonfire

Kajiya could hardly contain her excitement as she walked the last few tail-lengths into Palinda's camp. There were tons of feas milling about, and as the group entered, more than a few stopped to stare. Kajiya didn't pay them any mind though, and instead looked past them to the wagons and tents that littered the area. The tents appeared to be made out of various hides, and were held up with straight sticks that stuck out of the roof. A flap opened to reveal the interior, which was a cozy place, filled with mats, mattresses and other knick-knacks. Perhaps this was where they slept and lived. Kajiya thought that they looked very cool, and longed to go into one so that she could relish in its shade. But, she turned her attention elsewhere; Jiblin needed to be warned!

She started to look around again, and this time, her eyes settled on the wagons. They reminded Kajiya of the food carts in Animo, but much larger. They were set up on thick wooden wheels with sturdy spokes, so that they were nearly a tail-length off the ground. The wheel itself looked like it would come up to Kajiya's waist if she were to stand beside it. The wagons were covered with aimaia which had been finely woven into a solid material. Kajiya highly suspected that a large amount of strengthening magic had been applied to the weave to prevent it from fraying, and the separate aimaia stalks from coming apart. She wouldn't have even been surprised to find that the aimaia had been magically fused together in order to create such a large weave. Kajiya managed to catch a glimpse inside a couple of the wagons; one appeared to be used for storage, and lay nearly empty, revealing bent wood ribbing that gave the aimaia a form to adhere to, while the other appeared to be someone's home, housing a kitchen, bed and table.

No matter where she looked though, the feas were happy. There was no tension like there had been in Animo—but then again, these feas weren't under attack by spiedes. Yet. Kajiya's face fell. How long were these feas going to stay happy? If Turten had his way…

Kajiya shook her head; he *wasn't* going to have his way. She would stop him. No matter what the cost!

Finally, Coballen stopped at a large wagon with a wooden-plank door. The door was covered with a multitude of colours, mainly red and pink, and had a cutesy but elegant design carved into it.

"This 'ere is where Jiblin and Emera live," he said as he walked up the two wooden steps to the door.

"Emera?" Ainee repeated.

Coballen nodded. "Yeah, Jiblin's wife an' *my* sister," he added with a touch of pride as he knocked on the door.

Kajiya smiled, and breathed in deeply. Blood pounded in her ears as she waited, and she clenched the straps of her pack tightly. A sound came from inside, and the wagon shifted.

The door opened to reveal a slightly pudgy pale green-yellow fea with long blonde hair that curled at the ends. She had two blonde dots for eyebrows, and kind hospitable violet eyes. A stripe came off her left eye, and she had one stripe on each shoulder. The fea wore a light long sleeved–anfa hide dress which revealed the tops of her shoulders, and went down to her mid-thigh. She had two stripes on each thigh and two across her shins. In the centre of her chest, just under her collarbone, the dress had a triangle-shaped notch, and was held together with cross-stitched brown thread that Kajiya had no doubt was spun from pavoki fur. Over that, she wore a white apron with Palinda's tribal symbol, woven in yellow across the chest. The apron narrowed to a point, coming to just below her dress.

Palinda's symbol looked to Kajiya to be a leaf connected by the horizon to the sun, which had three sunrays coming off of it at different angles. It reminded Kajiya of her own green symbol, which was woven into the white loin-cloth she wore over her pants.

"Coballen! How was the hunt?" the fea greeted cheerfully, her voice strong, but with a touch of softness.

"It was good, Emera," Coballen said with a nod, "but that's not why I'm 'ere."

Emera turned, seeming to notice for the first time that she had an audience. Her eyes lingered on Kajiya's shoulder, and Kajiya felt her fur prickle uncomfortably. The confusion in Emera's eyes turned to joy however, and she stepped out of her wagon.

"Well I'll be!" she said. "Ta what honour do we owe yar visit, Magik?"

Kajiya was holding the straps of her bag so tightly she felt like she was going to snap them in half, "We need to speak to Jiblin right away!" she said, urgency, nervousness and excitement overwhelming her.

Emera's smile turned apologetic. "Well, that'd be a very hard thing ta do, seein' as he's not 'ere."

"What?!" Kajiya hissed in disbelief, and her

grip on the bag loosened with her shock.

She cast a glance to Coballen, but he looked just as surprised as her.

The female fea placed her hands on her hips, shaking her head as she continued, "Sorry 'bout that. Jiblin got summoned ta a Grand Assembly right after Coballen an' his team set out. He's been gone for almost two days already."

Kajiya's face fell, and her ears dipped behind her head. They had been so close!

"But if you need anything, jus' ask me. Palinda's always ready to help a traveller. Now," her voice turned serious, "may I ask your name? You couldn't be—"

"Kajiya," Kajiya interrupted sheepishly. "I'm afraid I am."

Emera went silent, and only her flicking tail tip betrayed her thoughtfulness. Kajiya glanced nervously at the others, not really knowing what to do or say. Fortunately, Emera decided to break the silence for her.

"You've travelled a long way," she said, then looked up at the sky, where Koiyan was starting to set. "Why don't you stay with us tonight? I'm curious to hear all about your journey."

Kajiya shook her head. "I don't think we should."

The others cast her curious looks, but Kajiya ignored them, instead looking up at Emera.

"We need to speak with Jiblin. A terrible catastrophe awaits all the tribes if we don't!" she blurted, tail flicking as her bell rang out.

Emera blinked. "What do you mean?"

Kajiya gulped; did she really have to explain

this all again? Fortunately Ainee stepped in for her.

"It's a very long story," she said, her own purple tail flicking. "But the long-short of it is that the Grand Assembly that Jiblin was summoned to is nothing more than a front for a certain power-hungry fea who wishes to enslave all women."

Emera's eyes widened, then narrowed. "That is a very serious accusation. And it would certainly be a catastrophe for the tribes, where is your proof?"

Kajiya sighed. "We don't have time for this," she hissed partially to herself.

Every second they spent here was one more when Jiblin could be getting closer and closer to the Grand Assembly. One more second that Turten could be manipulating feas to side with him. One second closer to when all feas needed to fear for their lives.

"Kajiya." Resurge's voice broke into her thoughts. "Look at the sky. It's getting dark. Midyan will rise soon." He stepped forward. "Who did Jiblin leave in charge of the tribe? What we have to say is not just for any ears."

Emera let out a small laugh. "Every time, I swear."

Resurge raised an eyebrow, but remained silent.

The green fea's mouth rose in a smile. "Why, me of course."

It took a moment for the shock to settle in. Kajiya looked over at Ainee; a *woman* in charge of the tribe?! That was unheard of in Mirabilia! Unheard of in Animo! In fact, Kajiya was the first female to ever be marked as a magik, so she had thought that she would also be the first female to ever lead a tribe. And here was Emera, not a magik, but his wife, and *she* was in charge?! Kajiya's jaw gaped, and Ainee broke out into a stunned smile. Even Resurge and Gaorun looked surprised.

A booming laugh rang out from Emera. "Y'all should see the looks on yar faces!"

Coballen joined her with a gentle chuckle, "Riiighht," he said. "I keep on forgettin' how *backwards* the other tribes are." He nudged his sister with an elbow. "Can you imagin'? Not lettin' women do any of the important things? I dunno how the tribe would get along without 'cha!"

Ainee stepped forward, tail bristling. "What's that supposed to mean?"

Emera held out her hands, attempting to contain her laughter. "Well dear, 'ere in Palinda, we do things a little differently. In the other tribes, some men protect the village, an' others go out to hunt an' bring the food on back, right?"

Kajiya nodded reluctantly.

Emera smiled. "Well, 'ere in Palinda, we don't have that luxury. The pavoki herds move with the seasons, and they move too far for us ta find one place and stay ta it. We have to chase them around, and even if we didn't need to, we still would. It's the way we've lived for generations."

Coballen broke into the narrative now. "But, well, you all seen how hard it is to *move* a pavoki—I can only let you imagine how difficult it is ta *catch* one, let alone kill it!"

Kajiya's fur rose as she imagined standing before the giant creature. Sure, she could kill it easily with magic if she needed to but... Not everyone was as skilled with magic as she was.

Coballen continued, "Oft'times a whole herd o'

us'll set out to catch 'em, and there won't be but four boys in the camp. Our women have to run the whole shebang."

Emera nodded, tail swishing. "We have ta milk the pavoki, feed the kivoltas that didn't go along, *defend* against any stray pavoki or kivolta silly enough ta try ta attack camp, and if things start gettin' rough, or there ain't enough aimaia for the pavoki, it's up ta us to move camp to a new spot."

Gaorun and Resurge nodded in unison, assimilating the knowledge seamlessly. Ainee looked like she was about to start dancing with joy. Kajiya still had no idea how to react. In a way, she was proud of Palinda for treating its women as competent, but in another, it seemed strange after so many years of watching the women of her tribe be pushed aside. An old darkness came to her stomach. The darkness that had come when Rotari had told them that the second rule of magic, that a woman's body was too weak to handle anything but low-level healing magic was false. Kajiya had always thought that her magik's mark made her special. Gave her the ability to do things that no other woman, or man, could. That no other fea could. Both Rotari's revelation and now, Emera's words, took that away. She wasn't special. Maybe it was just a fur marking. Nothing else.

No. You are special.

Kajiya stiffened slightly, but tried not to betray her surprise too much. She hadn't really heard the words, not from the world outside, or from inside her head like when Sarin or Ainee spoke to her silently. It was more of a feeling. A notion. Could it have been Rotari? Kajiya's heart filled with dread. What if the giant stone creature had found a way to communicate over the distance? Kajiya blinked; no, the communication would be, at best, one way. And she doubted even the blakeslee could find the strength to cast her voice that far. After all, it took both Kajiya and Ainee to be able to cast the sight and listening spell that they used to spy on Turten. So what had it been?

Emera's voice tugged at Kajiya's mind, bringing her back to the present. She sounded serious, in spite of the small smirk that had permeated her expression.

"But all that aside, I think y'all have a long story ta tell me."

*   *   *

Emera's violet eyes grew troubled. "No storyteller would dare make up a farfetched tale like that. Of course, that means y'all mus' be tellin' the truth. And that means that we are all in great danger." She moved over to the window above her kitchen counter, for the whole group had gone inside her wagon to talk.

It was a rather homey place, with a small rectangular table and booth seats. She had given them all pavoki milk to quench their dried throats, and as Kajiya clutched the wooden cup, she looked up at Emera. The pale green fea was staring at her tribemates. Clearly, she cared about them as much as Kajiya cared about her own tribe.

The idea stung at Kajiya's mind, and she cast her thoughts back to Mirabilia. How *were* her tribemates? Were they safe? Had Turten already passed his law there? Kajiya shook her head discreetly to herself; no, her father wouldn't allow it. And there was no way that he knew the purpose of the Grand

Assembly. She wouldn't, couldn't believe he did.

Emera's tail swished as she turned back to her guests. "I do not believe that my husband will stand for such a law ta be passed, but the spiedes provide a much more real threat. I will start preparing Palinda for such an attack at once. When they come, they will find Palinda more than ready," she promised.

She looked back outside the window, then smiled a little. "But, that's for tomorrow. For tonight, we have a bonfire planned, and I would be more than happy if you'd join us in our little celebration."

Gaorun's ears perked. "What are you celebrating?"

Emera leaned back against the counter. "Why, a good hunt of course. Coballen wasn't the only hunting group that jus' got back." Coballen beamed at his sister's words, and she continued, "We're ta have a feast tonight."

Kajiya shifted uneasily in her seat. "But, Emera, the sooner we leave, the sooner we can warn Jiblin about Turten. I don't want to waste—"

"Jiblin won't be travellin' at night, an' neither should you. He's only got a two day head start, I'm sure you'll catch up ta 'im in no time. Besides, what good is it if you exhaust yourselves before you even get a chance to stop that fiend? I won't take no for an answer, ya'll be spending the night in Palinda, and ya'll enjoy it too!" she said with a good-natured growl complimenting her smile.

Kajiya smiled weakly, but Resurge stood up from the table, and gave Emera a courteous bow. "We appreciate your hospitality."

Gaorun and the others followed suit, and Onta popped her head out from the open cupboard that she had climbed into and gave a small yap. Emera let out a little laugh and placed the onti back where she belonged, in Gaorun's arms.

"Now go on, Coballen will show you to the guest tents." She paused. "I do hope they're set up. Do you remember if they're set up?" she asked Coballen.

The cream fea shrugged. "I'm sure I can get someone to start setting them up if they aren't."

Emera nodded. "See ta it then." She turned back to the other feas. "For now, you can just leave yar things here; I'll see that they get put in the right place."

Ainee nodded, then appeared to be struck by an idea. "Actually, Emera," she began, "we have too many things to feasibly carry with us—it's really hampered our progress."

Kajiya nodded, catching onto Ainee's idea joyfully. When they were leaving Animo, they hadn't actually needed much, but the feas there had insisted that they take many different pelts, pans, cutlery and other things.

"Perhaps we can leave some of the stuff we don't need with you?" Kajiya interrupted, thinking gleefully of how easy it would be to travel without the stuffed-to-the-brim-and-then-some pack on her back.

Emera nodded. "Of course, we have quite a few wagons that are devoted just ta storage—but don't be surprised if what you leave isn't there when you get back. The stuff in there is fair game for anyone."

Kajiya nodded enthusiastically. "That's fine."

Resurge turned to them. "All the things we brought from home are to be kept of course."

"And we'll have to keep all my herbs…" Ainee began.

"We can sort this all out later," Gaorun interrupted. "Right now, my feet are hurting, and I don't know about you, but I'd like to just get some food, and some sleep. We'll probably be up early anyway."

Emera dipped her head in agreement, and Coballen stood from the chair he was sitting in.

"Well," he said, "I'd better get ta showin' ya yar new home."

Kajiya rose, and followed the cream fea outside, and the others followed suit. Coballen led them down paths in the aimaia to two empty tents that were just being finished. Pato and Napel were just tying down the last few hides with magic.

Pato noticed their arrival first, and waved a tan hand in greeting. "We thought y'all might like a place ta stay tonight!"

Napel smiled. "Can't believe 'em women forgot to set up the guest tents," he shrugged. "But then again, we don't get many guests do we?"

Pato shook his head. "Well, I bet your'a hankering to get some rest. We'll be off."

Napel nodded, and they started towards the main section of Palinda's camp. "But I reckon we'll be seein' ya at the feast?"

Gaorun nodded as his stomach rumbled. "I wouldn't miss it for the world! I expect you all to teach me the traps you use to catch pavoki!" he called out as they passed him.

Pato laughed. "It ain't easy stuff, but if your'a willing ta listen, I'm sure Tiu would be happy ta tell ya all about it!"

Napel turned around and started to walk backwards, cupping his hands around his mouth as he called back to Gaorun, "The hard part will be when ya want him ta stop! Once you get Tiu started, hoo boy!"

Gaorun laughed boisterously, and gave the pair a final wave. Kajiya smiled with a giggle. Something told her that Gaorun would certainly enjoy himself tonight—although with less sleep than he probably wanted.

"Are you two coming?" Ainee's sharp voice pierced Kajiya's ears, and the vibrant blue fea turned to her friend.

"Yes, just give us a moment!" Kajiya hissed back with a smile. "And to think, you once called *me* impatient."

Ainee rolled her eyes. "We need to decide what to keep and what to leave here. I would like to do this *before* the feast. I'm starved," she admitted, flicking her tail as she went back into the tent.

Kajiya's stomach grumbled, and she laughed sheepishly. They hadn't eaten since before the encounter with the kivolta pack, and she was starting to feel it. Nonetheless, Kajiya knew that Ainee was right. If they wanted to be able to leave as soon as possible, they needed to lighten their loads tonight.

"We shouldn't need too many furs," Resurge was saying as Kajiya walked in.

He and Ainee were both sitting on the floor, and Resurge was drawing in the dirt with a claw. Kajiya looked around; the tent was rather simple, there were four aimaia mattresses on the ground, and what looked to be a small fire pit in the middle. Light streamed into the tent from the hole in the top, and Kajiya joined Resurge and Ainee on the floor.

"…we'll have to keep all the meat of course," Ainee said, reaching over and making a mark on the floor. "And my herbs are a must."

"The same with water and my sword. And Gaorun's trapping supplies, but it'll be up to him to decide how much he wants to keep," Resurge said.

"I was thinking I'd stick to the basics." Gaorun held the tent flap open with a hand as he stood in the doorway.

One side of the flap was pinned back, but the other was loose, and he let it fly freely as he walked into the tent and joined the others on the ground.

"We should probably keep some of those pans as well, they're really high quality."

Kajiya nodded, thinking over all the supplies they had been given in Animo. The main source of extra weight was all the furs that they had been given. They had even given them a ball of spun taic fur that they referred to as yarn. It reminded Kajiya of Rosa, and she made a mental note to stick it in her yellow-shoulder bag when she got the chance.

"Knock knock!" Coballen's voice came from outside, and Kajiya blinked in surprise.

She hadn't even seen him leave. Kajiya got up, and held the tent flap open for him and his companions, some feas that she had never seen before. Before she could get a good look at them though, they walked inside, and placed the giant green backpacks on the floor.

Coballen wiped his brow with the back of his hand, and gave a nod to the other three feas who had come with him, and they left.

"I can see why'd ya want to leave some of yar stuff 'ere—them packs are hhheaavvy!" he said. "Anything else I can help ya with?"

Resurge stood and nodded at Coballen as he

went over to the packs. "We need to sort all this stuff out."

Coballen nodded, and the pair started to take everything out of the packs while Gaorun scooted over to join them. Ainee stood and looked over their heads as Onta jumped up onto her back, then settled down on the purple fea's shoulders. Kajiya smiled and took her shoulder bag away from the other things and set it down on a mattress. Yes, it had a lot of unnecessary stuff in it, but it was *light* unnecessary stuff, and after so many weeks of carting it around the continent, Kajiya couldn't imagine being without it.

"I think we have enough food for about a week or two," Ainee said as she watched. "We should keep a few pelts in case we reach Royalin before that and have to pay for a hotel again."

Resurge nodded, and tossed some over to Gaorun. "We'll want the highest quality ones."

"Of course, just keep tossin' 'em my way," he said as he moved the furs over to one of the mattresses where he sat down to look them over.

Onta jumped down from Ainee's shoulders and onto the mattress, settling down beside Gaorun for a nap. He smiled and ruffled her fur.

Kajiya smiled, and moved over to finish his pack; with all of them working together, Kajiya suspected that the task would take half an hour at most. A strange scent began to fill her nose as they worked, and it made her mouth water. She guessed that it was probably pavoki meat. They *did* say there was a feast. Kajiya's hands started to move faster as hunger spurred her on.

"Do we still need your 'Ruina' shirt?" Ainee's voice broke into Kajiya's thoughts as she picked up the anfa-hide garment.

Kajiya looked over to see the shirt that her friend was holding. Ainee had made it for her before they entered Animo. Back then, they didn't know that the other tribes thought she was reinstated, but dead. What they did know was that the other tribes would not easily accept a banished magik, and as such, they came up with a simple but effective disguise for Kajiya—a shirt that covered her magik's mark and a new name, Ruina.

The shirt had a collar similar to her signature half-tunic, but covered her midsection completely. The sleeves were very long, and split at the forearm, allowing her more movement while still completely covering her shoulders. On the shoulders, Ainee had put faux stripes, all completely straight of course.

Kajiya nodded after a moment of thought. "Yeah. We don't have any maps of Royalin, do we?"

Resurge shook his head. "I don't believe so."

"Then we should keep it. We don't want Turten knowing we're there before we crash the Grand Assembly," a touch of sadness entered Kajiya's voice.

She didn't particularly like being 'Ruina'; the previous time, it had almost gotten her and Resurge killed because she couldn't use her full magic capabilities while in disguise. The thought of playing that 'weak female' persona again disgusted her. Especially since the females of Palinda were so strong.

Ainee just nodded, then folded the garment and set it aside in what Kajiya guessed to be the 'to-keep' pile. Soon to follow was Resurge's chirpl-skin vest with its glittering bright green scales, and several carefully chosen anfa and taic furs. Next, the tents that they used for traveling, a few blankets, pillows, two woven mattresses that could be inflated by hand or with magic and some firewood, should they be unable to procure some in the future. A couple pots and pans, and all the meat and water they had also found their way into the pile, including some plants that Onta could eat should they start running low on meat. Finally, Ainee's herbs, other medical supplies, together with Gaorun's trapping supplies and Resurge's broadsword lay on one side of the room, with a large pile of furs and excess cookware on the other side.

"And I think we're done," Resurge announced, leaning back as he stretched.

Coballen smiled. "And it sounds like the feast jus' started. Good timin'!"

A grin broke out on Kajiya's face as she placed her shoulder bag with the expertly-stashed taic yarn on the 'to-keep' pile and started outside.

Ainee was still rummaging around though. "You go on ahead, I'll catch up."

Kajiya stopped and was about to say something when Resurge grabbed Ainee's arm good-naturedly. He smiled as he pulled her to her feet.

"You've been going at it pretty hard; we *all* deserve a break. You too," he said, and Ainee looked like she was about to protest, but he narrowed his eyes with a smile. "In the words of our host, 'I won't be takin' no for an answer!'"

Ainee let out a reluctant smile, and Resurge let go of her arm.

"Fine," she said, leaning up against him slightly. "But I expect *you* to repack all of this in the morning."

Resurge's eyes widened, but Ainee was already

halfway out the door.

"Ya comin'?" she asked with a smirk, tail curling with delight as she disappeared from view.

Kajiya nearly burst out with laughter as Resurge shook his head, smiled slightly and followed. Gaorun joined her in her giggles, and picked up Onta, carrying her like a baby as he exited the tent. Coballen walked beside him, and once they were outside, Kajiya could hear the two of them start to talk about different techniques to catch anfa. The subject didn't sound particularly interesting to her, and she tuned them out.

Kajiya cast a quick glance at the 'to stay in Palinda' pile. Mostly, the things they were leaving were furs; the people of Animo were much like those in Palinda in that they wouldn't accept 'no' for an answer. They had been given far more furs than they had needed or wanted. Kajiya felt slightly bad for leaving them behind, but she was sure that the feas of Palinda would make good use of them. There were also a few lower-quality pot and pans, and the original cooking materials they had brought from home. They had been good, but now that they had some better things, it was probably best to let them go.

Her stomach grumbled, reminding her of what was really important at the moment.

"Okay, fine!" she hissed to herself, heading for the tent flap again. "I'm going, I'm going."

By this time, Midyan had almost reached its full height in the sky, joined by the four moons, and the celebration was in full swing. The giant pile of wood and aimaia that Kajiya had spotted in what she now knew to be the centre of the village had been set fire to, and the feas were having a great time dancing around it. Collapsible wooden tables and benches had been set out, and everywhere she looked, there was food! Kajiya licked her lips, grabbed an empty plate and made her way down one side of the table. There seemed to be hundreds of different dishes, and not knowing what anything was, Kajiya decided to try a little of everything. The only thing she knew for certain what it was, was a small chunk of meat she ripped off of a hearty smelling roast-pavoki leg. At least, she thought it was a pavoki leg. She didn't believe it could be anything else. After all, the single exposed bone to which the meat clung had been just a little longer than her *arm*.

She tried the meat; it was much chewier than anfa or avian meat, and didn't quite melt in her mouth the way that taic meat did, but it held a savory tang that made her want to take the whole leg for herself. Somehow, Kajiya managed to restrain herself, and only took another piece off the leg, and continued her way down the table.

"I see you've found my pavoki curry," Emera's voice came from nowhere, and Kajiya froze for a second, fur rising as golden sauce dripped from the ladle she held over her plate.

Kajiya breathed out and dumped the rest on her plate before placing the ladle back where it belonged.

"I do hope you'll enjoy it," Emera continued, ignoring Kajiya's puffed-out state. "I spent most of the afternoon using the last of the pavoki from last week's hunt for it."

Turning to her, Kajiya let a weak smile surface on her face. "I'm sure I will." She gestured with her free hand to the entire table. "Everything looks so delicious. I don't think I'll be able to try it all!" A touch of concern entered her face. "Did you make all of this?"

Emera shook her head. "Of course not. Everyone pitched in. We do after every hunt."

Kajiya lowered the plate. "Why? Doesn't it get old? I mean, parties are fun and all, but…"

One of Emera's blonde eyebrows rose. "No, it may not look ta you like there's much reason to celebrate, now particularly," she set a hand on Kajiya's shoulder, "but it's the little things that need celebration. After all, no one knows how long they're goin' ta be alive, and each day could bring the end for someone. But that's why we celebrate, because we have life for one more day. Surely that's reason enough," she added, giving Kajiya a firm pat on the back.

Kajiya barely managed to keep all of the piled-up food on her plate, and she smiled back up at Emera as the fea started off towards her tribemates. Kajiya let the smile fade from her face as she picked up a piece of meat on a small twig. Her bell rang out as her tail flicked pensively and she bit the meat off the stick. It had a sweetness to it that was unusual, but delicious. A genuine smile surfaced to Kajiya's mouth, only to fade after a moment. Emera's words had put her in a more thoughtful mood.

Kajiya sat down at the edge of the bonfire ring, where the majority of older feas were eating and talking. The younger feas of Palinda ran around the fire, jumping in rhythm to the music played by a group on the other side of the bonfire. The drum was particularly upbeat, but the sounds did not overwhelm the air, so Kajiya could still hear herself think.

Not that she was really thinking, she was just sort of sitting, chewing away thoughtlessly. But, deep down, she knew there was something she was supposed to see. Except… She shook her head, and swallowed. What was it? What was it that kept driving her crazy?

She rested her head on her hand and stared into the fire, admiring the way the flames leapt and spun as she ate absentmindedly. What was it that had given her strength when the spiedes attacked? All the major events of the past few months, her befriending Sarin, meeting Rotari—that had been on a whim too! And her friends… Kajiya could still clearly remember meeting all of them: hanging upside down from Gaorun's anfa trap, being both defended and healed by Ainee after Kajiya had stood up to a bully at magic school, and even… And even the first time she ever truly regarded her brother as a friend.

It had been a few weeks after the whole 'trying to fly' incident at the cliff, and Kajiya was still under what her father called 'house arrest.' Essentially, she wasn't allowed to go anywhere without an escort. On this particular day, she was going crazy *with boredom. Gaorun had gone out with his father on an extended hunting trip, and Ainee was taking what seemed to be the thousandth test to get into the society of healers. And Proten, of course, was busy with his duties as a magik, meaning that the only one around who might* possibly *want to take her somewhere, was Resurge.*

Kajiya had hated the notion. Resurge used to be fun when they were kids, and they'd make-believe about fighting taics, and winning wars, but ever since he had started his warrior training, he had changed. He became serious, to the point of appearing to be constantly sullen. She could hardly get a word out of him, and it drove her nuts.

At this point, Kajiya had been in the tree-top hut that was her home, lying on her bed. Resurge was finishing packing his things; he had decided on the recommendation of his mentor to move out of the house and start living on his own. In some ways, Kajiya thought she might miss him. In others, she knew she wouldn't. But if she didn't do something soon, she was liable to do something she would regret, and get in even more trouble. She had sighed, and gotten up.

"Would you…" She hated the words that stuck in her mouth. She didn't really want to do what she was about to offer, but it was better than sitting at home alone all day; she had already read every book she owned—thrice. "Like some help?"

Resurge's ears had perked, and he turned to her. "I certainly wouldn't mind it. Can you take that bag over there?" he asked, pointing to a small backpack of clothing.

Kajiya's face had lit up; perhaps this would be easier than she thought! She nodded enthusiastically and raced over to pick it up.

Resurge let out a very thin smile, but a smile nonetheless, and Kajiya grinned back at him widely. He picked up the pack he was carrying and started out the door.

"Come on then," he said.

Kajiya blinked, then looked around for other packs. There were none. Then she noticed that her brother was already out the door, and raced after him, putting the pack over her head as she slipped it on.

"Is this all you're taking?" Kajiya asked as she caught up to him.

Resurge had nodded. "Yeah. My mentor says

I'm 'too caught up in the things of this world,' whatever that means. I'll show him!" he muttered under his breath.

Kajiya giggled, but a swift glance from Resurge's red-orange eyes silenced her. She twiddled her thumbs, and then let her arms fall to her sides. At least helping him move wouldn't take too long.

"So," she said, suddenly realizing something, "where are we going?"

Resurge shrugged. "Didn't get that far."

Kajiya's ears flattened as she padded across the wooden platform. "Resurge!"

The boy just shrugged again and started down the stairs to the forest. Kajiya stopped at the top of the giant tree which the stairs had been grafted into. She breathed out. She hadn't actually been into the jungle since the incident. Her claws scraped the tree's bark as her heart pounded. Should she use her normal way of getting down? Kajiya hardened her heart against herself, Resurge was probably already halfway down the tree, and she couldn't be afraid of heights forever. Especially since she still lived in the trees!

Kajiya's blue hands were already sweaty as she grasped the vine railing on the far side of the stairs. She had forced herself to smile, then, holding on for dear life, she jumped. The blue fea's tail hit a few leaves as she swung out, and back towards the tree. She let go of the vine at just the right moment, dug her claws into the tree and slid down to the next set of stairs, where she repeated the process.

Unfortunately, on the fourth set of stairs, Kajiya mistimed when to let go, and found with a sudden rush of fear and ice that she was still going away from the tree. She had been about to release the *magic that froze her veins, when she felt a sudden tug on her back. She looked up.*

Resurge had jumped over the railing and was holding onto the pack Kajiya was wearing with one hand, and the railing with the other. Kajiya let out a little gasp, and let the ice push them both up.

"What were you thinking?!" Resurge had gasped once they were back on the safety of the stairs.

"I-I," Kajiya stuttered, "I wanted to practice flying!" she blurted, ignoring the heat in her face that came with the lie. "My new mentor thinks I'm just about ready!"

Resurge leaned against the tree as he sighed and sank down to a sitting position. "Warn me next time, okay?" he said, still breathing heavily.

Kajiya bit her lip. He had thought she was going to die. She had thought she was going to too. He shouldn't have risked his life to try and save her! She bridled a little, and placed her hands on her hips.

After a few moments, Resurge rose. "Come on then. I'd like to get settled in by nightfall."

Kajiya had just nodded, and followed him down into the forest. He shouldn't *have risked his life to save her. She looked up at him with new respect in her eyes. He was her brother... Perhaps he did love her the way that family did after all. Her ears, head, and tail sank simultaneously.*

"Well," he said as they reached the ground. "I suppose you can leave that stuff with me and head back home now." There was a slight venom to his voice.

Kajiya flinched. She had preferred sulky silence to this! He knew perfectly well how much trouble she'd get in if she went home alone!

"No," she said fiercely. "I can't let you go off on your own after this! What if you get hurt?"

Resurge had rolled his eyes, then held up his hand. "I know how to use a few herbs."

Kajiya gripped the pack's strap. "According to Ainee, most herbs don't work without magic. I thought warriors didn't use magic."

"There are some that do work without it! I won't be tarnishing my honour!"

"But what if you need it?! I don't want you to get hurt!"

"I won't get hurt!"

"But what if you can't find a place to stay?"

"You don't need to worry about me, Kajiya!"

"I'm a magik—no, more than that, I'm your sister! *It's my* duty *to worry about you!"*

Resurge lowered his hand. "Heh, and I thought it was my *duty to protect you."*

Kajiya blinked away the tears that had threatened her eyes. "What do you mean?"

Resurge smiled. "Why do you think I wanted to become a warrior?"

Kajiya's tail flicked. "To fight n' stuff."

Resurge shook his head. "I want to protect people, Kajiya. That's why I'm doing this."

Her grip tightened on the pack. "But Resurge, who's going to protect you?"

He was silent for a moment, and Kajiya glanced up at his red eyes. He wasn't sullen anymore. He looked thoughtful. Kajiya didn't realize how much she had cared for him, and now it was all spilling out. She clutched the bag even tighter; how unbecoming of a magik.

"No one I suppose," he said at last.

Kajiya had gasped, but stopped when she saw the smile on his face.

"But that's the way it has to be. I can't live my life afraid of shadows. I want to help bring peace—order to this world. I want to make a difference, Kajiya. I can't just stand by and watch things happen."

Kajiya let go of the bag. "I feel the same way, a-about being a magik. I don't want to stand for injustice. I don't want to see my—our people hurt."

Resurge nodded. "Then you understand that sacrifices need to be made?"

"For the greater good?"

"For the greater good."

Kajiya's throat had closed, and she looked down at her feet. Then she had felt Resurge's hand on her shoulder, and she looked back up at him.

"Right now, I'm sacrificing my relationship with you and Dad so that I can serve our people better in the future. I suppose," he looked away for a moment, slightly purple in the face, "that you could say that I'm sacrificing the comforts of civilized life, but I don't think I'm actually going to miss living in the house. I am going to miss you and Dad though."

Kajiya's eyes burst with tears and she embraced her brother tightly. "I'm gonna miss you too," she managed to get out through his thick fur.

He had paused for a moment, then hugged her back, lightly, but sincerely. Then he pushed her away, and Kajiya wiped the tears from her eyes.

He looked up, then sighed, "Great. It's getting late, and I still have no clue where I'm spending the night."

"What about there?" Kajiya managed to get

past the block in her throat.

"Where?" he had asked, turning to her.

"You know," Kajiya had said, pointing in a familiar direction, "the clearing we always went to. Back when we were kids?"

A smile broke out on Resurge's face, and Kajiya's heart had filled with joy as he nodded. He may have said that he was sacrificing their relationship for the sake of being a warrior, but Kajiya had a feeling that their relationship was just starting to flourish.

"That," he had said, "just might work."

"Careful there, you might just get a splinter in your tongue if you keep chewing it like that."

Kajiya gave a little jump as Resurge's real voice shattered the memory, and she sheepishly took the heavily desecrated stick out of her mouth.

"What're you thinking about?" Resurge asked as he sat beside her, stealthily stealing a scrap of meat off of her plate.

"Nothing mu—hey!" Kajiya hissed, reaching for the meat, but it was already into her brother's mouth.

She pouted as he swallowed, then turned back to the plate herself, huffily taking a large bite of Emera's curry, only to discover it had quite the kick. She coughed, and summoned magic to her tongue, hoping to take away the sting of the spice as her eyes watered.

"Hot?" her brother asked with a silly grin.

Kajiya nodded as the magic began to take effect. Her brother held out a cup filled with pavoki milk, which Kajiya took gratefully. She downed the entire thing in four seconds, and breathed a sigh of relief. At last, she could breathe again, and she handed the cup back to her brother. What had she been thinking about again? It seemed important... Oh! Yes!

"Didn't save any for me, I see," Resurge said with a touch of disappointment to his voice.

Kajiya laughed sheepishly, and opened her mouth to say one thing, but as she did so, a thought struck her, and she blurted out another. "Where's Ainee?"

Resurge stuck his thumb over to right side of the fire, where a group of feas, mostly male, with a few females and Ainee were gathered. "Apparently she's dead-set on correcting some of their herb lore about jungle herbs. And they're dead-set on teaching her how to use plains herbs. I got out of there as fast as I could."

Kajiya giggled, ignoring her brother's look, then turned back to the fire. She did need to ask him about that. If anyone would know, she had a feeling it was him.

"Resurge," she began.

"Yeah?"

"I know this is sudden, and maybe a little weird, but..."

He sat up straighter, looking concerned. "What is it?"

Kajiya gulped. "Have you ever thought that maybe... Maybe there's something more out there?"

"'More' like what?" he asked, eyes narrowing.

"I-I don't know. More, like, like... More. Something purposeful. That all of this isn't just random."

"Like something that made everything?"

Kajiya nodded. "Yeah, like that."

Resurge shook his head, and Kajiya felt her heart plummet. Maybe she had overthought things. She looked at the ground. Yeah, that had to be it.

"Not something. Someone."

Kajiya snapped her eyes back up to her brother.

He gave a small laugh at her reaction. "Well, everything that's made is made by *someone* right? Your bell wasn't made by another *thing*."

Kajiya flicked her tail, and the bell gave an extended ring as it rolled in the dirt.

"I suppose you're right. But why—"

"Look around, Kajiya," Resurge said with a smile. "Everything is perfect. The way the suns and moons move across the sky, the way trees grow to give us shade, and even the food chain. Nothing is without sustenance. I can't believe this all just, is."

Kajiya looked down at the ground again, nodding.

"What about you?"

Her eyes darted back up. "I suppose, what— whoever it is…"

Resurge nodded. "Whoever it is…" he prompted.

"They gave me magic. Back when I was fighting the spiedes. They gave me back my water magic."

Resurge stiffened slightly. "What do you mean, 'gave you back?'"

Kajiya blushed. "Oh. I thought Ainee told you."

Resurge leaned in. "Told me what?"

Kajiya scooted away awkwardly. "Um, well. Back on Ainee—the island—I may have, lost the ability to use water magic."

Resurge just nodded, and Kajiya breathed a sigh of relief, remembering how Ainee had reacted when she found out that Kajiya had lost all her magic for a period of time. Resurge seemed to be taking it better.

"So when you caused that cave-in to protect Sarin and Rosa..."

Kajiya nodded. "I don't think that was me. Well, I mean it was me, but..."

Resurge held up a hand. "I think I get it."

"Why?" Kajiya asked, setting the plate of food down beside her, not caring it if got trampled or not.

Resurge shrugged. "I don't know. It could be that he cares about you for some reason."

"He? Can't it be a 'she'?" Kajiya blinked.

Resurge shrugged nonchalantly. "Why not 'he'?"

Kajiya sighed. "Good point." She paused, and put a finger to her lips. "Do you have a *reason* for saying 'he'?"

"Not unless you count gut instincts."

Kajiya cast her eyes down to her plate, then raised her head to the sky.

"How about 'they' then? It's a compromise."

"I can live with that," Resurge responded.

Kajiya smiled. Earlier. Those words. It couldn't be... Her fur rose.

"Hey, are you okay?" Resurge asked.

Kajiya forced her fur back down.

"I think. I think they do care. About all of us. I mean, if they made us... Why would they bother making us all special in different ways if they didn't care?"

Chapter 5: Faring Well

The embers from the fire still smoldered as Kajiya walked past. All throughout Palinda, snores echoed, except for the small group of feas that walked beside Kajiya towards the north end of camp. Emera had somehow been able to wake up before dawn, and subsequently awoken the rest of them.

Now, just as Koiyan was beginning to rise, and Midyan set, they were finally ready. Resurge had repacked the packs just as he had told Ainee he was going to, but Kajiya and Gaorun had taken pity on him and helped out.

With them was Coballen, and at his heels, Kip.

Emera paused at the far end of camp. "And it's 'ere I say 'goodbye,'" she said with a hint of sadness to her voice. "Coballen and Kip will escort you ta the end of the territory. Should only be a day or two's journey. Unfortunately I can't spare any more hunters, an' our warriors'll be busy pickin' up the slack. Don't have much need for 'em out 'ere." She looked back at the camp lovingly. "We still got a few, but I have a feelin' we'll need much more."

Resurge nodded. "Tell your warriors I give them my regards."

Kajiya stepped forward. "We can't thank you enough for your hospitality," she began.

Emera held up a hand. "Think nothin' of it. I was jus' doing what you would."

Kajiya blinked; if a dead magik was to show up at her door with some crazy conspiracy story, *would* she have welcomed them? She didn't know. She also hoped she never had to find out—it was hard enough to *be* that fea. And one major crisis in a lifetime was more than enough.

Emera let out a sigh and placed her hands on her hips, looking back over her shoulder at the sleeping camp. "I jus' wish I coulda sent some leftovers with ya'll, but I'm afraid we're clean out. Everyone was hungry last night."

Gaorun shook his head. "Don't worry about it; you gave us more than enough food already."

"Well, if you say so." Emera smiled.

Kajiya gave Emera a short bow, slightly fearful that her pack, while much lighter than it had been, was still heavy enough to topple her over.

The blue fea turned to the others. "Well, then, I suppose we'd best be off. Jiblin may be going at a slower pace, but he has a two-day head start."

Gaorun raised an eyebrow. "What makes you think he's going at a slower pace?"

"He doesn't know how important it is to get to the Assembly. We do." Kajiya said, flicking an ear.

"Not ta mention Jiblin's the type ta stop and smell the aika." Emera interjected. "He don't like rushin', not even for Grand Assemblies. It's parta what makes him such a good magik—he always spends hours figurin' out every last detail of a plan, and what ta do if something goes wrong."

Hours? Kajiya's plans usually took all of ten minutes. She suppressed a sheepish giggle, and started to turn around.

"Well, thank you again. I hope we get the chance to meet in the future," Kajiya said.

Emera nodded. "You an' me both. Oh! Wait!"

Everyone paused, and even Coballen looked slightly confused. Emera reached into the front pocket of her apron, and pulled out a rather large sphere. It was a transparent rich dark blue-purple, and the edges appeared more translucent than the middle.

"What is that?" Ainee wondered aloud as she stepped forward, peering into the ball's depths.

"This is a light sphere. It catches Midyan's or Koiyan's light and then releases it in darkness. Sometimes we use 'em to help see under the wagons when one of the wheels breaks. It's handier than you'd think," Emera said, holding out the sphere.

Kajiya took it from her gingerly, feeling the smooth crystal-like surface with her hands. "How do you activate it?"

Emera smiled. "Just a bit of magic, not much. Even us women have to use 'em now an' again. The guy who makes 'em knows how to make 'em do their job without any instruction from the fea who's usin' it. The more magic you use, the brighter it gets," she explained. "Why don't you give 'er a try now? Just ta get used ta it?"

Kajiya nodded, and summoned the ice to her body. She quietly redirected it to her right hand, where she was holding the sphere. After gathering a fair amount, she began to slowly feed the magic into the sphere, and it started to shine brightly. Kajiya looked away, and slowed the magic feed until it was just the smallest trickle, and the heat on her face subsided. She looked, the orb was still glowing brightly enough to cast shadows on their faces, and she was barely using any magic at all! She handed it off to Resurge, but kept her link open with the magic. Sure enough, it continued to glow. Now, as Resurge handed it off to Ainee, Kajiya cut her magic off. The orb dimmed slowly, and Kajiya could still feel the residue of her magic around it. Curious now, she summoned a large amount of magic, and placed it around the sphere just as Gaorun took it. It started to glow again, feeding off of the magic Kajiya had placed there. Kajiya stopped summoning the ice. The ball would glow on its own now for quite some time without Kajiya so much as having to numb a finger.

"That's amazing," Kajiya said at last.

Emera grinned. "O' course. Well, I don't know how much it'll help you on yar journey, but if you ever have to visit those spiedes again, I figure it should be a might helpful."

"Thank you," Kajiya said sincerely.

The pale green fea just raised a hand again. "Like I said, think nothin' of it."

Kajiya nodded, then with a wave of her hand, swept away the magic from the orb, extinguishing it. Then she took the orb from Gaorun and slid it into her shoulder bag. She then reformatted the cool chill in the air into strengthening magic instead and sent it into the dirt. Although she was sure the ground didn't need strengthening, Kajiya figured it was probably better to do something with the magic than just leave it. She didn't know what could happen to uncontrolled magic. She'd never seen any—not that magic was often visible.

What was it Rotari had said? That she believed there was an invisible force greater than magic? Perhaps she was trying to pin down the same entity that Kajiya and Resurge had talked about the previous night. Rotari was right about one thing; whatever, whoever it was, they *were* greater than magic.

"Well," Coballen's voice broke into Kajiya's thoughts, "we'd best be off." He grinned at Emera.

"See ya in a couple days, sis!" The cream fea spun around and started off without even a small goodbye wave.

Emera rolled her eyes and shook her head with a small smile. "Be seein' you!"

Kajiya and the others turned to follow, and a chorus of "Goodbye!" erupted from them as they waved.

This time Emera didn't say anything, and just waved back. Or at least, Kajiya thought she didn't, until, when they were a fair distance away, Kajiya's ears picked up Emera' soft voice on the wind.

"Safe journeys."

A quiet smile spread over Kajiya's face, and she gave the pale green fea one last nod as they set out.

Onta, who had been sleeping on top of Gaorun's pack, had been awoken by the light sphere and was now out and about, running. She and Kip seemed to have become friends, and the two of them darted through the aimaia, appearing to Kajiya to be playing hide and seek. One minute they'd be out in front, and then the next, behind them, and in the next, Kip would be chasing Onta as she jumped from fea to fea as if they were branches. Kip barked and Onta yapped. For a second, Kajiya longed to join them in their play, as if she was a child again, but then she remembered her purpose. She needed to find Jiblin and put a stop to Turten's plans.

While Coballen and the others talked, Kajiya hung at the back of the group in silence. So, Jiblin spent hours on his plans. Kajiya knew her father often sought council when making his plans, but she didn't know how long it took for him to make them. Perhaps, it would be good for her to actually plan out what she was going to do when she got to Royalin in detail. She nodded to herself. Yes, it would be good to do that.

If they were to somehow get there before Jiblin, how would they know? Kajiya's stomach clenched. They wouldn't. She supposed they would just have to crash the Assembly anyway. Kajiya's mere existence should, at the very least, prove that Turten was a liar, and the note for Beifin should prove that what she said was the truth.

Suddenly, Kajiya was struck by another thought. How would they prove to Jiblin that they were telling the truth? She suppressed a gasp as her eyes shot to her bag. Of course! The light-sphere! Kajiya's expression softened; the real reason that Emera must have given it to them was to prove to Jiblin that they were friendly. True, they could have stolen one, but it was obvious to Kajiya that only Palinda feas knew what they were, or how to work them. To know both would prove that they were friends to the Palinda tribe. Kajiya smiled at Emera's tact. She probably hadn't had the time to write out a letter detailing everything like Sai had, but she didn't need one to communicate with her husband.

Would Kajiya ever be able to communicate with someone like that? Heat filled Kajiya's face; she was far too young to even be *thinking* about marriage! She shook her head fiercely and forced her thoughts elsewhere.

But what would happen if they did find Jiblin? They would still make the trip all the way to Royalin, but there would be no need for a disguise. Turten wouldn't be able to touch her if the other magiks already knew she was there. Was the disguise even necessary? Yes, Kajiya decided at once, remembering her reasoning for keeping it in the first place. Although, if she were to come across her father or Turten in the open… It wouldn't be much of a disguise at all. All it did was cover her mark. Maybe she should cut her hair… Kajiya cast the ice-blue locks a swift glance and didn't entertain the notion.

She sighed; if she was to be caught out in the open by Turten, the results could be disastrous. But… What if she were to cast an invisibility spell? She nodded to herself, that would work, but it would be a difficult thing to maintain… Or, she realized suddenly, they could just keep to the poorer section of the village until they were ready to crash the Assembly. She remembered Turten saying something about wanting to put the poor under the same slavery-law as the women. There was no way someone so pompous would be going to the place he was about to enslave! At least, she sincerely hoped not.

The morning was starting to wear thin, and the group stopped for a short breakfast. After they finished Kajiya continued to trail after the others, only to pause.

She counted silently, eyes jumping from fea to fea. There was no doubt about it; Gaorun wasn't in front of her. Kajiya turned back to the small clearing where they had eaten. There, Gaorun was examining something on the ground whilst Onta tilted her head at different angles, apparently trying, as Kajiya was, to understand what had caught the green fea's interest.

"You coming, Gaorun?" Kajiya called back.

His ears twitched and he looked up at her. "Yeah, I'm coming." He reached down, grabbing a small stone as he rose, and jogged to catch up.

About halfway through the day, the wind picked up, sending waves through the aimaia. Kajiya could have watched the rippling field forever and been satisfied, but as it was, she barely even noticed it. The treeline, a green and blue smudge on the horizon grew ever closer and larger, but Kajiya was restless in spite of her steps. No matter her plans, the sooner they found Jiblin, the sooner they got to Royalin, the sooner they would stop Turten. She hoped.

There was one other possibility that Kajiya had not considered yet. Had not dared to. What happened if Jiblin arrived before they did? What happened if Turten had already passed the law? Could she get them to renounce it? Kajiya's heart filled with dread, and she looked at her feet as they padded over the hardened brown dirt. That couldn't happen. She couldn't let it.

She pursed her lips; what of that being that had given her magic back then? Rotari had called magic a 'survival instinct,' but Kajiya knew it was much more than that. And if this being could give it and take it away… Kajiya looked up at the sky, where Koiyan was crossing overhead; there had been a time when she had almost completely lost her magic. Had that been their work as well? She thought back to when she first lost it; it had been right after she had attacked the Mirabilia Assembly. And when she had fully regained it, it had been when she didn't care about her own safety. In that moment, all she had cared about was getting Rosa and Sarin out alive. Could it be that the entity knew her motives? And gave more powerful magic when she was putting others first? She didn't know, but it certainly seemed like it. Actually, now that she thought about it, Rotari *had* said something about magic to that effect—that mothers and fathers protecting their children often used magic that surpassed masters or something? It had been so long ago that Kajiya could barely remember.

The group in front of her stopped and Kajiya nearly bumped into Ainee.

"What is it?" Kajiya asked, a tinge of trepidation entering her voice.

Ainee looked at the sky, then turned to her. "It's lunch time."

Kajiya let out a small growl, had the day really gone by so quickly?

"Can't we walk and eat?" she asked.

Resurge, who had been setting out the firewood from his pack looked at her, then turned to Coballen. The cream fea shrugged, and Resurge placed the firewood back into the murky green of his canvas.

"I don't see why not."

Kajiya smiled, and Gaorun approached with a pan. She nodded, if they were going to eat on the road, then her magic would be needed to ensure that the meat was properly cooked. Kajiya created a hot blue flame, and set it under the pan as Ainee slid the meat from Gaorun's pack into the pan. She reached into her herb bag and took out a small shaker to add some seasonings. The purple fea then nodded to Gaorun, and went up to Resurge and Coballen. Suddenly Coballen froze.

"Kajiya," he said, turning back to her.

"Yeah?"

"Can ya make it so that the scent don't travel? I don't want another kivolta pack thinkin' there's food 'round." Coballen's dark violet eyes looked serious.

Kajiya nodded at once, and commanded the air around the pan to go straight up, remembering all-too-well the adventure of the previous day.

After a while, the meat was cooked and they all ate heartily. Gaorun cleaned the pan quickly with magic, and Kajiya helped him replace it in his pack. Now that they had eaten, Kajiya was delighted to find that they were picking up the pace, so that even Kip and Onta had to work their short legs a little faster to keep up. The sun crossed overhead, and just as Koiyan started to set, Kajiya could start to make out individual trees in the treeline.

"We're almost there!" she cried out happily as the air started to cool before Midyan's arrival.

Coballen stopped, then surveyed the area. It was another pavoki grazing ground, so the land was relatively flat and aimaia free. He nodded to himself then turned to Kajiya.

"We'd best stop here for the night. Ya don't want to catch a kivolta pack after dark. They can get vicious."

Kajiya let her disappointment show, and pointed to the treeline. "But—"

A vibrant purple hand appeared on her shoulder. "Kajiya," Ainee's face was stern when Kajiya turned to her, "we've been on our feet all day. It won't help us if we're too tired to continue, even if we did make it to the forest."

Kajiya sighed. If there was one thing that she had learned during this whole trip, it was that Ainee was usually right. She gave in with a shrug.

"Alright then, shall we set up camp?"

*   *   *

Kajiya couldn't help but smile as she listened to the boys complain. They had just finished packing up the camp, and thanks to a slight lack of foresight from Coballen, all three of the boys had had to share the same tent. As it was, in Kajiya and Ainee's tent, there was enough space for the two of them, their mattress and a little bit of elbow room. Kajiya could only imagine the kicking and squishiness of theirs. And, from what they were saying, it sounded like they had all somehow managed to sleep on the thin floor of the tent rather than the mattress!

"...and he snored all night!" Gaorun was hissing about Coballen, prominent bags beneath his eyes.

"I snored? What 'bout you two? Ya both were louder than a pavoki during a stampede!" he retorted.

"If both of you can *shut up*, maybe we'll get some ground covered," Resurge growled, his tiredness evident in his voice.

The hunters both crossed their arms and started to mutter, but neither stopped for a second. Kajiya grinned to herself; this was straight out of one of her books! But her smile faded as the treeline on the horizon drew ever closer. What if the boys stayed angry at each other? Kajiya didn't want Coballen to leave them angry; she had hoped to stay friends with Palinda. Kajiya tightened her grip on her pack as her mind raced to think of ways to make them make up. All she succeeded in doing was giving herself a headache. She sighed; it looked like they were on their own. *And besides,* she realized, *just because* they're *grumpy doesn't mean I have to be!* A small smile broke out on her face; perhaps *her* relationship with the feas of Palinda hadn't been jeopardized at all.

With the jingling of her bell, she bounced up to Coballen. "Have you ever been in the forest before?"

He turned to her, and loosened his shoulders. "It depends on which 'forest' yar talkin' 'bout."

"The one we're going to go into, I guess,"
Kajiya said, looking at the green-blue smudge ahead.

She could almost see individual leaves. A
twinge of nervousness caught her off guard; they
would reach the treeline today for sure. That meant
that they would be leaving Coballen and Kip behind.

"Nope." Coballen's matter-of-fact voice
brought Kajiya back to the present. "I've been in many
a forest, includin' yar jungle. Sometimes I gotta chase
an anfa into the forest so I can catch 'em."

A movement in her peripherals caught Kajiya's
eye. Gaorun's ears had perked. Kajiya's heart leapt
with joy as he turned to them.

"Why would being in the forest make them
easier to catch?" he wondered, arms still crossed.

Coballen smirked. "'Cause these be *plains*
anfa. They don't know the forest like yars do. They're
used to runnin' as fast as they can in the opposite
direction, they don't know what ta do when there's a
tree in the way."

Gaorun nodded, and lowered his arms. "I
suppose our anfa wouldn't know what to do without
trees. They would stick out like a torn claw."

Coballen laughed, and Kajiya smiled as she
quietly dropped back. The two feas were being
friendly with each other again, and she hadn't even
tried!

Kajiya fell to the back of the group again, and
returned to her silence. It was easier to just look
around this way.

Then, among the white aimaia, close to the
ground, she spotted a small golden flower mid-bloom.
Kajiya gasped, and swiftly nudged Ainee.

"What?" the purple fea hissed.

"Isn't that an aika flower?" Kajiya wondered aloud as she raised a claw to point at it.

Ainee's eyes widened and she hastily scanned the field, letting out a small yelp as she spotted the flower. Kajiya smiled; Ainee did love her herbs.

Ainee dashed over to it, only to skid to a stop and kneel down in front of the plant. After a quick, but intense examination, Kajiya saw Ainee sever the flower-head with magic, holding it in the air above her hands. Flecks of dirt flew off the flower as Ainee cleansed the plant with magic, then, holding it with one hand, she reached back into her bag and pulled out two jars. One was empty, and the other was filled with some sort of oil. After putting the flower into the empty jar, she poured oil over top of it, then sealed the jar with a cloth and magic as she rose and started back to the others.

"I'll start studying it as soon as we camp for the night," she said, a twinkle in her eyes.

Kajiya smiled to herself, it wouldn't take Ainee very long at all. Kajiya remembered back when she was captured by the spiedes, she had been able to get a stone that the giant creatures actually lived off of, known, strangely enough, as 'Ainee's blood.' When she and Ainee had trained with Rotari, Ainee had objected to the deep-red stone's name, but for Kajiya at least, the name had stuck. Thanks to Rotari's tutelage, once Kajiya had given Ainee the stone, the purple fea was able to study it with ease, and finished her experiments before Kajiya's wounds had even thought about healing. Kajiya wondered if she still had it. She couldn't see Ainee throwing it away.

"Well," Coballen's voice broke into her thoughts once more, and Kajiya felt a sting of sadness, "it looks like we're 'ere."

The treeline loomed in front of them, and Kajiya cast a sidelong glance at Coballen. Even Kip looked somber.

"Thank you for everything," Ainee said as she dipped her head.

"It was nothin'." Coballen returned the gesture.

"Are you sure you'll be okay on your own?" Resurge asked, a note of worry in his voice.

Kajiya blinked; she hadn't even thought of that. Would Coballen be able to return to his tribe before sunset? They had gone a long way... And without the proper camping supplies... But at the same time, they couldn't really go back with him. It would undermine the entirety of their journey so far!

"I'll be fine," the cream fea insisted, then bent down to pat his kivolta. "Kip 'ere'll protect me from anything, and if his barks don't scare it off, I've always got this." He pulled the beater stick off of his back and stroked it with his free hand.

Kajiya blinked as she actually noticed what the stick looked like. It had been painted a light blue-silver colour, and narrowed to a point at one end. The other end was large and thick, with a darker blue coloured knob that looked like it could do some serious damage. Coballen put the stick back in its sheath on his back, with just the pointy end sticking out.

"An' besides, it don't matter if I'm exhausted tomorrow. I ain't goin' nowhere," he said with a touch of glee.

Kajiya shook her head. "Then I guess we should all get going." She bowed, and couldn't help but notice the unease that infiltrated Coballen's expression when she did so.

In a way, she understood; she was a magik. Magiks weren't supposed to bow to anyone except other magiks and high ranking officials. It was fine for her to bow to Emera, but to the magik's brother-in-law? Kajiya just smiled.

Coballen bowed deeply back, and then turned towards the prairielands. A chorus of goodbyes rang out as Kajiya and the others moved forward, into the shade of the trees. Resurge and Gaorun even gave a few little bows of their own. Coballen raised a hand, and Kip seemed to nod at them before vanishing between the stalks of aimaia. Onta's tail drooped, and she jumped back onto Gaorun's shoulders. Then they entered the trees, and the cream fea disappeared from sight altogether.

Silence filled the forest, aside from the occasional buzzing of insects as they flitted by. Onta managed to snap one up that had wandered too close to her flower-patterned muzzle, and she crunched away happily beside Gaorun's ear. Kajiya didn't know how he put up with it.

Before too long, the shadows of the forest began to lengthen. Kajiya looked up to catch snatches of the golden sky behind the canopy. Was it already so late?

Resurge signaled with a raised hand for the group to stop. He pulled out the map from one of the pockets on his pack, and Gaorun stepped forward to help him distinguish landmarks. Finally, after a bit of murmuring the boys put away the map.

"We'll carry on a bit farther tonight," Resurge said.

"And when we set up camp, I'll take a look around for signs of feas," Gaorun said. "Now, we may not have even entered the same part of the forest as them, and it has been a couple days, so it is a bit of a long shot—don't get your hopes up."

Kajiya nodded, and the group started off again. They climbed over trees and roots, until finally, just as Midyan started to rise, and the blue light hit the tops of the leaves, they found a clearing just large enough to fit the tents. Their food would have to be cooked with magic fire again, unless, of course, they felt like setting fire to the forest.

Kajiya, Ainee and Resurge set up the tents while Gaorun went off to get firewood to sustain the magic flame, jointly looking for signs of Jiblin and his entourage. Kajiya grimaced as the tent spike reverberated against a large rock hidden below the topsoil. Unlike her jungle, where the ground was moist, the heat here had made everything dry and powdery.

For a moment Kajiya wondered if the ground would be be able to hold the spike. Her brow furrowed; if they couldn't set up the tent, where would they sleep this night? She had slept outside before, but always on her own terms. And even then, she had often awoken with a crick in her neck.

A sound from the forest caught her ear and she leapt to her feet, fur bristling. A soft breeze carried Gaorun's scent to her, and she relaxed.

"Any signs?" she asked as he entered camp with an armful of firewood.

The dark green fea shook his head. "Not a one."

Kajiya let out a sigh, and Ainee stood from where she was working with the mattress. Resurge walked over, having finished his tent already, and kneeled down beside Gaorun to help arrange the firewood into a cone shape.

"Well, I guess there's nothing that we—" Ainee's words were cut off by a sudden flurry of yapping from Onta.

Everyone looked at each other confusedly, and Gaorun went over to the pacing onti.

"What is it, girl?" he asked, trying to hold her, but she kept sliding out of his grip like water.

The onti's yapping grew more frantic and she kept her eyes focused on one spot in the forest. While the others tried to calm her down, Kajiya cast a glance to the trees. There was nothing—a movement. Kajiya's fur rose at once. It wasn't so much a movement she had seen, rather than a distortion. The same kind of distortion she had seen when untrained feas tried to make themselves invisible. But it had lasted only a second, and she had often seen the same sort of waves with the jungle heat. But… No! There it was again!

Kajiya bristled. "Who's there?!" she yelled out, and the others turned to her worriedly, then followed her gaze.

"Kajiya," Ainee's voice had adopted a healer's tone, "there's nothing there."

Kajiya's heart wrenched; Ainee thought she was seeing things!

"We aren't going to hurt you!" Kajiya called, thinking it best to show her friend rather than try to insist that she wasn't crazy.

Ainee's hand found its way to Kajiya's shoulder, but Kajiya shrugged it off fiercely. Onta's yapping grew even more furious as the wind changed direction, and Kajiya knew why. The shift brought the invisible fea's scent with it. Even magic couldn't take away scent. She could feel Ainee stiffen beside her, and the purple fea's fur started to puff out. Resurge rose, and bared his claws, his sword being on the other side of camp. Gaorun also bristled, and was about to advance when Kajiya put out her hand.

"We don't know what they want yet," she hissed.

They could be a fea from Jiblin's entourage that got separated, and could indicate which way he was going. They could be a loner, a fea who chose to live on their own, and perhaps she and her friends were accidentally encroaching on their territory. That seemed the most likely scenario in Kajiya's mind, and if that was the case, they needed to handle the situation with tact.

The invisibility faltered and a decidedly Mirabilian fea collapsed to the ground. Kajiya let out a gasp and charged forward with Onta.

The fea was similar in colour to Resurge, to the point where Kajiya could barely tell their fur apart when Resurge helped the fea up. Even their stripes appeared to be the same. However, he had a similar build to Gaorun, and was quite lanky in spite of obvious muscles. But unlike Resurge or Gaorun, this fea had a scruffy chin, and wild hair that stuck up all over the place with overly long bangs that fell in front of his eyes. His eyebrows were marked by his stripes, and there was one under each eye and on each side of his neck. A row of stripes ran down one side of his tail, and he had three stripes on each forearm, and on each side of his stomach, something which struck Kajiya as unusual, but she didn't give it too much importance. He wore nothing but a pair of anfa-skin slacks with an avian-skin belt around his waist.

Ainee was the last to reach him, as she had retrieved her herbs. He was clearly in need of medical attention and already had a bandage across the bridge of his nose. However, when Ainee reached him, he managed to open up his orange eyes and shake his head.

"Food," he croaked out. "I just need food."

Ainee shook her head as she started readying the various plants. "You're injured."

"No!" he said vehemently as Resurge lowered him into a lying down position beside the fire that Gaorun started. "No healing."

Kajiya's stomach clenched. If he kept this up, he could be seriously hurt.

Ainee sighed, and reached over. "At least let me—"

The stranger grabbed her wrist before she could get any closer, and looked at her fiercely as Onta sniffed about. "No examinations. Food. Just food."

Ainee tried to pull her arm away, but the stranger held it fast. At once, Resurge grabbed the stranger's wrist.

"Let her go," he hissed.

"No examinations," the stranger insisted.

Ainee's pink eyes hardened. "Fine! No examinations! What's it to me if you die!?"

The stranger released Ainee's hand and she clutched it close to herself. Resurge was a bit slower in letting go.

The stranger smiled. "Good."

Kajiya felt her fur bristle. There was something off about this stranger, but she couldn't quite put her claw on it. What sort of fea refused healing?

The scent of pavoki meat started to fill the air, and Kajiya turned her attention to the fire. Gaorun was cooking. She padded over to his side of the fire, and her bell rung as her tail flicked uneasily.

Gaorun flashed a glance to her. "I figured we could all use some food. We haven't eaten since lunch."

Kajiya nodded, then went over to Ainee's pack.

"Do you still have those powdered avian teeth?" she wondered, looking into the bag's recesses.

Ainee's tail flicked huffily as she bridled. "No, I used the last of them healing *you*. Not that I would give them to this ingrate anyway!"

Kajiya flinched. She had never seen Ainee so riled—but then again, she had also never seen Ainee *not* heal someone. The fea must have been stronger than he appeared. Perhaps though...

"What about the Ainee's blood?" she asked, carefully moving jars of herbs and putting them back exactly as she found them when they didn't contain the red gemstone.

The stranger's ears perked at the words.

Ainee rolled her eyes, then sighed. "Move over," she said as she opened a hidden flap and pulled out the deep crimson stone.

Kajiya looked over and saw the stranger's orange eyes widen.

"Where did you get that?" he asked, a slight hint of awe to his voice.

Kajiya shuddered. "You don't want to know."

The fea's eyes narrowed. "You've been with the spiedes."

Chapter 6: Chase

Kajiya stiffened; that was it! The thing she couldn't place her claw on. The haunted look in his eyes, this fea had escaped from the spiedes as well!

Suddenly, Kajiya was back in that tunnel, screams, spiede and fea alike around her. Sarin was pulling her through the total darkness, and her feet stepped on things of which she never wanted to know what they were.

As soon as the memory began, it was over, and Kajiya placed her hands over her ears, shivering. Ainee was at her side at once.

"It's over, Kajiya. They're gone. You're on the surface, you're safe," Ainee whispered in her ear.

Kajiya gulped, and her eyes watered. She had gone so long without a flashback. She couldn't be relapsing now!

The stranger grunted as he pulled himself to a sitting position. "I'm sorry, I didn't mean to dredge up unwanted memories."

Kajiya forced herself to breathe, and took her hands away from her ears. "It's fine. I just. I just need some time."

The stranger nodded weakly, and Gaorun passed him a slab of meat. Resurge's face fell into a barely discernable scowl as he subtly watched the stranger eat.

Ainee wrapped Kajiya in a cocooning hug. Kajiya didn't hug her back, but she didn't try to resist either. Eventually though, Ainee let go, and gave Kajiya a small nod. Kajiya nodded back, and walked towards her tent. She needed to lie down, to rest. A thought struck her, and she cast a glance back at the stranger. He had made no mention of her magik status. Had he not seen her mark? In a way, Kajiya was glad that he hadn't, and went into the cool darkness of the tent. But even this darkness was not absolute like the cave, and as Kajiya slid under the blankets, she listened to the conversation outside. It was better than trying to think. She was sure that her thoughts would turn to more unpleasant things.

"…and that's essentially what happened," Gaorun was saying.

The stranger let out a low whistle. "Harsh. I can only imagine. A brother of mine was taken by the spiedes."

"Did he escape?" Gaorun wondered.

The stranger paused. "Not really."

"Not really?" Resurge's suspicious voice chimed in. "How does one 'not really' escape from the spiedes?"

"He got out for one day, and they got him back the next." The stranger seemed to become choked, and the pitch of his voice started to rise.

"I see," Gaorun said quietly.

There was a long pause and Kajiya could hear the fire crackle in the background. The familiar sound was soothing. It felt like she was being held in a warm embrace. She curled up in the bed and slid an arm under her pillow. She was almost asleep when the conversation began again.

"So," Resurge said with slightly less suspicion in his voice, "what's your name?"

"Er," the stranger paused, "didn't I tell you earlier?"

Kajiya's ear flicked, and she turned her head.

Was he stalling for time?

"No," Ainee said bluntly.

"Oh, well, how rude of me," the stranger said, and Kajiya let out a small laugh; the stranger hadn't been anything *but* rude! "My name is Chase."

Kajiya resisted the urge to sit up—Chase was the name of one of the humans in her book. Could this fea have read the same book? He did appear to be Mirabilian, and Kajiya *had* taken the book out from the library to read a few chapters before she bought a copy for herself. It was a best-seller in Mirabilia for a few years, but Kajiya only got into it after the height of its popularity.

"Chase?" Resurge said. "That's an odd name."

"Try telling that to my mother," Chase said. "What are you bunch doing out here anyway? And if you're from Mirabilia, why'd you go to Animo?"

Ainee sighed. "We're trying to stop Turten from passing a law that will turn every woman into a slave. And failing that, we're trying to stop him from taking over the world with the spiedes. Although, Kajiya says that the spiedes plan on betraying him and will try to take over regardless."

"Kajiya's the one… in there, right?" Chase said uncertainly.

"Yes," Ainee laughed. "Now look who's being rude. We haven't introduced ourselves either. I'm Ainee, that's Resurge, and this is Gaorun."

"And that's Onta," Gaorun piped in.

"And Onta," Ainee said, a touch of warmth to her voice.

There was a pause.

"It's getting late," Ainee's voice said. "We should all turn in. We have a long journey ahead of us."

"Where are you going?" Chase asked.

"To Royalin. That's where Turten will be. I mean, where else are you going to get a law passed but the Grand Assembly?" Gaorun said with a growl.

"Ah, yes, the Grand Assembly. Right, right." Chase didn't sound very certain of himself.

No, he sounded more like he had never heard of the Grand Assembly before.

"And I take it that feas from all over will be there?"

There was silence, and Kajiya guessed that her friends were picking up on his fishing comments as well.

"Yes," Ainee said simply, but confusion with a hint of suspicion laced her voice.

"Then would you mind if I joined you?" Chase asked. "I have some business I need to attend to in Royalin. But I seem to have lost my way. I'm not familiar with these woods."

Kajiya could just imagine everyone stiffening, but Resurge jumped in at once.

"If you were to come, you'd be expected to carry your weight. Since you clearly *don't* need medical attention," there was a slight venom to her brother's voice, "I suspect you'll be perfectly capable of carrying Ainee's pack. That way she only has to carry her herbs."

Kajiya nodded to herself, what Resurge was saying made sense, in more ways than one. Firstly, Ainee's was the lightest pack, so it wouldn't hamper Chase too much if he should prove weaker than he let on, and secondly, Ainee's herbs were heavy and the bag for them cumbersome. It would be easier for her to travel if she only had to worry about the one bag. Not that Chase would know any of this.

"Of course. I wouldn't expect anything less," he replied without missing a beat. "And where should I sleep tonight?"

"Right where you are," Gaorun hissed, and Kajiya suspected that memories of the previous night's attempt to get three feas in the same tent had made him vehemently opposed to the idea. "I'll get you some blankets," he said in a much gentler tone.

There was some rustling and movement around the camp as her friends presumably made Chase somewhat comfortable. Finally, they bid each other goodnight, and the tent flap opened.

Ainee padded in quietly, and used magic to ensure the bed didn't move as she climbed under her own blanket. Kajiya relaxed, and let the warmth of the embrace that held her lull her to sleep.

*　　　　　*　　　　　*

Kajiya awoke slowly, becoming aware of the sounds around her long before she could actually think clearly. She rose cautiously, trying not to awaken Ainee. Koiyan was starting to rise as she exited the tent.

Kajiya bristled for a moment as she saw the fea from the night before, but she relaxed when she saw that he was just staring upwards as he sat.

"It was Chase, right?" she said quietly as she sat down beside him.

He turned to her with his piercing orange eyes and nodded.

"I'm sorry about last night. I didn't mean to—"

Kajiya raised a hand, then smiled. "I told you. I'm fine. You just caught me off-guard is all."

Chase smiled back. "Your friends said you were called Kajiya?"

Kajiya nodded in response, and a smile broke out over Chase's face.

"I'm glad to see my memory isn't broken!" he laughed.

"We should get the others up soon," Kajiya said, biting the inside of her cheek as she looked around.

They couldn't waste daylight.

"You guys really are in a rush, eh?" Chase said with a sidelong glance as he stood and stretched out his arms.

Fatigue pulled at her body as Kajiya stood, but she nodded regardless.

"If we can catch Palinda's magik before he gets to Royalin, we can put a stop to Turten once and for all."

"Catch?" Chase turned to her. "What do you mean?"

There was a clink as Kajiya cleaned the pan from the previous night. There were still small red granules from the ground Ainee's blood mixed in with the pavoki grease.

"He started out from Palinda two days ahead of us, but he doesn't know about Turten or his plot. We're hoping to overtake him and warn him."

"Ah, of course." Chase nodded as if this was something he knew all along.

Kajiya raised an eyebrow as she put away the pan. "Fold those blankets will you?"

Chase nodded, and together they carefully put away the exterior of the campsite. Kajiya knew from her own experience that being woken up on travel days was never pleasant. As long as she could be merciful, she would, but the sun grew ever higher, and it was time to set off again before long.

Kajiya walked back into her tent. "Ainee, it's time to get up."

The purple fea rolled over once, and off the mattress. Kajiya cringed as Ainee fell with a thump onto the floor.

"Morning," the purple fea hissed sleepily.

Kajiya grinned, and edged out of the tent.

"Chase," she said as she rounded up the salvageable pieces of firewood, "could you get Gaorun and Resurge up?"

Chase paused for moment from where he was putting away the blankets. "Er, well…"

Kajiya raised an ear. "Something wrong?"

"Oh, no, nothing. Nothing at all," he said as he stood abruptly and started over to the tent.

Before he could reach it though, a rustling came from within, and Resurge emerged with Gaorun in tow. Kajiya's eyes narrowed confusedly as she saw Chase sigh.

"Don't worry about getting us up," Resurge said. "You two could wake up a taic colony!"

"Sorry," Chase laughed.

Resurge eyed him suspiciously as he turned back to the tent and started to pull the spikes from the ground.

Gaorun shot Chase an apologetic smile and shrugged as he went to help Resurge.

"I don't think Resurge likes me very much," Chase commented as he walked back to Kajiya.

Kajiya shook her head. "You can't blame him. I'm afraid we don't really know you."

Chases flinched. "Don't trust me, eh?"

Ainee's tail flicked as she exited the tent. "Like Kajiya said, we don't know you. And the last time we trusted someone we didn't know, we almost got killed."

Kajiya put her hand out. "Now, Ainee, I didn't know Sarin that well either when we went to war against the spiedes and I *would* have died if it hadn't been for him." More quietly she added, "We need to at least give him a chance."

"Hah!" Ainee bridled, tail flicking as she set off to put away the last of the tent materials.

Kajiya flinched, and reached out her hand, then set it back down. They really *didn't* know him. But that only meant that he could be the key to stopping Turten, or the key to his success. They couldn't know.

"We're ready," Gaorun said as he stood from where he and Resurge finished putting away their tent.

"I'll be just a minute," Ainee said, stuffing the girl's tent into her pack violently.

After sealing it shut with large aggravated motions, she held the bag out to Chase, a smug sneer on her face.

"This is yours, I believe?"

Chase ignored her expression and took the bag from her hands. "I'll do my best."

Kajiya sighed and picked up her own pack. Something told her today was going to be a long day.

Fortunately, with packing finished, they were able to set out at once. Kajiya relaxed as the group began to focus on the task at hand. Gaorun would run ahead every few hundred tail-lengths and look around, sniff the ground with Onta by his side, or even climb up to the lowest branch of a tree. Kajiya was pretty sure that he was looking for signs of Jiblin and his entourage, but she didn't know. Meanwhile, Resurge had the map out, constantly verifying their path through the trees with Ainee at his side. Since Gaorun was preoccupied, Kajiya could only guess that Ainee took it as an opportunity to help find the way. Either that, or as a chance to get away from Chase.

Chase hung behind them, never more than three steps away. His footsteps were quick, and his tail hardly swung at all. He glided over the forest floor as if it were a flat field. Kajiya walked a few tail-lengths behind him, watching. He didn't seem dangerous, or suspicious now. Maybe he was like Resurge, a warrior of some kind with an aversion to magic… No, that couldn't be it; he had used an invisibility spell to approach them. Why wouldn't he let Ainee heal his wounds? Kajiya blinked, then squinted as she looked at him. He *had* no visible wounds. Why had he collapsed the previous night then? A sigh left her lips as she opened her eyes fully; had it just been exhaustion? She had heard that feas could faint from exhaustion, but she had never seen it happen.

She quickened her step. "If it's not too personal," she began, keeping her voice soft, "what was your brother's name?"

Chase turned back to her. "What?"

Kajiya's shoulders rose slightly. "You know, the one who got captured by spiedes?"

Chase blinked. "Oh! Of course. Orn. His name was Orn." He looked at the ground.

"Was?" Kajiya repeated as gently as she could, moving a little closer to him.

Chase smiled weakly as he turned to her. "I don't know. Like I said, he was recaptured by the spiedes."

"Ah, of course."

Kajiya drew back for a moment, then leaned forward again. "Did you ever try to find out?"

Chase looked back at her. "If he was alive or not?"

Kajiya nodded. "Yeah."

His long bangs shook with his head. "I couldn't."

"Why not?" Kajiya pressed.

"I, er, I couldn't bring myself to go into the caves. Surely you understand?"

"No, I don't," Kajiya admitted. "I mean, I do, but… I can't leave them there."

Chase turned his head to her fully. "Can't leave who where?"

Kajiya swallowed. "All the feas the spiedes have captured. It's not right, and I intend to free them. Somehow…"

Chase turned his head back, and looked at his feet again. He wasn't gliding much now.

Kajiya looked away. Had she crossed a line? She did barely know him—what if he thought she was condemning him for not being brave enough? She didn't want that! She hadn't meant that. She only meant that…

"Sorry," the word found its way out of her lips before she could even bring herself to look at him. "I didn't mean to bring up painful memories…"

Chase touched her leg with his tail, and shook his head. "It's only fair. I did the same to you last night."

"But you didn't know! I did. What sort of magik am I?" she whispered only partially to herself.

Chase turned to her again, but he kept silent.

Finally, Kajiya found words again. "Will you forgive me?"

A smirk came over his face, and the bright light of the sun shone down through the canopy. "Of course. Anything to help a fe—riend. Do you mind if I call you that?"

Kajiya shook her head, but unease found its way into her stomach. Perhaps the thing that was off about this fea wasn't that he had seen a spiede after all. Perhaps she was just hearing things. Perhaps he just got tongue-tied. Perhaps. Perhaps.

"So where are you from?" Kajiya blurted, attempting to hit a less touchy subject.

Chase smiled, and Kajiya guessed he was enjoying the change. He looked forward again.

"My family didn't live in a tribe," he began, and Kajiya's ears perked, "but I know we lived in Animo territory. I wouldn't say we were from Animo though."

Kajiya shook her head. "Yeah, no. Your parents were from Mirabilia right? Maybe they knew my dad."

"Y-Yeah. It's a possibility, I guess," he laughed, but it sounded to Kajiya like more of a giggle than the loud laughter she was used to from her brother and Gaorun. "And you're Mirabilian of course," Chase said, leaning towards her.

Kajiya nodded. "We all are."

"So tell me," Chase said after a moment, "what's it like to be a magik?"

Her fur rose a little at the unexpected question. "Well, um… I can't really say."

Chase blinked in surprise, and he paused for a

moment, then said, "Why not?"

A faint purple hue infiltrated Kajiya's cheeks. "Well, I've lived as one my whole life. I don't know what it's like to *not* be a magik. So, it's just... Normal."

Chase nodded understandingly and reached up to push his bangs out of his eyes. "I see."

"Kajiya," Resurge's voice floated over from where he and Ainee had stopped. Onta ran about at their heels, yapping contentedly. "I think it's about time we took a lunch break, unless you feel like eating while we travel again."

"We probably should," Kajiya said, putting a hand to her chin. "Jiblin will be stopping to eat and do other things along the way."

"See? Told you," Ainee's voice interrupted before Kajiya could finish her thought. "Now get Gaorun over here, and I'll cook up the last of that avian meat."

Kajiya bristled slightly; how rude could they be? Asking for her opinion, and then not even letting her say it. She snorted, and stuck her snout into the air as she began to stalk forward. But she had barely taken two steps before her anger died. Sure it was rude, but was it worth the time it took to argue? She could simply remind Ainee of her manners, and they would be on their way.

She breathed out, then put her hands on her hips as she followed Ainee. "Did you have to cut me off?"

"Oh, sorry! It's just—Resurge and I were having an argument. I guess I was a little eager to see him be wrong for a change," she said with a small nod in his direction.

Kajiya let out a small laugh and held a hand to her head. "But Ainee, *you're* the one who's usually right."

She blinked. "Really? Sure doesn't feel like it some days." Venom shot from Ainee's eyes straight to Chase, who grinned sheepishly in response.

Kajiya put her hand on Ainee's shoulder. "Ainee!" she said, keeping her voice low. "Look, I know he hurt your feelings, but this is not the way to go about it. You need to let it go. You're acting positively childish!"

Ainee blinked multiple times as she processed what Kajiya was saying. The anger and shock faded from her pink eyes to be replaced with the warmth that Kajiya knew and loved. She dipped her head, but just then, Resurge and Gaorun returned with the meat, primed and prepped.

Resurge gave an exaggerated bow. "We'll leave this to you ladies today."

Gaorun copied the bow, and Onta took the opportunity to jump up on his back. He laughed as she settled down for a nap, leaving him stuck in the bent-over position.

Kajiya snickered and Ainee joined her.

"Problems, Gaorun?" Kajiya asked.

"Maybe." Gaorun smiled.

"Let me help you with that," Chase said as he walked over and took the onti off of Gaorun's back, and placed her on his own shoulders instead.

Onta flipped her snout at the back of his neck, and settled down again. Gaorun straightened and started to laugh.

"She likes you," he said, putting his hand in his pocket. "I can still remember the first time I met her.

Saved her from a chirpl—and I've got the scars to prove it!"

Chase grinned. "Now *that* sounds like a story."

Gaorun started to walk forward, joining Resurge and his map at the front with Chase in tow. "It is. Now, you've gotta picture the scene. It was just dusk, you know, that time when both suns are visible in the sky…"

Their voices got quieter and quieter as they walked further away, until finally, it was just Ainee and Kajiya left. Kajiya looked over to where Ainee was pulling out the seasoning herbs to bring out the flavours of the meat.

"Ainee," Kajiya began, and this time, she knew what she was asking. "Have you ever thought that there was something more out there?"

Ainee blinked and turned to her, ears erect upon her head.

Kajiya's face went a little red. "I've been asking everyone."

"Rotari right?" Ainee said as she turned back to her herbs, pinching her fingers to grab the smallest amount possible to sprinkle over the meat.

Kajiya blinked. "What do you mean?"

Ainee dusted off her hand on her dress, and moved the leaf bracelet on the hand that held the meat slabs further down her arm so that water the boys used to rinse off the preserving salt wouldn't dip on it.

Then she straightened up and passed the seasoned meat to Kajiya. "Well, when Rotari said that there was a force greater than magic, I couldn't get her words out of my head."

The duo started to walk forward to follow the boys, and Kajiya began to warm her hand with magic to cook the meat.

Ainee held her hands around the strap of her herb bag. "So, I started to think. What if she was right? Where was the evidence?"

"And?" Kajiya prompted. "You're smiling, you found something. What was it?"

Ainee laughed, and her face turned a bit redder, "I didn't have to look far. Kajiya, think for a moment about our bodies. I know you don't know much about them, but… They're perfect, Kajiya. They work more efficiently than anything we could ever build or create with magic. The way they defend against disease, the way they heal when they're broken? Simply amazing. And that's even before we start to interfere with magic. And really, all we do is speed up the process."

The wind blew through the tops of the trees, creating a pleasant rustling, and sending shadows everywhere.

Ainee looked up, and a thoughtfulness came into her eyes. "It's too perfect, Kajiya. I had no choice but to conclude that Rotari was right. And, well. Whatever it is…"

"Who," Kajiya interjected.

Ainee looked at her in surprise. "Who?"

Kajiya nodded. "Who. Resurge and I determined it was a 'who' when we spoke." Had that really only been a few days ago?

Ainee tilted her head. "How?"

Kajiya smiled. "Well, when you read a book, do you ask *what* wrote it, or *who* wrote it? 'Whats' cause things," she said, thinking of the ocean that had caused the cave-in as she tried to escape the spiedes, "but they don't create them. It must be a 'who.'"

Ainee nodded. "Whoever it is then," she smiled

as she turned to Kajiya, "is greater than magic."

Kajiya nodded. "Then I guess we all agree."

Ainee turned to her. "Gaorun too?"

"Gaorun too." Kajiya's tail flicked, and her bell rang out.

"What about him?" Ainee jabbed her head in Chase's direction.

"I don't know. It's not really a 'get-to-know-you' question." Kajiya said. "So what got under your fur?"

"I guess it was just the way he refused. Couldn't he see I wanted to help?"

Kajiya nodded, and passed the cooked meat over to Ainee, and started on the next slab.

"Well, there's a first time for everything, I suppose," Kajiya said as the new slab's scent started to waft. "Do you have some rags or something I could wipe my hands on afterwards? This avian was plump."

Ainee reached into her bag and pulled out a square of bandages and put it over Kajiya's shoulder. "All the extra fat will taste good though."

"Yeah. So, what do you think? Friend or foe? I want to say friend, but there's something about him…"

"That just doesn't seem right, right?" Ainee finished.

"Yeah." Kajiya let her chin sink to her chest.

"Maybe that's part of why I can't stand him. He just rubs me the wrong way," Ainee said as she put her hands on her hips. "As much as I hate to admit it, you're right, I do need to give him a chance."

Kajiya beamed.

Ainee shook her head, laughing, "It's funny, but, when you said that, I realized how much you've grown. There was a time when I was the one who had to tell you that."

"Really?"

"Really."

Kajiya pursed her lips slightly, and flipped over the piece of meat in her hand; was she even the same person that set out on this journey? Well, her goals had certainly changed. She was no longer on a quest to regain her honour; in fact, she didn't even really care about that anymore. What she did care about, was stopping Turten and saving her people! From the spiedes, from all of it.

"Do you think I'm cut out to be a magik?" Kajiya asked quietly.

Ainee blinked, then turned to help her over a large fallen tree. "Of course you are! You have your mark…"

"But what about it? What is it than just a fur marking? It doesn't mean I'll be a *good* magik. Admit it, there have been plenty of bad ones!" Kajiya hissed as she balanced on top of the trunk.

Ainee smiled. "Kajiya, you're not like them. You care. You care about your tribe, the other tribes even. I mean, look at what you've done! You almost single-handedly stopped the spiede invasion of Animo, and now we're going to put a stop to Turten. You'll make a great magik Kajiya, when the time comes."

A weak smile surfaced on Kajiya's face, and she nodded, then passed the fully cooked slab of meat to the purple fea.

It felt for a moment, as if the entire continent of Mysterium was upon her shoulders, and Kajiya's smile faded. There was so much to do, and so little time. And the what-ifs… Could she really…

Kajiya squinted, focussing on the ice that held

her hand numb; right now, she only had one task. And that was one task that she could do. One thing that she could accomplish. Sure, it wasn't big, exciting or substantial, but her grumbling stomach informed her that it was still important. The next three pieces of meat practically flew out of her hands, and the boys dropped back for their shares when a change in the wind brought the scent to them.

Gaorun held out his hand, and Kajiya placed the final slab of meat she'd been cooking in it. He immediately ripped it in half, giving a portion to Onta. Her purple snout practically smiled as she snatched up the piece. Gaorun laughed, and took a bite of his own as he turned back to continue forward. Resurge held his hand out to Ainee, and gave her a small bow as she placed the meat in it. Chase held back, fiddling with the straps of his pack. Ainee rolled her eyes, and held out another slab with a smile. Resurge bristled a little, but stepped aside as Chase took the meat.

"Thank you," Chase said, holding it between his first two fingers and thumb.

"It's nothing," Ainee said as she turned to Resurge.

Chase smiled, and looked at Kajiya excitedly. Kajiya smiled back, and the group started off again. Kajiya snatched one of the last two slabs back from Ainee, and popped it into her own mouth.

"Who's that last one for?" Chase asked as he split the meat the same way that Gaorun had.

"Gaorun and Onta," Kajiya said. "Gaorun likes to share his food with her, even when we make her her own piece."

"Gaorun's interesting, isn't he?"

Kajiya smiled, mouth full. "A little bit, a little

bit. He's had Onta as long as I can remember. She's practically family to us both."

Chase nodded.

"So," Kajiya said after she had swallowed. "What's your business in Royalin?"

Chase stiffened. "It's difficult to explain."

Kajiya's bell rang out as she accidentally hit it against an exposed root. "Try me."

"What is that?" Gaorun's voice cut into the conversation, and all eyes turned to him.

"What's what?" Resurge asked, surging forward with the map.

Ainee cast Kajiya a worried glance, and the two of them jogged forward to see what the boys were going on about. Chase was only a step behind.

Right as they arrived, Gaorun's orange eyes widened, and a smile broke out over his face. Even Onta yapped happily.

"It's the beach!"

Chapter 7: Rebel

The group was out of the forest and on the white sand in moments. Kajiya couldn't help but stand amazed as the ocean took her breath away. Unlike the other side of the continent, where the island of Ainee was, here the ocean lay flat on the horizon, and it felt to Kajiya as though she could see to the end of the world. The others stood, likewise awed, until Gaorun spoke.

"Footprints! I see footprints!" The green fea pounded along the forest at the edge of the beach, sending sand everywhere as Onta jumped off his shoulders and onto the ground.

He knelt down beside the vague prints, and as Kajiya walked up to him, she wondered what had tipped him off to the fact that they were footprints rather than a few strange depressions in the sand. Probably his years of hunting experience.

Onta sniffed the sand around the prints, tail held high as Gaorun observed the depressions from different angles, carefully avoiding going within a tail-length of them, as to not replace them with his own tracks.

"We've missed them by a couple of days," he said at last, looking up. "It had to be them—the wind would have taken out most of the prints, but Pato told me that Jiblin took the entire Palinda Assembly and a few others, just over a hundred feas in all. For a print to stay on the beach this long, it must have been one of many. Either way, I think we're gaining on them. And if they've reached the beach…"

"Then they'll continue along it to get to

Royalin," Ainee finished.

Gaorun nodded and stood. "While there aren't very many prints left to follow, I don't think we'll be needing the map anymore."

Resurge shook his head. "I disagree. If we're not careful, we could easily lose time here, thinking we're getting places, but not going as fast."

Kajiya stepped forward. "Then we'll leave it up to you to make sure we're making good time?"

Resurge took the map out and looked around. Finally he nodded, and flicked his tail. "Let's go."

Kajiya broke out into a large smile, and looked upwards. Koiyan was beginning to descend, but she had the feeling that they were progressing nicely. They would have to stop for the night soon though. She turned back to Chase.

"So," she said, dropping her pace to join him at the back, "you never answered my question."

Chase blinked, then looked forward. "I'm afraid you'll have to remind me what it was."

Kajiya started to try to hold her hands behind her back, but stopped as her backpack got in the way. Instead, she flicked her tail irritably, and her bell let out a jingle.

"What are you going to do in Royalin?" she asked, shaking out her hands as she remembered the white cloth on her shoulder.

She took it down and started to wipe the grease off of her cooking hand as Chase began to speak.

"I'm going to approach the Grand Assembly as well."

Kajiya looked up in shock, and her ears perked. "About what?"

Chase looked out at the ocean. "About the

rebellion."

"The *what?*" Kajiya hissed, nearly dropping the clothe.

Rebellion!? Who was rebelling against what? Turten hadn't even imposed his law yet, so there was no reason for feas to already be rebelling against him.

"You don't think my brother escaped from the spiedes by accident do you?" Chase said nonchalantly.

Kajiya's brow furrowed; where was he going with this?

"Well, he was actually set free temporarily." Chase turned to her, his orange eyes intense. "He was sent to be the slave of a spiede who does *not* believe in slavery!"

Kajiya gave a little jump, and her eyes widened. "What? Those exist?"

Where were those spiedes when she was in that cavern? Kajiya's fur rose, and a small memory came back to her, probably the only memory she had of a spiede that didn't terrify her. A mother spiede nuzzled her child as she sent it inside their home. They could love. And if they could understand what was good, then surely they understood what was evil.

"Yes, they do. And they set my brother free to be a liaison to the feas, and tell them that the spiedes who do not believe in slavery are planning to overthrow their king. He was recaptured shortly after he told me. I figured it was my duty to finish what he started."

She nodded hesitantly to Chase; it was possible that some of the spiedes were good. At least, Kajiya hoped they were.

"And what do they plan to do once their king is overthrown? Will they appoint a new one?" Kajiya asked.

Chase shook his head. "No, they want to use what they call a 'democracy'—they'll take a vote to determine their leaders."

Kajiya raised an eyebrow. "Vote? Not sure how well that's gonna work. But then again, I guess they don't have fur to be marked, eh?"

Chase blinked, then smiled and nodded. "O-of course."

Kajiya turned ahead; the others were out of earshot. They wouldn't have heard about Chase's purpose. Kajiya's mind began to race; if there were spiedes that were trying to overthrow the king, then they could fight alongside them when the spiedes attacked. And Chase's story would lend her accusations against Turten some more credibility. It could even help the Grand Assembly come up with a plan of attack. The rebelling spiedes would have to be utilized to their full potential—Kajiya cast her eyes down to the sand beneath her feet. Was she *actually* thinking about a full-out war? She *hated* war. But, as she looked up to the sky, she realized, that at this point it was nearly unavoidable. She sighed, then turned to Chase.

"As soon as camp is set up, you need to tell the others. We need to start thinking about how to contact the *right* spiedes, mobilize the captured feas. Start unlocking shackles—"

"Whoa, whoa, whoa!" Chase held out his hands. "You're getting a bit ahead of yourself there, Kajiya. First we have to get to Royalin, and then the Grand Assembly will decide what to do, right? And I'm sure that if we manage to stop Turten from *helping* the king, it'll be a major blow to their plans. One step at a time."

Kajiya lowered her ears sheepishly. "Of course. But the next step is still to tell them," she said, signalling towards the others with her snout. "They need to know."

"Once camp is set up then."

Kajiya didn't have to wait long. With Midyan rising, the group ahead decided to stop for the night quickly, and they set up camp near the treeline.

"It'll be best if we don't set up too close to the ocean," Gaorun explained as they put the finishing touches on the campsite. "The sand will never hold the tent spikes, and we don't want to wake up in the tide."

Resurge nodded in agreement as he brought out a pan from his pack. "I think we made good time too. We should be in sight of Royalin by tomorrow."

Kajiya's stomach clenched. "What about Jiblin? Will he have made it there before us?"

Gaorun looked at her and nodded. "Based on his tracks, they'll make it to Royalin sometime tomorrow, if they're not there already."

Kajiya gulped. "We're not going to catch them are we?"

Gaorun shook his head. "No, we're not. If we had another week, we might be able to…"

Kajiya sighed as Ainee took the pan from Resurge and brought out their meat. Ainee created a small flame and set fire to the wood that Chase had artfully arranged.

"I think it's time we came up with plan B, *Ruina*," she said as she slapped the first piece of meat onto the pan.

"Before we do that," Kajiya interjected, "Chase has something he needs to tell you guys."

Chase stiffened slightly, then relaxed. He gave Kajiya a short nod and stepped over to stand by the fire.

"According to my brother, there are some spiedes that are planning a rebellion. They want to overthrow their king. I'm going to the Grand Assembly to seek the tribes' help in making sure that they are successful."

Resurge narrowed his eyes. "And why should we help the *spiedes*? They nearly killed my sister!"

Chase turned to him. "Because when they overthrow the king, one of the first things they will do is free the slaves! They believe that spiedes and feas can live in peace."

Kajiya nodded, and Gaorun turned to her.

"Kajiya," he began. "You were down there. Are they capable of this?"

"Not the ones I saw the most, but… I believe so," she said honestly.

Gaorun dipped his head. "If you say so." He turned to Chase. "We'll trust you on this, but why didn't you tell us about this from the beginning?"

"Only Kajiya asked," he said with a shrug. "I also wasn't sure how well you would take it after hearing about what happened in Animo."

"I'm still curious as to why you wouldn't let Ainee heal you. What else aren't you telling us?" Resurge asked, a hint of a growl to his voice.

Chase stiffened, but Ainee rose. "That's enough Resurge. I'm sure Chase had his reasons." She smiled at him. "And I won't pry. But if you ever get *seriously* hurt, you need to let me heal you, okay?" she said, putting her hands on her hips as her tail flicked sharply.

Kajiya let out a small gasp as the meat fell out of the pan that Ainee had apparently forgotten she was holding. Ice filled Kajiya's hand as she held it above the ground. She sighed in relief and turned to Ainee.

"And you don't forget what you're doing Ainee!" she chastised.

Ainee blinked, then scooped the piece out of the air with the pan. "Whoops," she shrugged.

Kajiya rolled her eyes and let the ice melt. As she did so, she became aware of Chase staring at her. She raised her shoulders and flicked her tail. Her bell rang out, apparently snapping him out of his stupor. He cast a frenzied glance at Resurge and Gaorun, then clasped his hands in his lap, staring at his feet. Kajiya's ear twitched and she turned back to the others. Resurge looked slightly taken aback, but otherwise fine, and Gaorun and Onta were both watching the pan with the anfa meat hungrily.

Kajiya relaxed her shoulders and sat down on the ground. "Alright, so now that that's all sorted out, shall we go to that plan B?"

Ainee nodded. "I think we'll need to change Resurge's name too this time."

Resurge stiffened. "Why?"

Ainee turned to him. "Because if we use your name, they might figure out that you're related to Proten and tell him. If he finds out you're there before we figure out where the Grand Assembly hall is, he might try to find you, and if he finds Kajiya before we intend, then he might let it slip to Turten that she's there, even if we *do* tell him everything!"

Kajiya sighed and leaned back, flopping down on the ground. "Well, at least we can be siblings again. Ruina and... Voi?"

Resurge crossed his arms and raised an eyebrow. "Voi? No offense, Kajiya, but I'd like something a bit more impressive."

Ainee shook the pan. "What about Nijiru? I've always liked that name."

"Or Heka? Or Dereen?" Gaorun chimed in.

"Dani?" Chase said so quietly that Kajiya was sure Resurge didn't hear him.

"Or even just Surge?" Gaorun said again.

Resurge raised a hand. "Nijiru sounds fine," he said and Ainee beamed.

Kajiya smiled; Ainee had given her Ruina for a name as well. Of course, she suspected that Resurge had other reasons for choosing that name.

"So I guess I was right about needing that shirt, eh?" she said as Ainee took one of the pieces of meat and gave it to Onta.

The purple fea nodded, "I'm glad you decided to, it would be annoying to have to make another one. Although, I must admit, I want to try a pattern like Emera's dress."

"But, all of that aside, what are we going to do in Royalin?" Gaorun asked.

Resurge stepped forward and joined Kajiya on the ground. "Our first objective will be to find the Grand Assembly hall. If we can't find that, we've lost everything."

Kajiya nodded, then sat forward to put her hands on the ground in front of her. "There should be some maps in the library if we aren't able to find it by asking. I mean, most feas should know where it is."

Resurge nodded. "And what if there's no Assembly that day? They'll want to give Jiblin a day or two to rest after he arrives."

Gaorun nodded. "He might even request it. It's a bit of walk from Palinda to Royalin."

Ainee laughed. "My feet agree with you."

Kajiya nodded, drawing in the dirt with a claw. "So, with any luck we should arrive when the Assembly starts. But, most Assemblies take place in the morning, and try to wrap up by late afternoon. If we arrive in the evening, we should try to find a hotel that'll take us. Or if the Assembly's is taking the day off. And… Actually, I don't think just covering my mark will cut it this time guys," Kajiya said with sudden apprehension. "If Turten's around, he won't be looking for me, but if I could change my appearance more drastically this time—"

"Why don't you use an illusion spell?"

Everyone turned to Chase in surprise, and he looked around awkwardly.

"You know illusion magic?" Gaorun blurted.

Chase nodded. "If you're just going for being unrecognizable, I find changing the colour of your fur often works pretty well."

Suddenly, before their eyes, his fur shifted from blue to green then to orange, red, and yellow, and then finally back to blue. Kajiya's jaw gaped, and the scent of cooking anfa started to get a smoky charred tinge to it.

Kajiya jumped up at once. "You've got to teach me how to do that!" she held her fists in front of her chest, and her tail swung about wildly with excitement.

Chase laughed and held his hands up. "Of course, of course!"

Kajiya nodded. "Well then?"

"Now? Right now?" Chase drew back slightly.

"Yes right now! We haven't a second to waste!" Kajiya said, and her tail's flicks grew sharper with her impatience.

Chase nodded hesitantly, and stood beside her. "Summon the magic," he instructed, "and send it out as a sort of aura around your entire body."

Kajiya nodded, taking her normal magic using position, an old fighting stance that Resurge had taught her many years ago. She stood with feet shoulder width apart, and arms at her sides, fists clenched. The ice filled her body, and she held herself perfectly still as she sent it just beneath her skin. She pushed it outside of herself, and nodded.

Chase nodded back. "Now focus on the colour you want your fur to become."

Orange would work nicely for a trial run. Kajiya breathed in, closed her eyes and focused on the colour.

"And now imagine it settling onto you. Bring the magic closer to yourself when you're ready. Now, it might take a few tries to get it—right."

Kajiya had been doing as he instructed as he spoke, and now she peeked open an eye. She looked down, and her heart skipped a beat. Sure enough, her fur was bright orange, and her stripes a white-pink. She blinked a few times and could still feel the magic just above her fur. She reached out it, and shifted the colour to green. She couldn't help but laugh as the colour changed.

"This is amazing!" she said as she spun around.

She looked back, smiling, and released the magic, causing her fur to shift back to its natural blue.

Chase let out a small cough. "You're talented. It took me at least three tries before I got it right. The first time I was half-purple."

"Half purple?" Ainee inquired.

Chase nodded. "The left half to be specific."

Resurge let out a laugh. "Sounds about right. Magic never works the way you want it to when you need it."

Kajiya rolled her eyes. "It's worked pretty good for me."

"But you're a magik," Resurge retorted.

"I should try that out—" Gaorun said, "it'd be great to be able to camouflage myself into my surroundings, no matter what those surroundings are."

Ainee stood up and began to pass out the meat, starting by walking over to Resurge.

"But what about you?" she asked concernedly. "You wouldn't use magic to change your fur colour like Kajiya's, would you?"

Resurge shook his head. "Never. I will never use magic unless it's absolutely necessary. It would tarnish my honour."

Gaorun pursed his lips as he took two pieces of meat from the pan. He let one drop and Onta leapt to catch it.

"But what if Turten sees you?" he wondered.

Resurge shook his head again. "They don't know we left with Kajiya, we should be fine. He might just think that I came to see Dad."

Kajiya nodded. "I'd feel better if we could disguise you a little though. Make sure you wear your vest. You didn't have it back in Mirabilia, so even if Turten sees you, it should put him off a little, hopefully."

Gaorun smirked. "And failing that, the light reflecting off the scales'll blind him!"

Kajiya giggled. "I doubt that, Gaorun!"

"It's possible." He grinned, leaning forward.

Kajiya pushed him away playfully and took her piece of meat from Ainee's pan. She gobbled it down in two swift bites, and started for her tent.

"Well, then, we'd best get some sleep. We have a long day ahead of us tomorrow."

*   *   *

Kajiya tried her best to stretch her back in spite of the bag she wore. Walking along the beach in the early morning air had been nice and peaceful at first, but by midafternoon Kajiya had grown exceedingly bored of the shoreline. No matter where she looked, it was all the same: white-beige sand, bright blue ocean that seemed to be endless and harsh sunlight that reflected violently off the waves into her eyes. Kajiya had to watch the treeline for any signs that they were making progress. Resurge had been right about keeping the map open, and was constantly pushing them to go faster in order to keep their progress consistent.

Kajiya had given up any hope of catching Jiblin, and instead focused on getting to Royalin as fast as she could. What would she say when she got there? Would the proof they brought, her being alive, the letter for Beifin, the light-orb, and Chase's tale be enough to convince them? It had to be. But could it be?

Kajiya shook her head, and sped up her pace. Overthinking wouldn't help her; moving faster would.

The others gave her curious stares as she powered through to the front of the group, but kept their thoughts to themselves. Kajiya nodded to her brother as she reached him.

"How much farther?" she asked, tail tip twitching.

Resurge happened to have the map open in his hands. "At least another day."

Kajiya let out an exasperated growl, but didn't say another word. Complaining wasn't helpful either, no matter how much she felt like it.

Resurge raised an eyebrow, but a small smile surfaced on his face regardless.

"Impatient?" he wondered.

Kajiya rolled her eyes and hunched her shoulders. "And you're not?"

Her brother's smile faded. "Anxious. That's a better word."

Kajiya sighed, nodding, and she let her pace drop again. As she slowed down, Ainee passed her with a smile, and Chase and Gaorun as well. Kajiya blinked as Gaorun passed her, and sped up to keep pace with the others again. As she did so, she saw Gaorun cast a glance to the forest. His tail swept from side to side slowly, and Kajiya couldn't help but watch. His tail only moved like that when he was hunting or thinking hard. He clearly wasn't hunting.

He moved over to Chase, and started to speak to him in a low voice. Kajiya's ears perked, and she moved closer, hoping to catch a snatch of their conversation. Chase didn't look comfortable. In fact, the colour had drained from his facial fur.

Suddenly, a screech rang out from the forest, and the sun disappeared. No! Not now! Except... Except... she heard that. She really heard that! This was no memory.

A shadow passed over Kajiya and all of her fur stood on end as she looked up. It couldn't be. There was no way!

But it was. The spiede skidded on the sand and crashed into the ground, sending a spray of powder into the crashing waves. It scrambled to its feet, and Kajiya found herself sending up puffs of sand as she headed for the safety of the forest. Gaorun, Ainee and Resurge wasted absolutely no time in joining her, but Chase hesitated, and his fur shifted to purple. Kajiya gasped, and spun back around. The spiede got to him first. Kajiya had no choice to but to watch as Chase turned into a pink blur above her head. A resounding thud echoed as he hit a tree and vanished into the bushes.

Kajiya turned back to the spiede, breathing heavily as magic froze her to the spot. Her heart pounded in her ears as they fell beneath her head. This couldn't be happening!

"*Yaaa!*" Resurge's voice brought Kajiya back to her senses, and she snapped her head to the side to look at him as he charged from the forest, broadsword in hand.

Unfortunately, the spiede heard him as well.

The ice within Kajiya changed in an instant from paralyzing to mobilizing. She flung her hand out to the ocean; if she had defeated them with water before, she could do it again. She made a fist and threw it over her head, creating a giant wave of water that loomed over the beach.

Ainee and Gaorun were by Resurge's side as soon as he stopped, and they held out their hands to the sky. Kajiya saw them out of the corner of her eye. They would keep him safe; there was no reason to hold back.

The spiede thrust its head up as it listened, but,

with its eyes closed, Kajiya knew that it had no way to predict what she was doing.

The wave crashed into the sand, producing a satisfying crunch, but as Kajiya released the magic, and the last shreds of water disappeared from the magic-bubble that Gaorun and Ainee had cast, her eyes widened and a dark pit opened in her gut. The spiede was still standing.

Resurge leapt without hesitation, while Gaorun gave a low whistle for Onta, who promptly ran out from the safety of the forest to begin to deliver vicious poisonous bites to its thin legs, nipping and jumping away before the spiede could attack. Gaorun then summoned one of his nets from his pack with magic, and flung it over the spiede's abdomen as Resurge copied Onta's tactic of attacking the legs, then jumping back before the spiede could counter. Kajiya suspected he didn't fancy being thrown like the last time he had fought a spiede.

Even Ainee was running around, yelling at the top of her lungs, and Kajiya knew that she was trying to give the boys some cover. Every now and again, she'd even send a small fireball towards it. If the spiede so much as opened its eyes it would go blind, so it chose to rely instead solely on its hearing and perhaps the vibrations of the ground.

The vibrations of the ground! Now that was an idea. Kajiya threw herself back into the action, summoning all the magic she could. She had to protect them! The ice solidified, and Kajiya recognized the feeling. This, *this* was the magic that had saved her in the tunnel.

She knelt to the ground, careful to keep her knee off the sand so she could rise quickly if she needed to. She touched the beach with one hand, and sent all her magic through it, feeling her way down until she hit solid dirt, stone and vast quantities of salt. She moved the magic over below the spiede, and happily discovered a large patch of salt. Then, she felt her way around with the magic; there wasn't enough water in the surrounding area to dissolve it all! But, there was plenty water in the ocean.

Kajiya grinned, and tightened her hand in the sand, causing her magic to draw the water down through the sand and into the salt, and then to percolate into the dirt below. Just a moment more…

"Get away, now!" she screeched as she pressed her hand into the sand, giving the new cavern the push it needed to collapse in on itself.

She looked up, breathing heavily. Sure enough, the feas had jumped away just as the sand began to give in order to fill the new cavity. The spiede tried to scramble away, but the shifting sands were too fast, and it soon found itself sinking into the ground.

"You won't get away with this!" it hissed in its grating claw-on-rock voice. *"The king's armies are almost ready! The surface will be ours by the end of the week! My death will change noth…"*

Kajiya shuddered as its head went under the sand. Soon, only the tops of three of its bent legs, and one uplifted leg were visible along with the dark brown mound that was its abdomen. Green ooze flowed from the wounds that Resurge and Onta had inflicted, and one of its hind legs had been bound to its body with Gaorun's net. Kajiya could even see singe marks from Ainee's fires.

But what about Chase? At once, the relief that she had felt was gone, and Kajiya began to look for the missing fea.

"I'll put it out of its misery," Gaorun was saying as she twisted and turned. "I would never want to be buried alive."

Kajiya's fur prickled and her breath grew ragged. "Ch-Chase!" Kajiya shouted once she found her voice again.

There was no response, and Kajiya's tail puffed out. She could hear her heartbeat in her ears, and her red eyes darted about from the forest to the sea and back again.

Ainee jogged over to her. "Kajiya!" she hissed sharply. "You need to calm down!"

Kajiya's breaths were short and shallow, but she nodded and gulped. Hysterics were never good for anyone.

Ainee lifted her hand, and Kajiya nodded, breathing in when the purple fea raised her hand, and back out when she lowered it. Once her pulse had slowed, she repeated herself.

"We need to find Chase," she said, starting towards the forest.

Now that her mind had cleared a little, she remembered seeing him being hit by the spiede's leg and go flying into the trees. Her brow furrowed at the memory. Why had he been pink? Was her memory messing with her again?

Kajiya ran up to the tree she had seen him hit. Sure enough, a groan came from the tree's base, and she recognized his voice, although it seemed higher than usual again.

Kajiya moved the bushes that obstructed her view of him to the side. She stopped at once, and her jaw went slack.

Where Chase should have been, in his place was a pink female fea she had never seen before.

Chapter 8: Break Down

Kajiya couldn't do anything but stare. The fea wore a sleeveless magenta jumpsuit with large puffy pants. A light beige cloth that bore a slight resemblance to a skirt was wrapped around her waist, held together in the front by a purple stone clasp. A similar material covered her arms from just below the shoulders to slightly past the crook of her elbow. It was also suitably puffy. Her long hair fell past her shoulders, spreading out on the ground to frame her face. Her bangs were parted to both sides and her ears had one stripe each. Her face stripes went from the middle of her cheeks down her neck a ways. There was one stripe right over top of each of her shoulders, and Kajiya could see three stripes on each of her forearms. Starting at her wrist though, the striping appeared to create what seemed to be fingerless gloves. Her tail, which had many stripes, told Kajiya that she was most likely from Animo; it was thick and fully furred, although a little scraggily, and tapered to a sharp point.

But what really caused Kajiya to stare, was the girl's fur colouring. She was a dull light pink, with *darker* pink hair and stripes. Kajiya had heard about such feas existing, but she had never seen one. Everyone knew that only males had darker stripes than the rest of their fur. Females always had *lighter* stripes.

Suddenly, Kajiya became aware of Ainee at her side.

"Oh my," she said as she kneeled down to check the fea's temperature. "Go get my herbs."

Kajiya nodded in a daze. "R-right."

The blue fea turned around and started towards the beach without a word. She found the herb bag from where Ainee had abandoned it, and as she picked it up, raised voices reached her ears.

"You *knew* we were being followed?!" Resurge was hissing at Gaorun, throwing his hands into the air.

Kajiya nearly dropped the herbs.

"I didn't think that it was by this! I thought—" the green fea responded.

"You didn't think Gaorun! What if it had been—" Resurge began.

"Been what?" Gaorun hissed, crossing his arms as his eyes narrowed.

Resurge growled and stuck his sword blade-first into the sand. It promptly fell over, but Kajiya could see that her brother's tail was still thrashing.

"Look," Gaorun said, gesticulating, "I thought it might have been a spiede sent to *escort* Chase to the Grand Assembly. Let's face it, if he had approached with the spiede, it stands to reason that we would have freaked, right?"

"This didn't look like an escort to me," Resurge growled as he crossed his arms, fur bristling as he raised his shoulders. "And why wouldn't he tell us about it then?" Resurge's face became positively contorted with anger. "Where is that ungrateful spiede-lover anyway?!"

Gaorun looked around, and it appeared to Kajiya that it was occurring to both of them for the first time that Chase was gone.

She looked towards the forest, then back to the boys; Resurge was stalking towards the trees, arms held rigid at his sides. Gaorun followed at a respectful distance in spite of his apparent anger, well out of the way of Resurge's powerful tail.

"Look, I was just about to ask him about it when the spiede attacked! How was I supposed to know it wasn't friendly?"

"What on *Mysterium* made you think it was?!" Resurge roared. "Well?" he growled as he reached the forest. *"Come on out, Chase!"*

That was it. Kajiya tightened her grip on the bag and stalked over to her brother.

"Resurge!" she hissed.

He whirled around to face her, his red-orange eyes far more red than normal. "What?" he snarled.

Kajiya stiffened. In all their years of being siblings, she had never seen him like this.

"Get a hold of yourself, Resurge. You need to calm down," she said in a tone that she hoped wouldn't invite contradiction.

"I will, as soon as that *idiot* gets out here and explains what that was!" he said, stomping forward towards Kajiya.

The breath caught in Kajiya's throat as she stepped back. She was frightened. Frightened by her own brother. No. No this wasn't her brother. This wasn't him at all. It was as though something else had taken his form.

"Heh, you wouldn't hit a girl now, would you?" a strange voice said.

Kajiya was only too happy for the distraction. Ainee had the strange girl's arm draped over her shoulder, and was helping to carry her to the beachside.

"Kajiya!" Ainee hissed. "Where were you?!"

Kajiya looked over her shoulder; Resurge

showed no signs of calming down.

The only way she could respond was with magic, *I don't think—*

"And just who are you?" Resurge roared, shouldering his way past Kajiya harshly.

Ainee's eyes widened, and she quickly put herself between Resurge and his new prey.

"She's my *patient,* Resurge," she said as she stared into his eyes.

Kajiya could do nothing but step back as Resurge drew himself up to his full height. Ainee wasn't backing down.

No, no, this wasn't working. The anger, it fed off of itself. Maybe… Maybe if she could project her thoughts, then maybe she could project her feelings too. Kajiya summoned the ice, and it came with all the strength she had felt battling the spiede. She held her hands tight against her chest, and gathered the magic there. This was from her heart, not her mind or throat. Tears started to form in her eyes.

Resurge had just opened his mouth to speak when the magic reached them. He faltered, and stepped back. He looked over as Kajiya started to sob; but now that she had started, she couldn't stop pouring out her feelings with the magic. Everything came crashing down at once, and the others started to look around uncomfortably. Kajiya didn't want to share this. Not with them. She was supposed to be their leader. Not their weakest link. But the magic wouldn't stop, and she doubted she was even in control of it anymore. So, she did the only thing she could and sent it up to the sky. Perhaps whatever being was there could understand; could make it all right. Perhaps they wouldn't be overwhelmed.

Finally, the magic faded, and Kajiya found her facial fur flatted and spiked by her tears. Resurge had walked up to her. He looked at her with the guiltiest, most repentant gaze she had ever seen, and as he held his arms out, Kajiya buried herself in her brother's fur.

"I'm sorry. I lost control," he said. "I never meant to—to scare you."

"Just don't do it again, okay?" Kajiya whispered between sobs.

The group was silent, and Ainee walked over to take the herbs from where Kajiya had dropped them. She sat the pink fea down on a log.

The pink fea's ears were low. "I'm sorry I caused so much trouble. I didn't expect any of this to happen."

Kajiya wiped the tears away from her eyes, and pushed her brother away to look at the stranger.

"What do you mean?"

The stranger cringed as Ainee applied some herbs to her arm. "I'm Chase."

Kajiya shook her head in disbelief. "You can't be."

The fea looked up and smiled apologetically. Suddenly, her fur shifted colours, just the way that Chase had taught Kajiya. Before Kajiya's tired mind could even comprehend what was happening, Chase's image had formed around the stranger.

"See?" she said, and Kajiya could now hear how she had skillfully lowered her voice to sound masculine. "This is why I didn't want Ainee to heal me. She would have recognized me as a girl right away."

Kajiya sniffled and wiped her face with the back of her hand. "But, why did you pretend to be a guy? Is 'Chase' even your real name?"

"No," she said in her natural voice, letting the illusion fade. "My name is Sarka."

Kajiya looked behind her. Resurge had placed one arm against a tree, and his head against his forearm. His tail drooped, and was still. Kajiya's heart ached. This wound would take time to heal no doubt. But for now…

"And, in the city, all the other slaves looked down on me for using magic."

Kajiya's ears perked at once. City? Slaves?

"You were the one captured by spiedes," she thought aloud.

Sarka nodded, and pulled sharply away from Ainee as the purple fea tied a bandage around her arm.

"Yeah. My whole family was. I don't know what happened to them. I was lucky enough to be given to one of the rebellion's leaders. He was born without eyes, so they elected him to talk to the feas, to us. But when he was given me, he figured that I would do a better job of it. You know, one of their own? I tried to tell him that they wouldn't listen to me," she looked away. "That's the curse of my family."

"What do you mean?" Gaorun asked with his arms still crossed.

Sarka looked up at him. "Can't you see?!"

"I see your fur's strange," he said.

"Well," Sarka spat, "according to the other everyone else, my fur makes me inferior. They talk as though I'm not even there. My whole family is like this, so, we moved away from Animo. Started a circus outside town for travellers. I was the acrobat. I mean, we're all oddities, so why not?"

Kajiya held her stomach; she remembered Sai

talking about when the feas started to disappear after the spiedes began their attacks. The ones outside the city limits were the first to go. Even so...

"No. You're not. You're just different," Kajiya said. "Like me."

Sarka raised her ears inquisitively. "You don't look that different to me. I mean, yeah you've got that strange fur marking, but at least it's the right colours."

Kajiya blinked; strange marking? Her magik's mark!

Ainee gave a little gasp. "Don't tell me you've never seen a magik's mark before?"

Sarka turned to her. "They have marks?"

Kajiya nodded. "We do. And, I'm the first female magik. Ever. I'm different too."

Sarka lowered her eyes. "But you don't know what it's like. To be ridiculed by your *own* kind?"

A breath left Kajiya's lips. Sarka was right, she *didn't* know.

"I didn't think so." The pink fea pushed a stray lock of hair out of her face.

"No, you're right, you *are* an oddity." Ainee's voice sounded unnecessarily harsh, and Kajiya was about to rebuke her when she saw a smirk spread across her friend's face. "Where did you learn to use magic like that?"

Sarka leaned back. "See? This is why I pretended to be a guy. Everyone *freaks* when a girl uses magic. I mean, even when I turn my fur the proper colours! I was so shocked when I saw you two use magic freely, and these guys didn't bat an eye."

Gaorun blinked in surprise. "No wonder. The second rule of magic is that woman can only use low level healing magic—anything else could put too much strain on their bodies and kill them. The only exception is Kajiya," he said, gesturing to her, "and that's because magic favours her."

Sarka blinked. "Magic has rules?"

Kajiya nearly fell over. "You didn't know?!"

Sarka shook her head. "My brother never taught me about them."

"Your brother taught you?" Ainee said with a touch of shock to her voice as she began to put away her herbs.

Sarka nodded. "Yeah. Almost every chance he got. The colour-changing trick was a favorite of his," she said with a reminiscent smile. "I just modified it once Sharack decided to send me to be the rebellion's voice to the feas. I knew that they wouldn't listen to a girl. Let alone one like me."

"Sharack?" Gaorun repeated incredulously.

Sarka nodded to him. "That's the spiede I was given to. I got really lucky with him too. He had lots of candles lit all the time so I could see what I was doing. I mean, he was blind anyway, so it didn't really matter."

There was a long pause. No one seemed to know what to say, until finally, Sarka shrugged and stood up.

"But neither of us expected me to be followed. I'm sorry, and I can understand if you want to continue without me," she said, bowing to Kajiya.

Kajiya shook her head. "No, Sarka. You need to come with us."

The pink fea lifted her head, confused, and Kajiya continued.

"This is bigger than either of us." She cast a fleeting glance to Resurge.

She didn't think he had moved an inch.

"…Than all of us." Kajiya turned back to Sarka. "The safety of so many is at stake. No," she held out her hand, "we'll be just as glad to have *Sarka* by our side as we were to have *Chase*. Just, no more lies, okay?"

A smile broke out on Sarka's face as she took Kajiya's hand. "I wouldn't dream of it."

Kajiya smiled as they shook hands, but her smile faded as she looked back at Resurge.

Sarka followed her gaze, then looked away, and stepped back.

"Well," Gaorun said as he walked to Kajiya, "shall we set up camp and call it a day?"

She was tempted to say 'yes,' but as Kajiya looked up to the sky, she realized that Koiyan had only begun to fall. She shook her head.

"We keep going. Like I said, stopping Turten is bigger than us."

*   *   *

Kajiya breathed in the pre-dawn air deeply. They had made considerable progress the previous day in spite of… Kajiya looked down at the sand. She couldn't bring herself to name it. She didn't want it to be true. Her tail flicked and the bell jingled across the beach.

She drew her knees up to her chest as she sat down, and began to doodle in the sand with her claw. A sound came from the forest behind her, and she looked up hopefully. *Resurge?*

No, it was Gaorun, and Kajiya let her disappointment show. Onta came up beside her with her ears flattened sadly. She nudged Kajiya's arm, and Kajiya lifted it so the onti could settle down beside her.

"Thinking about yesterday?" Gaorun asked quietly as he sat down.

"Trying not to," Kajiya said, hugging her knees ever tighter.

Gaorun put a hand on her back. "A while back, you asked me if there was something else out there, do you remember?"

Kajiya looked up. "I do."

"And you believe there is as well?"

She nodded. Where was he going with this?

"That magic you used yesterday," he said. "What was that?"

Kajiya's face flushed. "I-I don't know. I just couldn't. I couldn't stand watching."

"Do you think it was that?" he wondered.

Kajiya opened her mouth, then closed it again. The magic… It had been exactly like in the tunnel. Exactly like when she had wanted to protect them. It was the same. It was her magic, but it wasn't.

"Yeah, I think so," she said. "What about you?"

Gaorun shifted his weight, turning to face the ocean. "I've seen a lot of magic, heck, I've *performed* a lot of magic, Kajiya, but I have *never* felt something like that, ever. Not when Rotari or you guys spoke with that weird thought-magic, not when I cast a spell. Nothing."

Kajiya sighed as she looked out to the ocean. "So what? Even magic can't change history."

Gaorun grabbed her hand, and held it tight. "Well no, but I learned something. Whoever this being is, he *cares.* About you at least. I mean, why else would he let you do that?"

Kajiya smiled a little, and shook her head. "Not just me, all of us. I only get that kind of magic when I'm trying to protect something."

"If he's so caring," Ainee's voice floated from the forest, "then why did he let Resurge go off like that?"

Gaorun dropped Kajiya's hand like a piece of rotten meat, and Kajiya drew it back to her chest.

"Why would they care about us if we were just pawns in some sort of game?" Kajiya asked aloud.

Suddenly a thought struck her, and she blinked. Maybe Resurge was right. Maybe they were a he. She gulped, and found her closed throat opening just enough for her to speak freely.

"They remind me of my dad. I mean, Dad always insisted that Resurge and I make our own mistakes. He was ready to help any time we asked, but…"

The ocean crashed against the sand. There were no words for what Kajiya was feeling. No words to even try to speak. But yes, Resurge was definitely right. This being was most certainly a he. Her shoulders rose, and Kajiya let out another sigh, then stood.

"Come on, words aren't going to stop Turten unless we can get to the Grand Assembly," she said as she walked back into the forest.

Resurge was up, quietly tending the fire as Sarka slept on. Kajiya smiled to herself, she knew from experience that it was impossible to perform magic while sleeping. She wondered if Sarka had been able to sleep at all while maintaining her male persona. Gaorun and Ainee immediately set about putting away camp, and Ainee awoke Sarka to help her. Kajiya looked around, and then, seeing nothing for her to do but wait, retreated to the safety of the trees. Away from the tension. Away from all of it.

She walked a fair distance, but tried to keep within shouting range. At least then, if they finished and she wasn't around, they would just have to yell for her.

Her feet padded aimlessly, until at last she stopped beside a rather thick tree. She placed a hand against it, and summoned the magic. It was cold, but purely hers. No hint of the strength that had come. Her face fell.

She leaned up against the tree. Earlier, when she had likened him to her father… She looked up and opened her mouth.

"I feel like an idiot doing this, but, if you're out there… If you're out there, I—" she sighed, and Koiyan's light seemed to fade.

She had no clue what to say.

Go on.

Kajiya gave a little jump. She looked around her, but there was no one. Had she even heard it? Was her imagination messing with her? Well, it certainly couldn't hurt.

"I'm worried about Resurge," she said to the sky. "I don't know what happened. But he's still my brother. I-I don't know what to do."

Silence. Maybe he wanted her to keep going.

"I mean, thank you for the magic. For helping me. Why don't you help them? Why just me?" she wondered.

The leaves rustled. She listened harder, but there was nothing. Another sigh left her mouth.

"Okay, I give up," she said, throwing her arms

into the air as tears threatened her eyes again. "I hope you know what you're doing. Because I don't."

She started to walk away, but stopped. "Just. Just make it all alright. Okay?"

The wind blew gently, rustling her fur, but there were no words resting on its ribbons. How much could she take of this? This silence?

Trust me.

Kajiya didn't move. A single tear flowed down her snout.

"I'll try," she whispered. "I'll try."

*   *   *

Koiyan beat down on them relentlessly, and Kajiya stumbled for what seemed to be the fortieth time that day. She looked up; Gaorun was leading the pack with Sarka, referring to the map they had borrowed from Resurge. Ainee hung in the middle, watching Resurge concernedly. Kajiya didn't think that Resurge had looked up since the previous night. His tail dragged in the sand.

Suddenly, she felt like she needed to speak to him. Enough was enough! Even if he had messed up, he wasn't the first to snap. She had too at one point. And if they could forgive her, treat as their leader, and help her to see that it wasn't the end of the world, then it was time for her to return the favour. She broke into a light jog, and signalled to Ainee with her tail that she wanted to be alone with her brother.

"Resurge," she said after Ainee had left.

He didn't respond.

"Resurge, you need to look at me."

Nothing. Kajiya bit her lip; what had brought her out of her depression when she had snapped? Ainee had something that had completely shocked her.

Maybe that's exactly what she needed to do. But what would shock him? That, she had no idea. Maybe if she just spoke, something would get through.

"You know we love you, Resurge. All of us, we can't stand seeing you like this," she said as she placed a hand on his shoulder.

Kajiya took a breath. "We forgive you. Look, none of us can change the past, Resurge, but you have the power to change the future."

"Do I?"

Kajiya smiled in spite of his words; it was a response.

He looked at his hands. "That's what they told me when I started out my warrior training. I'm supposed to protect feas, Kajiya! Not scare them."

Kajiya nodded. "I know what you mean."

His ears perked and he looked at her skeptically. "I doubt it."

"Are you really so thick?" Kajiya hissed. "I don't know how I'm going to face Dad after what *I* did."

Resurge looked back at her and a glimmer of understanding came into his eyes. "Your banishment."

Kajiya nodded. "You didn't see me. I was far worse than you."

Resurge swallowed. "So, how do we get past this? They certainly never covered it in warrior training. As far as I'm concerned, my honour may as well be nonexistent."

"Why?" Kajiya asked. "Because you were mad that the attack could have been prevented? You can't blame yourself, Resurge. You messed up once," Kajiya laughed. "One mistake…"

Resurge smiled weakly. "Does not an unfit

leader make," he finished. "Dad always says that, doesn't he?"

Kajiya nodded. "Because he makes mistakes almost every day. I think if that messenger didn't pop up everywhere, he would probably get lost."

Resurge snorted. "The purple one with the black stripes?"

Kajiya nodded. "Yeah, him." They giggled together for a moment.

It felt good to laugh.

Kajiya forced herself to breathe again. "But Resurge, my point is, even magiks aren't perfect. I mean, you should know that after living with me and Dad for so many years. But warriors and generals make mistakes too. As a wise fea once told me, 'It doesn't matter how you fall; it matters how you get back up.'"

Resurge's ears perked. "Who said that?"

Kajiya smiled. "You did."

Resurge leaned back. "When?"

Kajiya's face flushed. "You remember back when you first started training in the clearing, and I would come and watch?"

He nodded.

"And there was that one day that you were trying to learn a jump-kick and you kept falling on your tail?"

His tail swished. "How could I forget? My backside hurt for a month."

"I was laughing at how much you were falling when you said that," Kajiya admitted sheepishly. "It's always kinda stuck with me."

Resurge smiled at her. "Thank you. I guess I just have to get back up now, eh?"

Kajiya dipped her head, then jumped forward and held out her hand. "Yeah, but no one said you had to do it alone."

Resurge stopped, then smiled back at her and grabbed her wrist, and Kajiya grabbed his back.

"Besides," Resurge said as they started to walk again, "I gave up my honour the moment I decided to come on your quest. When your honour is restored, mine will be as well."

Kajiya shook her head. "No, Resurge. Honour isn't something that can be taken from you. It's something you decide to keep. And you're the most honourable warrior I know."

Gaorun's excited voice rang out through the air. "I see it!"

Kajiya turned to Resurge with a smile on her face, and he smiled back. They ran up to the trio at the front together. There, out of the heavy fog that lay on the horizon, was a cluster of islands. Royalin.

A whoop went up from Resurge, much to the surprise and amazement of the others. Ainee nearly broke into tears as she laughed, ditching her bag and practically knocking Resurge over as she embraced him. He hugged her back, then practically turned red as Ainee kissed him on the cheek. Gaorun burst out laughing, and grabbed Sarka's hands and whirled her around in a little jig while Onta held on for dear life to his pack. Kajiya joined in their laughter, and grabbed one of each of their hands to join in on their dance.

They had finally made it.

Chapter 9 : Royalin

Kajiya could hardly believe her eyes. Koiyan was just beginning to fall, and they had run as a group the last few hundred tail-lengths, so she was quite out of breath. But, as she grasped her knees, she stared up at the great bridge of Royalin. It reminded her a little of the bridge to Rotari's island, except far better maintained. The wooden platform was large enough for them all to walk side-by-side comfortably, and led out to the first island of the Royaliste Crescendo. Giant tree trunks that rose out of the channel of ocean that separated the island from the mainland supported the pathway from underneath.

She looked at the others with anticipation in her eyes. She was here. The end was in sight, as soon as they got to the Grand Assembly, they could put a stop to Turten! Then she remembered that the Grand Assembly only operated in the *earlier* half of the day. Today's delegation would be long done.

She gave a nod, and the group set off without a word. Sarka had already used her illusion magic to turn herself back into Chase, and now Kajiya realized, it was time for her to use it herself. With everything that had happened, they hadn't had time to convince Resurge to learn the spell, and with the way things were, Kajiya didn't even bother trying. With so much of his ego deflated, there was no way he'd even consider tarnishing his honour. He had however, taken Kajiya's suggestion and was wearing his chirpl-skin vest.

Kajiya pursed her lips, what colour could she change and still pass for his sibling? Emera and

Coballen were yellow and green… She smiled to herself; did it even matter? The Royalin feas would just assume they had taken after different parents. Kajiya had already changed into her Ruina shirt, so all she had to do was summon the ice and change her fur colour. After a moment's consideration, she focused on the colour pink. The same hue that lit up the sky when Koiyan set. She smiled as her colours shifted. She was as good as unrecognizable.

Chase-Sarka looked her over. "Really?"

Kajiya hunched her shoulders. "What?"

"I'm pink."

"So?"

"I turned blue. You turned pink."

Kajiya rolled her eyes. "Why did you choose blue anyway?"

Chase-Sarka blushed a little. "Well, when I performed in my family's circus, there were always spotlights on me. The only guys I ever saw clearly were my dad and my brother. I tried very hard *not* to look at customers outside of there. I thought if I made eye contact that they would make fun of me. But, that aside," she said hastily, "how would you like to masquerade as your dad?"

Kajiya shuddered. "Good point. But what about in the spiedes' city? Didn't you see anyone there you could base your form on?"

Chase-Sarka shook her head. "No, only Sharack's house had any light. I mean, yeah there were candles here and there, but never enough for me to see the other captives clearly."

Kajiya nodded, then stared at her, remembering how she had thought Chase's colours were similar to Resurge's. "So… You based that form, on those two?"

she said, pointing to Resurge and Gaorun.

Chase-Sarka laughed sheepishly. "Yep."

Now that Kajiya was looking closer, it was very obvious that Sarka had taken Resurge's colours, mixed them with Gaorun's build and added a few creative liberties of her own; the elongated neck, the hairstyle, the stripe pattern and the bandage over the nose. Even made the chin a little scruffier.

"Well," Kajiya said as she put her hands behind her back. "For being based on those two, it's not bad. Not bad at all."

Chase-Sarka laughed and readjusted Ainee's pack on her back.

Kajiya giggled as well, then looked to Resurge. He still looked a little down, but with his normally serious personality, Kajiya found it hard to tell if she should be worried or not. Chase-Sarka moved up to chat with Ainee, and Kajiya almost slowed to a stop. Her talk with Resurge—it was like when she had been in Animo. She had known just what to say.

Kajiya looked up. "Thanks," she whispered.

Kajiya caught up to the rest of them as a guard, a dark orange fea with darker stripes held out his hand. The entrance to Royalin was nothing like the entrance to Animo. Yes, there was a guard, but his hand seemed to be on the hilt of his sheathed sword more out of habit than anything else. He wore a formal tunic with a high golden collar and a pale blue fabric.

The actual entrance wasn't a gate like there had been in Animo, instead, it was an elaborate gate*way*. It arched high above the bridge, and from where Kajiya looked through it, she could see stairs down to the streets below.

"Ahem," the guard said. "What is your purpose

here?"

Gaorun begun to advance when Resurge stepped forward hastily. Gaorun shot him an inquisitive look, but said nothing and dropped back.

"We're travellers from Mirabilia. We've set out to learn about the other tribes," Resurge said stiffly.

The guard looked them over. "Names."

"I'm Nijiru, this is Ruina, Chase, Gaorun and Ainee," he said, pointing to each of them in turn.

The guard looked them over once more, then waved a hand nonchalantly as he turned away, looking as though they were nothing more important than an onti that had wandered across his path.

Kajiya eyed him as she passed. What was with that attitude? Who did this guy think he was? She rolled her eyes as they passed him. It wouldn't matter.

Kajiya's heart pounded as they descended the wooden steps into the village. The jungle reminded her so much of Mirabilia, but it was different too. The village was on the ground to begin with, and the paths were clearly worn into the forest floor. Giant leafy plants sprung decoratively from the sides of the path, and there were many feas walking about. Almost all of the males wore similar formal tunics to the guard, and the woman wore long flowing conservative dresses with golden trim along the neckline. A few even had intricate gold embroidery on their long sleeves. Some glanced their way, then promptly stuck their noses in the air and hurried past.

Kajiya blinked at them. Was everyone in Royalin like that? Kajiya remembered being visited by Royalin officials back in Mirabilia. They had acted the same way, *even* to her father and Turten.

"So," Ainee said as they got down to the dirt, "where should we go?"

Gaorun looked around, then pointed off to the right; the majority of the Royalin feas were going the opposite direction.

"I'll bet that that's the market. Everyone who lives here is heading home," he said.

"So, there should be hotels there?" Chase-Sarka said happily, not even bothering to disguise her voice.

Gaorun nodded. "Or at least someone who'll be able to tell us where to go.

Kajiya grasped the straps of her backpack and started off without warning. Ainee smiled and walked briskly beside her. Kajiya grinned back, and Resurge and Gaorun followed, with Chase-Sarka close behind.

"Sarka," Kajiya said as they walked.

"Yes?" Chase-Sarka replied.

"I think you should ditch the illusion when we get to the Grand Assembly."

Chase-Sarka stiffened, and her fur went slightly purple before she apparently regained her concentration and it returned to blue.

"Why?" she wondered.

Kajiya looked at her out of the corner of her eye. "Well, I'm going as myself, and I'm supposed to dead. Besides, trust me, lying brings nothing but trouble."

"But will they listen to me?"

Kajiya smiled. "I'm not going to give them the option."

Chase-Sarka laughed. "I could learn a thing or two from you, Ka—"

"*Ruina.*" Kajiya interjected, hissing.

"Ah, right. Ruina." Chase-Sarka laughed embarrassedly.

Kajiya looked down at her feet as a twinge of guilt panged in her stomach. Lying brought nothing but trouble—and here she was, lying about her identity again. Just because it was necessary didn't mean she had to like it.

As they went further and further down the path, buildings started to become apparent. They appeared to be made out of large wooden planks, like the buildings in Mirabilia, except that they were far more square, reminding her of Animo's stone buildings. Some buildings had been painted different bright colours. Blues, greens and faded yellows were common. However, the further into the village they got the more run-down the marketplace seemed to become.

The crowd was dying down, just as Gaorun had predicted, and Kajiya began to spot feas who stood out. These feas wore wearing clothing similar to their own, and every now and again, there would be a fea that sat against one of the buildings. These feas appeared to do nothing and often had large bags beside them.

Kajiya couldn't help but stare curiously. What were they doing? A memory found its way into her mind as she stared. The first time she had spied on Turten with the sight spell, one of the feas attending his meeting had asked what was to become of *beggars.* Sure enough, as they passed, a dingy moss-green fea held out his hand. Kajiya's heart went out to him, but they didn't have any money either.

What she didn't understand, was why he didn't get up and go hunt or something to get some furs to trade. Maybe he wasn't physically able to. Maybe he was untalented with magic. Kajiya didn't know, but while she silently resolved to help him and the other feas like him when she could, she was sure that the spiedes wouldn't care that he was a beggar; they would just see him as another slave. Their plight would have to wait until after she had taken Turten and the spiede king down.

While she had been thinking, Gaorun had approached a shopkeeper wearing a formal tunic. He took one look at Gaorun, then pursed his lips and raised his head. Kajiya didn't catch their conversation, but it was obvious from Gaorun's expression that he had been less than helpful.

"Can you believe that guy?" Gaorun growled as he returned. "He 'only accepts *Royalin* currency'. He didn't even *look* at our furs!"

He signalled for the others to follow him down the street with a sharp flick of his tail. In his current state Kajiya thought it best not to argue and complied.

Every place they visited was the same—they only accepted *Royalin* money. Kajiya was beginning to lose hope. Maybe they'd just walk all the way to the Grand Assembly hall and sleep on its porch—if it had one—tonight. Kajiya forced herself to smile. At least they wouldn't miss the meeting.

Koiyan had almost completely set by the time that they reached a section of the market that was far more decrepit than the rest, but full of similarly dressed feas.

At last, they entered a rather nice-looking hotel that had been painted pure white. The inside was all white as well, and there were large circular columns scattered throughout the room. There were at least three storeys, and a stairwell to the left of the front desk.

Kajiya looked around, her enthusiasm dampened by her tiredness. Almost everything in the lobby was white: the desk where the innkeeper sat, the large thick armchairs, and the square shelves attached to the wall behind the desk. The innkeeper was a crimson fea with even deeper red markings and shoulder-length hair. He smiled toothily at them. Even his teeth were a pristine white.

"Welcome travellers! How can I help ya?"

Gaorun walked over to the desk and wasted no time in getting to the point. "Look, it's been a long day. How much for a pair of rooms?"

"Well, that depends," the innkeeper said stroking his chin. "What do you have?"

Kajiya thought Gaorun was going to start flying from the elation that showed on his face. "Taic pelts, avian skins and anfa pelts."

The innkeeper whistled. "Taic? Let's see them."

Resurge had stepped forward and brought out the thick white furs from his pack before Gaorun could even signal for them. They put them onto the desk, and the innkeeper ran a hand over them.

"And how long are you folks planning on staying?"

"Just a night," Gaorun said.

The innkeeper nodded to himself, and examined them further for a long, nerve-racking moment. "One pelt per room seems like a fair price to me."

"Deal!" Gaorun said, stretching out his hand before they even had a chance to discuss the trade.

Kajiya shot Ainee a short glance, but the purple fea shrugged. They were all tired.

"Here you are," the innkeeper said as he reached below the desk and brought out a couple of room keys while Gaorun retrieved a second fur for him. "Rooms four and five, ground floor. They'll be just down the hall," he pointed to a doorway next to the stairwell.

They all nodded their thanks, and Resurge passed Kajiya the key for room four; it was a simple silver key with a pale wooden keychain and the number painted in bold red on both sides. She quickly passed the key to Ainee and followed her into the hallway. Ainee had let the boys go into the hall first, and Kajiya quickly realized that this had been a wise decision. The room numbers got smaller the closer they were to the lobby, so the group reached their rooms at the same time.

As soon as Ainee opened the door, Kajiya rushed in and let go of the magic, turning back to her natural blue while releasing the shiver that she had been itching to give for the past ten minutes. The illusion spell felt like it had left a covering of frost over her entire body. Sarka also released her magic to show her true form as Ainee closed the door behind them.

"How on Mysterium do you do it?" Kajiya hissed as she abandoned the packs and whipped a blanket off of the bed to wrap around herself until only her head peeked out.

Sarka grinned. "Cold?"

"Frozen!" Kajiya retorted as her tail flicked sharply, but the blanket muffled the bell.

Sarka laughed. "Well, I suppose my clothes

help a little," she said, stretching the tight magenta fabric off her chest. "Taic fur is a great insulator."

Kajiya smiled. "I know. There were days in Animo when I wanted to take Rosa's fur and wrap myself in it."

"Rosa?" Sarka asked as she set down Ainee's pack.

"The taic that helped her and Sarin escape from the spiedes," Ainee clarified with a grin as she took the bags and started to unpack.

"Oh. I see," Sarka said as she moved over to help.

Kajiya smiled. "We should all try to get some sleep tonight, we'll need it. Big day tomorrow."

Ainee's face grew concerned. "But what about the Grand Assembly hall? We still don't know where it is."

Kajiya sighed and leaned back. "We'll figure something out. But for now, we're all tired. We should sleep."

      *   *   *

Kajiya woke up in a cold sweat, her breathing ragged. She clutched the blanket tightly, and waited until her heart rate had slowed to a reasonable pace before she swung her legs over the side of the bed. She bent over and stared at the floor. She had gone so long without any nightmares, and now, just this night, this was third time she'd awoken from them. Maybe it was the stress. Maybe she wasn't tired enough. Maybe the spiede that had attacked them was causing a relapse. Maybe she was seeing what would happen if she were to fail.

She gulped, and moved to the window, careful not to disturb Ainee. There were only two beds and a small closet in the room, so Ainee and Kajiya decided that Sarka would get her own bed. After all, they had been tent-mates for long enough to know that they wouldn't bother each other. Sarka had tried to make one of them take a bed for themselves, but they had insisted.

Kajiya moved the sheer curtain over to the side slightly. Midyan was still high in the sky, partially obscured by Admirai, but there was no way that she could get back to sleep.

She had to find something to do. She had walked all the way to the door and had her hand on the handle when she remembered that she had entered the hotel with a different fur colour. She closed her eyes and focused on the shade in her memory as she summoned the coating of ice. She thought she saw her breath as she opened her eyes. Then she opened the door, and nearly walked into Resurge. They both jumped.

"Couldn't sleep?" she asked quietly as her fur began to settle.

He shook his head. "How can I? There's too much to be done."

Kajiya nodded. "Do you think there'll be someone at the desk?"

They started down the hall.

"I hope so," he said, "you had mentioned going to a library to look up a map. If they don't have one here, that's a good idea. We should at least be able to get directions and the hours from the innkeeper."

Kajiya nodded in agreement. "You should do the talking. It'll make more sense."

Resurge looked puzzled for a moment, then nodded.

They approached the lounge area, and Kajiya took a seat on the armrest of a heavily padded armchair while Resurge went to the desk. There was a small hand bell on the desk. He looked around, then picked up the bell, but Kajiya beat him to it as she flicked her pink tail, creating a jingle from her own bell. He shot a short glare at her, but she just smiled impishly. The innkeeper appeared at once.

"Well, you folks are up late. What can I do for ya?" he asked, leaning on the counter with one arm.

"We were wondering if you had a map of the city?" Resurge asked. "Since we're new, we figured it best to try *not* to get lost."

The innkeeper laughed appropriately. "Wish I could help ya, but I'm afraid we're fresh clean out of maps."

Resurge shrugged. "Then could you give us directions to library? And when's it open?"

The innkeeper whistled. "Well, what do you know? A fea with a head on his shoulders! The library's actually open all day *and* night."

Kajiya shared her brother's smile and she bounded over to the innkeeper. "That's great! Where is it?"

The innkeeper pulled out a piece of parchment, ink, and an avian-feather quill. "We may not have maps, but I can make you one for anywhere on the island."

Kajiya blinked. "Then maybe you could direct us to the Grand Assembly hall?"

Resurge stiffened, but didn't say a word. Kajiya knew asking would arouse suspicion, but if he could give them directions, their searching time would be cut in half.

The innkeeper shook his head. "I'm afraid not. The Hall's a couple of islands over, and I wouldn't know where to find my own tail there!" he laughed. "Sightseeing?"

Kajiya nodded hastily. "Yes."

The innkeeper smiled. "Can't tell ya how many feas come through looking for that place. Of course, most of 'em are feas from other tribes. My establishment is the only one that accepts furs within half-an-hour's walk of the main market," he said with a smile. "I get all the tourist-y types. If you want to know anything about Iota, just ask. Chances are I've looked it up at one time or another. Ah! And there we go!"

While Kajiya hadn't been paying attention, the innkeeper had been using magic to control the quill and create the map, which he now handed to Resurge.

"Now, you two have a good night, but try to get back by checkout, okay?"

Kajiya smiled. "We have friends sleeping here. Trust me, we won't be leaving without them."

The innkeeper laughed. "Sounds good."

Resurge gave the innkeeper a little bow, and the duo set out. As usual, Resurge's map reading skills were superb, but even Kajiya recognized the paths they were to take.

Sure enough, Royalin's library was the only building with fires lit. The trees on either side almost blended into the gloom of the night. The building itself was up on a platform with wide stairs leading up to a porch that extended to the street. It was difficult for Kajiya to distinguish colours thanks to Midyan's blue tint, but it looked as though the wooden building had not been painted. As she and Resurge started up the steps, Kajiya looked up. It appeared to be a large circular building with a hut-like roof. Kajiya thought it looked cozy.

On the porch there were tables set out, she assumed so that patrons could sit outside and read when the weather was nice. Kajiya nodded to herself; she would like that. Resurge pulled open the door for Kajiya, and she gave him a small curtsey as she walked past, snickering to herself.

The interior of the library was as grand and orderly as the exterior. Tall shelves lined the walls from top to bottom, and there was a large circular desk in the middle, with a kind-looking dark-green fea with even darker green stripes on the other side. He sat on a chair of some sort, and was rummaging around below the desk as Kajiya and Resurge walked up.

His ears swivelled towards them, then he sat up hastily. He pulled at the collar of his formal tunic with one hand, which indicated to Kajiya that he was not quite used to it. The collars of most formal tunics she had worn had been quite stiff as well. They always made her feel like she was choking or something.

"Welcome to the library!" he said happily, then his dark pink-red eyes flashed to Kajiya. "From Mirabilia I see," he said with a smile.

Kajiya nodded; he must have seen the tribal symbol on her loin-cloth.

"What can I help ya with?" he wondered, leaning forward in his seat.

Resurge put his hand on the desk. "We were hoping you could point us to some maps of Royalin."

The librarian nodded sympathetically. "Ah, yes. Royalin is a little hard to get around the first time through. Don't worry, you'll get used to it eventually," he promised with a smile. "The maps are just over there, next to the family trees."

He pointed over to the left, to a small corner of the library that looked a little dustier and a little darker than the rest.

"Oh," he said, reaching below the desk once more to pull out a torch, which he quickly set flame to. "You might need this. It's sometimes hard to read when Midyan's out. There'll be a stand for it on the table. And don't worry—everything in here's been fireproofed. A little magic goes a long way in preserving our collection."

Resurge took it with a small nod. "Thank you."

Kajiya nodded as well, and they set out. The flame from the torch proved to be most helpful as they entered the space between the wall-shelf and the freestanding one. Finally, they reached a table stained a dark brown colour. There was a thin layer of grime on the table, and Kajiya blew at it, sending up a cloud of dust. Resurge shot her a quick glare, to which she merely grinned sheepishly.

There was indeed a metal stand for the torch, and Resurge put it in carefully, then began to scan the shelves. Kajiya also started to look around, and found that the majority of the maps weren't for Royalin. Or, she'd find one for an island, but be unable to figure out which island it was.

As the looked-through books began to pile on the desk, Kajiya began to pick up on some things. Firstly, the Royaliste Crescendo, where the Royalin tribe was situated, was made of five islands: Ovis, Aria, Zaylene, Volmari, and Iota, the island where they were currently residing. Secondly, the maps always classified the different winding paths in two ways: high or low class. Kajiya gritted her teeth when she saw that; the low class streets were often the oldest, and, Kajiya could tell from the drawings in the map-books, the most run-down. Why were they in such disrepair?

In Mirabilia, the entire tribe would band together to fix the tree-top village after every storm. Her father was proud of the fact that everyone had a place to call home, and if anyone ever needed help, they only had to come and ask for it. Kajiya had never really understood that pride before, but now, she was starting to. There was no doubt that Proten had recognized the problem in the other tribes, and then had taken steps to ensure that Mirabilia was better.

Kajiya closed the map book with a thunk. This was getting too heavy for her. She sighed, and wandered away from the table, where her brother was still skimming the maps. She moved over to the nearest window, and looked outside. Midyan had hardly moved at all, so they couldn't have been looking for more than an hour. She sighed again when she heard a sound behind her. It sounded like something had fallen over.

She turned around, wondering if she had accidentally brushed a book over with her tail or something, but the book that had fallen off of the shelf was about halfway down the aisle. Curious now, she wandered over and picked it up.

Her fur prickled. The book was cold. But not a normal cold, *magic* cold. Not the kind of magic that she had come to associate with the being either. No, there was no doubt about it. This was Rotari's magic.

She looked around and gulped. If Rotari could move something all the way over here, on the other side of the *continent*... She grasped the book tighter. It was probably best if she didn't finish that thought. However, her interest had been peaked; the stone giant hadn't made any move to try and contact her before, even though there had been plenty of times when she could have used the blakeslee's help. Clearly, Rotari felt that whatever was in this book was important for her to know.

Kajiya looked at the book's spine. It was a record-book. She opened it up. Her fur rose. It was a record for her family tree. She walked over to the small desk below the window, and sat down as she began to flip pages. She started at the end, where her and Resurge's names had been written in ink. Both her and her mother's had been crossed out with a single line.

Kajiya put her hand over Karei's name, and then slid her fingers down the page.

A small star beside a name denoted a magik, and Kajiya soon found that, while it had skipped a few generations before her father, on his side at least, she came from a vast wealth of magiks. The record went back to almost before the Great War. There had been at least seven magiks in her family in the past four hundred years. But, what about on her mother's side? Were there any magiks there?

She flipped back to the space where she and Resurge were, and then carefully followed her mother's family tree. She had just discovered one magik who had married into the family when she saw something on the next page that made her heart stop. Her great-times-fourteenth grandmother, had a sister.

Kajiya stood. There was no way. It couldn't be! She looked to the sister's husband. It was. Rotari and Gakkar were her and Resurge's great-times-fourteen aunt and uncle. She looked again; they had had no children. Suddenly, it clicked, why Rotari had taken such a great interest in her, why she thought it was important for her to know.

Kajiya closed the book and walked back over to Resurge. Why hadn't she taken as much of an interest in him? Kajiya thought back to her time on the island. It would have seemed strange if she had taken an interest in him, now that she thought about it. Firstly, he was a warrior, and Rotari was teaching her and Ainee magic. She wouldn't have anything to really teach him. Certainly she would have known many fighting moves after watching the other feas for centuries, but with her body, how would she properly demonstrate them? And Kajiya couldn't imagine *Resurge* taking fighting instructions from a girl, even if she *was* a returned blakeslee.

She set the book on the table, and Resurge looked up at her.

"You won't believe what I just found," she said matter-of-factly.

"What?" Resurge put his elbows on the table.

"Rotari is our great-great-great-great-great-great-great-great-great-great," Kajiya paused for breath and reconfigured her hands as she'd been counting to fourteen on her fingers. "Great-great-great-great, aunt," she finished with a large breath.

Resurge raised an eyebrow. "Seriously?"

Kajiya opened the book. "Seriously. Look," she said as she found the page and pointed to it.

Resurge flipped over a couple pages to where the more recent names were. "Well, I'll be…" a smile spread over his face. "And that means Gakkar was our uncle!"

"Great-great-" Kajiya started to correct.

Resurge held out a hand. "I get the point Kajiya. But you're not the only one who's found something interesting. Look." He pointed to the map he had been studying.

Kajiya set down the book and sat on the table so that she could look over his shoulder without actually looking over his shoulder.

"It appears that the Grand Assembly hall is over on Volmari," he started, pointing to the map.

Kajiya broke out into a smile. "Great! I'll go get some parchment and a quill from the librarian."

"Ah—not so fast there, Kajiya," Resurge said, grabbing her wrist as she slid off the table.

Kajiya's bell rang out as her tail flicked curiously.

Resurge moved his finger north of the hall, "See this hill? The hall's also right below the *only cave on the islands.*"

Kajiya's fur rose. "Oh no."

Resurge nodded. "Turten could have been using it to communicate with the spiedes this entire time. He might know you're alive."

Kajiya shook her head. "I don't think so; I mean, I was wearing my Ruina shirt the whole time and, well, the only time I ever said who I was, it was to Sarin and Rosa."

Resurge didn't loosen his grip. "But Kajiya, that doesn't change the fact that you escaped with magic. Turten will know that it had to be you. You're the only girl who can—"

"No, I'm not," Kajiya interjected, prying her brother's hand off of her wrist. "Sarka can too. Maybe there have been others down there as well."

Resurge drew his hand back. "I certainly hope so. Now, that parchment?"

"Coming right up!" Kajiya twittered as she started for the desk.

*   *   *

Kajiya blinked groggily. After she and Resurge had gotten the directions, they had returned to the hotel. Kajiya wondered if he had been able to get some sleep as well. She had laid down, and soon found herself falling to a silent sleep. No dreams bothered her at all.

She yawned, and looked over. Ainee wasn't there. Perfect. She grabbed the majority of the blankets and rolled over, wrapping them around herself.

"Glad to hear someone's awake. Sleepyhead." Ainee's voice floated over to her sharply.

Kajiya sighed. Maybe if she pretended that she was really asleep, she could go back to actually being. But her mind was quick to remind her about Turten, and she opened her eyes reluctantly. She couldn't stop him if she was sleeping. She sat up and yawned.

Ainee raised an eyebrow as she looked Kajiya over. "Long night?"

Kajiya nodded. "Couldn't sleep," she said simply.

She didn't want Ainee to worry about her nightmares. The healer had done enough of that back in Animo.

Kajiya sat crossed-legged under the sheets, and stretched out her arms. "Where's Sarka?"

"She said something about rocks and rushed off to the lobby," Ainee said nonchalantly as she ran her fingers through her hair.

Kajiya blinked, noticing for the first time that her friend's hair wasn't tied up. Kajiya blinked again, then squinted at the back of her head; it almost looked like Ainee's hair was slightly longer on the right side. Kajiya shrugged, it didn't matter. But...

"What are you doing?" she asked.

"Why, this is *Royalin,* dear! One just can't go around looking like they got mauled by a taic. And, they actually gave us a mirror. It's been forever since I've been able to work with my hair."

Kajiya looked past Ainee and into the eyes of her reflection. It had been a while, certainly.

"Wouldn't a brush work better for that than your claws, though?"

Ainee sighed. "Well, yes, but when I was packing for this little 'expedition,' there happened to be a limit to how much I could carry. With just some food, blankets, and my herbs, that was already pushing it. Of course, we've all gotten a lot stronger since then, but I can't say I mind having Sarka around to carry my pack for me."

Kajiya laughed. "Now we just need someone else to join us so they can carry *my* pack!"

Ainee's reflection smiled as she shook her head. Kajiya grinned, and got to her feet as a knock sounded at the door. With a calm movement, Kajiya coated herself in the illusion-creating ice, moved over and opened the door. Gaorun was there, smiling happily.

"Hurry up you two! You're going to miss breakfast," he said as he started down the hall, to where a strange but mouth-watering scent emanated.

Kajiya swiped her tongue over her lips; it *did* smell delicious. She followed at once without even bothering to look at Ainee.

"Ruina—Ruina! Wait for—" The door closed.

Kajiya snickered and ran down the hall to catch up to Gaorun. "What sort of breakfast is it?"

Gaorun smiled. "The best kind, hot and free! Sort of."

Kajiya tilted her head to the side. "What do you mean?"

Gaorun laughed. "Right! I forgot that the only hotel you've been to is the one in Animo—right?" he added hastily.

Kajiya's shoulders rose. "It's not the *only* one. Just, one of the more recent ones," she said, pursing her lips as her snout rose a little.

Gaorun chuckled to himself and continued, "Well, some hotels like to make breakfasts for their customers, included in the price of the room, and this is one of them!"

Kajiya looked at him as they entered the lobby, and smiled. "Really?"

Gaorun gestured with a hand to three small tables that sat against the lobby's far wall, each one filled to the brim with different dishes. "Really."

Kajiya's stomach growled hungrily, and Kajiya went to grab herself a plate. The way it was set up reminded her of the feast in Palinda, but in miniature.

"There you guys are!" Chase-Sarka said as she turned to them. "You've gotta try these rockras! They're delicious!"

Kajiya's ears perked. "Rockras?"

"These," she said, using two long thin wooden sticks to pick up a very small piece of meat. "Just watch out for bones. I heard it's impossible to get them all out."

Kajiya walked over, grabbing a pair of food-sticks for herself. Long ago, her father had taught her how to use all the different cutlery of all the different tribes, in preparation for a trip to the other tribes. However, the trip was cut short by a fierce windstorm that forced all of Mirabilia to live on the ground for a few months. Kajiya still preferred using her hands to eat anyway.

Curious, she picked up the meat and put it on her own plate. It was a light pink colour, and not very thick.

"Rockras are a type of water-animal," Chase-Sarka said, taking another three for herself. "There were some captives from Royalin who wouldn't shut up about them. Or anything else," she added quietly. "Apparently they can't hunt them, so they have to trap them with a net, or on a hook."

Kajiya sniffed the meat, and sure enough, it was the source of the mouth-watering scent. She plopped the meat in her mouth. It seemed to flake apart on its own as she chewed, and it reminded her of the sea. Her mouth was sad when she finally swallowed, and she hungrily piled a few more on her plate as Gaorun reached them.

"Good?" he asked, reaching down to take a few with his hands.

"Wonderful," Kajiya confirmed.

She almost stopped for a moment; Gaorun was eating with his hands, as usual. Kajiya bristled slightly—it seemed so disrespectful, especially when the food-sticks were provided. Her fur smoothed as she considered it a moment longer; perhaps he had never learned to use the utensils. She turned back to Sarka curiously; she was using them well, but it looked as though she were practicing. Perhaps the innkeeper or the captive Royalin feas had taught her how to use them.

"Ruina!" Ainee's voice broke into her thoughts and she cringed. "I'll have you know that was horrendously rude," she said as she took a plate.

Kajiya lowered her head sheepishly as she moved onto the other dishes. There were some anfa stews, anfa and rockra stew, boiled rockra, fried rockra, the list went on and on.

"Sorry, but what can I say? I can't wait for you forever—and besides, I was hungry." Kajiya smiled sheepishly.

Ainee snatched two of the food sticks and pointed them at Kajiya as she deftly grabbed a plate of her own. "Even so, if you're going to be—" she cut herself off, and Kajiya saw her flash a glance over to the innkeeper, "…what you're going to be, you're going to have to work on that."

Kajiya snatched up another piece of rockra meat. "Duly noted."

Ainee sighed with an eye roll, took a piece of the meat herself and placed it on her plate with a lot more elegance than Kajiya or Sarka.

"We shouldn't tarry here long," Resurge said as he appeared at the end of the table and grabbed a plate of his own. "If it weren't for the fact that we need to eat, I'd say that we should head out now, but…"

Gaorun smirked, plopping another strip of meat into his mouth. "It smells too good, right?"

Resurge broke into an exceedingly small smile. "Indeed."

Kajiya giggled a little and found a seat beside Chase-Sarka. The currently-dark-blue fea grinned at her, and Kajiya grinned back.

"Regardless," Resurge said as he sat down with them, a slightly more modest portion of food on his plate, "we should eat quickly."

Kajiya nodded as Ainee and Gaorun joined them. In spite of the bright sunshine that shone through the thin slit-like windows of the hotel, a heavy sense of foreboding hung over her. Today, she went to the Grand Assembly. Today, she confronted Turten. Today, she either saved the tribes, or doomed them.

She shook her head. They just had to get to Volmari, which was two islands over, by noon. She looked at the windows, the sunlight in particular. It came down as a long shaft on the ground. It couldn't have been more than an hour or two past sunrise, but Kajiya began to realize that her brother was right. They needed to get going.

Kajiya scarfed down the rest of her food as fast as she could. The others shot her questioning looks.

"Maybe not so fast that you'll choke," Resurge said as he raised an eyebrow.

Kajiya swallowed the last strip of meat and stood up at once. "Where do you want this?" she asked the innkeeper, holding out her plate.

The red fea blinked at her suddenly curt tone, then pointed to an empty spot at the end of the table. "Over there will be fine."

Kajiya swiftly set her plate down, hand trailing on the white tablecloth.

"I'm going to make sure we've got everything ready to go," she announced as she walked towards the hall.

Gaorun nodded. "We're ready to leave at any time."

Kajiya paused as Ainee tossed her the keys, and her strange pink tail flicked as she caught them, causing her bell to ring out. Kajiya swiped her bangs out of her eyes and walked down the white hall.

She entered the room without trouble, and found that Sarka and Ainee had already started to repack their things. Kajiya let go of the magic and turned back to her natural blue. She kneeled down on the ground and started to finish shoving the numerous bottles on the floor back into Ainee's bag. Kajiya believed she had been checking her stocks. It wouldn't matter for much longer. Kajiya's stomach twisted itself into a labyrinth, and her chest felt tight. Nervousness couldn't be helped. She'd only been preparing for this for a couple *weeks.* She forced herself to slow down and take a breath.

You can do this Kajiya, she told herself. *You have your friends, Resurge is here… What is Dad gonna say when he sees me?*

Kajiya froze, hand halfway in Ainee's bag as she bit the inside of her lower lip. What *would* her father say? Would he be happy? Elated? Scared? What if they thought she was a ghost? She shook her head; unlike the spiedes, she *knew* ghosts didn't exist. Besides, if feas could return from the grave anyway, why would anyone bother giving them life as a returned?

She blinked; what would she tell him of Rotari? Rotari was a returned.

A sigh left Kajiya's lips and she returned to her task. The fact was, she didn't know. She couldn't know. And right now, none of that mattered. She would have time to consider those things when she was there, but for now, she just had to get there.

A knock came from the door, and Kajiya's heart stopped. What if it was the innkeeper? She began to summon the magic and focused on her fur colour.

"Ruina! You *could* let us in," Ainee's voice came through the door, and Kajiya breathed a sigh of relief as she jumped over to it.

The door unlocked with a click and Chase-Sarka and Ainee came in without a second of hesitation.

Ainee's pink gaze flashed over to her. "Almost ready?"

Kajiya nodded. "I think so."

Chase-Sarka picked up Ainee's pack while Ainee finished what Kajiya had been working on.

"Not bad," she said with a smile as she closed the herb bag. "You even got most of them in the right places."

Kajiya laughed, and turned to her own bag. She hadn't bothered unpacking it last night, so it was still fully travel-ready. With a quick flourish, she swung it over her shoulders and settled it onto her back.

She started for the door, but Ainee held out her hand, raising an eyebrow. Kajiya stopped for a moment in confusion, then blushed as she summoned the magic. Her fur shifted to pink.

"Better?"

Ainee nodded. "Better."

Kajiya stepped out the door, and looked down the hall towards the boy's room. They were just locking the door. Kajiya tossed her own key to Chase-Sarka.

"Ready?" Resurge asked.

Kajiya nodded. "Let's go."

They left the keys on the innkeeper's desk, and

Kajiya gave him an appreciative nod as she passed. He raised a hand and smiled back.

Now that it was morning, the market was bustling with feas. The majority of them wore some kind of tunic, and a few male feas wore anfa-skins accented with chirpl skin overlays.

Kajiya found it difficult to get through the crowd at first, but as they reached the end of the market, where large wooden platforms had been built over the water, they finally were able to start moving a bit faster.

There were five platforms, one leading to the next island, the others, to nowhere. Some feas with nets were starting down the long platform, while those on the shortest one carried poles.

"What are they doing?" she asked Gaorun as they started to cross the bridge.

Gaorun looked over, and his eyes widened. "Oh! I think they're water-hunting!"

Kajiya blinked. "For rockras?"

Gaorun nodded. "And other aquatic animals. The nets are to catch the creatures that swim through the water in giant groups. They catch other lone animals as well though," he said as a group of four men tossed the net into the water. "Sometimes they go out on rafts or boats and toss them from there. And those guys," he pointed to the feas with poles, "put bait on a really thin vine they enhanced with strengthening magic and tie a rock at the end so it sinks to the bottom. They then toss it into the water, and if they get lucky, something bites. It's a hunting technique that requires some patience."

Kajiya nodded, then blinked and looked at Gaorun incredulously. "How do you know all this?"

Gaorun laughed. "A couple of reasons actually. My grandfather was from Royalin."

"Really?" Kajiya interjected.

Gaorun nodded, and stroked Onta's head as she rested on his backpack. "Yeah. My dad thought I should know about," his face became stern as he imitated his father, placing his fists on his hips, "'our heritage.'"

He broke out laughing, and Kajiya joined him until he began to speak again.

"And, well, you know how I am about hunting. I've always kinda wanted to try water-hunting. But no one's ever taught me how to do it. All I really know are the basics."

Kajiya blinked. "Why didn't you try when we were on Ainee? The island, I mean," she added hastily.

Gaorun smiled sadly. "I wanted to, but I couldn't figure out how to make a line that wouldn't snap."

"Why didn't you ask Rotari?"

Gaorun flushed. "It was kinda embarrassing. I'm sure once we stop Turten I'll get a chance to figure it out, don't worry."

Kajiya nodded, and stared back over the ocean as her feet padded over the boards. Her fur chilled again, but as the sun began to heat up the sky, Kajiya welcomed the coolness.

The next island looked about the same to Kajiya, and she was glad for Resurge's clear directions as they turned through street after street. Her heart pounded each time she looked up at the sky. She bit her lip again. Would they make it to the Grand Assembly hall in time?

"K—Ruina," Chase-Sarka said, coming up

from behind her. "You, well, someone, mentioned that magic has rules. What are they?"

Kajiya blinked. She had completely forgotten that Sarka didn't know the rules of magic. The idea still seemed utterly foreign to her, having had it drilled into her by years of magic mentors. Nevertheless, she could at least share with Sarka what she had learned about the rules.

"Well," Kajiya said. "if you ask anyone besides me and Ainee, you're going to get a different answer."

Chase-Sarka's ears perked. "Oh? Why?"

Kajiya smiled meekly. "We, trained under a really good mentor who disagrees with some of the conventional rules."

Chase-Sarka nodded. "And you agree with him?"

"Her. But yes, we do," Kajiya said.

Chase-Sarka smiled, then signalled with her tail for Kajiya to continue. Kajiya nodded; reciting the rules was something she had done for years, perhaps it was just the distraction she needed.

"Rule one," she began, and she smiled, "with enough practice and some determination, anyone can become talented with magic."

Chase-Sarka nodded. "With you so far. Will you tell me which rules have been changed?"

Kajiya dipped her head. "That one was. The conventional rule is you either have talent with magic, or you don't."

Chase-Sarka's nose scrunched up. "I like the first one you said better. I certainly had a hard time working it out to begin with."

Kajiya took note that the street was becoming slightly more crowded as they entered a busier section of the village. She lowered her voice.

"Rule two," she faltered; could she really say this?

Didn't Sarka's mere existence contradict it? And according to Rotari, *Kajiya* herself contradicted it. It was Ainee who had said that the rule still applied. She modified it as she spoke.

"Some females should only learn low-level healing magic, it puts too much strain on their bodies for them to use anything more difficult."

"Now that you mention it—didn't Gaorun say something about that earlier?" Chase-Sarka laughed. "I guess I misheard him—I thought he said women *couldn't* use magic."

Kajiya's face flushed; Gaorun had mentioned it, hadn't he? But he didn't know about the changed rules. Still, it was amazing what adding the word 'some' to a sentence could do. Sarka didn't need to know that one had been changed.

"Er, yeah." Kajiya looked up at the sky. "Something like that."

"I would have asked what he was talking about before, but well...You know."

Kajiya smiled at her, then continued. "Rule three; if you want to bring back someone from the dead, you have to die."

Chase-Sarka gave a little jump. "What?! I just always assumed you couldn't bring back the dead."

Kajiya shook her head; something caught the corner of her eye as they exited the large crowd. Perfect timing. She pointed back to the dark blue fea. He wore a blue-white tunic with a red band pinned on his left arm just below his shoulder.

"It's possible. You see that fea?" she said.

"The one with the red band on his arm?"

Chase-Sarka turned her orange eyes to the crowd and looked around. "No."

Kajiya pointed. "The one leaning against the tree back there."

Chase-Sarka squinted in the direction Kajiya indicated, until at last she pointed to the fea. "Oh! There he is. What about him?"

"Her."

Chase-Sarka turned to her with a very confused look on her face. "I know I may be representing the spiedes, but my vision isn't *that* bad—unless they're using illusion magic too?"

Kajiya shook her head, "No, the band indicates that that fea's a returned. Returneds have to wear them so others don't get confused. It also indicates what gender they were, that doesn't change just because they switched out of their original body."

Chase-Sarka's ear flicked. "How can you tell?"

A corner of Kajiya's mouth jumped up. "A full red band for a female. A red band with two blue stripes is a male."

Chase-Sarka nodded, then turned to Kajiya again. "But why do they have a different body? Why couldn't they just keep the one they had to begin with? And why do you have to die to bring someone back?"

"Because it's impossible to have two feas in one body," Kajiya said with a shrug. "You have to die so that your body will be available for possession."

Chase-Sarka's fur rose. "So you die and give the other fea your body? What if they don't want to come back?"

Kajiya grinned sheepishly. "Then you're already dead. Sorry, I'm kinda jumping all over the place with this one, just listen for a moment."

Chase-Sarka pursed her lips, and Kajiya took a deep breath. It would be easier to explain this one by reciting it from the beginning.

"Rule three," she repeated, closing her eyes, "in order to bring back the dead you must die. Then you will traverse to the realm of the dead and *ask* that fea if they want to return to the world of the living. If they say no, then you're already dead and there's nothing you can do about it, if they say *yes*, then they will possess your *former* body, and you will stay dead." Kajiya creaked open an eye. "That clearer?"

Chase-Sarka's tail flicked. "A little bit. Is that it then?"

Kajiya laughed. "Oh no, there's eight rules in all. We've only just begun!"

Chase-Sarka's ears drooped. "I'm beginning to regret asking."

Kajiya clapped her on the back. "Relax, the others are a little more straightforward. Rule four, magic is conducted purely by feeling."

Chase-Sarka's ears rose with her smile. "Knew that."

Kajiya smiled back. "See? Easy. Rule five," she stopped short.

Chase-Sarka turned to her. "What is it?"

Kajiya looked at her feet, heart pounding. Rotari *had* been right. Magic *didn't* have a mind of its own. But its distribution was clearly controlled by something more powerful.

"Ruina? You feeling okay?" Chase-Sarka lowered her voice.

Kajiya shook her head. "I'm fine. Rule five, magic can seem to have a mind of its own at times."

"Seem?"

"Seem. There's actually something, some*one* far greater at work. And well, He chooses who gets extra magic."

Chase-Sarka's eyes widened. "Really?"

Kajiya nodded, a strange calmness filling her. "Really," she stuck her snout in the air as she continued, and the calmness vanished instantly. "Rule six, and you know I've broken this one a few times."

Chase-Sarka grinned. "Ooh, I'm really curious now!"

"Trans-species intercommunication is forbidden," Kajiya said.

"Why?"

Kajiya rolled her eyes. "Because we can't eat plants. I mean, well, I would never be able to eat Rosa—she's my friend! Or Onta either—not that Gaorun would ever let us, but can you imagine if someone talked to all the animals they came across?"

"They would starve," Chase-Sarka realized.

Kajiya nodded. "Yeah. Rule seven's one of my favorites."

"What is it?" Chase-Sarka was lapping up the information like a taic seeing water after walking over a mountain.

"You're only limited by your imagination," Kajiya answered.

Chase-Sarka laughed. "Another one I already knew!"

Kajiya giggled as well. "I bet you'll know this one too. Rule eight, always, *always*, be ready to learn something new."

The ground under Kajiya's feet changed back to wood. They were on the second bridge already?!

She looked up over the ocean, watching the sun reflecting off the waves. Her nerves came back to her all at once. She was sure her stomach had gotten lost in the maze it had created of itself. She gulped.

Kajiya felt a hand on her shoulder.

"Thanks for the magic lesson," Chase-Sarka lowered her voice. "You'll be fine."

She turned to Chase-Sarka, surprised by the warmth in her artificially-orange eyes. "Thanks."

Chase-Sarka nodded, then kept walking on, catching up to Ainee. Kajiya allowed her pace to lengthen for just a moment. Then, holding her voice at a whisper so small she could barely hear herself, she began to speak.

"Thank you. For everything you've done," Kajiya said. "Could you...Could you help with this too?"

There was no answer. Kajiya twitched an ear skyward, but nothing came. Still... Before He hadn't said anything but to trust Him. Maybe He was working in a way she couldn't see. Perhaps everything she had been through up to now had been to prepare her for this moment. She just had to trust.

Kajiya's pace increased with renewed strength. Even if she failed, He could make it all right in spite of her. She had felt the strength He could give enough to know that He was far more powerful than even Rotari. She had nothing to fear.

She was still afraid of course, but the idea that she didn't need to be was comforting, and she clung to it as she caught up with the others. She looked up at the sky, and her heart nearly stopped. The sun was hitting noon.

"How much farther?" Kajiya burst as her heart

threatened to explode inside her chest.

Resurge turned to her. "Not much farther now. Maybe half-an-hour?"

Kajiya's heart sank. Half an hour? That could be too late! But, she knew that they were already going at a pace that would confuse anyone who happened to pay attention to them. They were practically running.

Kajiya focused on her magic, extruding it from herself, and her bag started to glow, startling her. She sighed as she remembered Emera's gift laid within, and she realized that she had nothing to worry about. *Actually,* she thought as she looked back at it, *I completely forgot about it. It'll certainly come in handy now... If we get there in time.*

The streets and feas passed by in a blur, but as they speed-walked down the dirt paths, Kajiya noticed a few things. First, that compared to the feas of this island, the rest of Royalin was underdressed, making her and her group stand out even more. She held her head down as yet another set of feas turned to stare. And second, she noticed that Royalin's forests, with their tall towering straight trees, and almost no shrubbery, created a thick canopy that held out most of the sunlight. Kajiya may have come from the jungle herself, but Mirabilia had been built *in* the canopy, not under it. The darkness made her jumpy.

Finally, Resurge stopped, and everyone almost crashed into him as he spoke.

"We're here."

It was here. This was it. Kajiya's heart felt like it had found a permanent resting spot in her throat as she stepped around the four-fea pile-up of her friends to get a better look.

The Grand Assembly hall was the biggest

building she had ever seen, looking exactly like a larger version of the assembly hall she known in Mirabilia. The middle was a large circular building made up of many large wooden planks, with two rectangular sections coming off it. It was even raised on a platform above the street, and framed with trees.

Kajiya walked up to the double doors. There were sounds coming from inside! They weren't too late! But before she could relate this information to her awe-stricken friends, she heard a loud banging. *Turten!*

His voice floated through the doors loud and clear to her ears.

"Alright then," he began, "all the sides have been argued. All those in favour say 'I.'"

Chapter 10: Party Crashing

"Stop!"

Kajiya threw open both doors at once just as the others came running to her, seamlessly shifting the magic around her body to her throat so that she could call out with both magic and her voice. She knew it would be the only way to get their attention before anyone could say anything. Her fur shifted back to blue.

The entire room was silent. Until…

"K-Kajiya?!" Proten stood from his seat, fur completely puffed out.

A ripple of shock went through all of the feas present, and they turned to each other in confusion. Even *Turten,* that sleazy no-good-*liar,* looked startled. However, he recovered far faster than Kajiya would have liked.

Sorry Ainee, Kajiya said with magic as she slid her claws between the seams of the sleeve on her left shoulder, and ripped it off to reveal her magik's mark.

A collective gasp went through the Assembly, and Kajiya took the moment to introduce herself, dumping what remained of the sleeve on the floor.

"I am Kajiya, daughter of Proten, and future magik of Mirabilia!" she declared as her heart pounded.

She turned as the others padded in behind her, and then flinched as her father cried out again.

"Resurge!" Proten's red eyes were completely filled with tears of joy.

Kajiya smiled back at him; how could she not? Suddenly, he jumped out of his seat, and with magic obviously fuelling his jumps, bounded down to sweep both her and Resurge up into a giant hug.

"I thought I lost you both forever," he said.

Kajiya let him embrace them just a moment longer than she should have, but secretly, she was overjoyed to see him as well. To see him safe, and sound, and here. She pushed him away though.

"Not now, Dad," she said, "we'll have plenty of time to chat later. I promise. But for now," her voice grew dark as she turned to face Turten.

"Kajiya," the sickly smooth voice slid throughout the room to her ears.

Turten was just as Kajiya remembered him. Blue fur, black stripes, and slicked-back hair.

"It is good to see you again," he began, waving a hand about nonchalantly. "I was so grief-stricken when the warriors said you were dead."

"Couldn't kill me you mean," she interjected.

She felt every gaze snap to her, and she forced herself to breathe. How many times had she imagined this moment? How many times had seen Turten tremble at the mere sight of her in her mind? He wasn't trembling now.

"Kill you? Oh no, those warriors were sent to *find* you. There has been—"

"I didn't misunderstand!" Kajiya hissed stepping forward. "We know about the spiedes, Turten!"

Another magik stood. "Spiedes? What are you talking about?" His brown fur puffed out.

Kajiya blinked. "You must be Beifin."

The magik nodded. "What was that you said?"

Kajiya felt a hand on her shoulder.

"Kajiya." Her father looked concerned.

Fortunately, Resurge stepped forward and

walked over to the seats. He held a piece of parchment in his hand.

"This is from Sai," he said as he held it up to Beifin.

Beifin stiffened, and his fur fluffed out even further. "You've been to Animo?"

Kajiya shrugged her father's hand off her shoulder gently. "Been to and below."

Beifin took the paper from Resurge and started to read as Kajiya spoke.

"After my exile from Mirabilia," she began, "my companions and I travelled to Animo. There we came to a village under attack."

The darkest feas all started to look around worriedly. Clearly, this was Animo's delegation.

"What were they under attack from?" the haughty voice came from the very head of the circle, just above Turten.

"Spiedes," Kajiya said simply.

"The spiedes are just a legend!" a voice from the Mirabilian section called.

Kajiya turned to him with the harshest glare she had ever used. "Tell that to my scars!"

"She speaks the truth," Beifin said, rolling up the parchment briskly, tears in his eyes. "And thank you for giving my son back his voice," he added quietly.

Kajiya blinked, then turned to him, "Son? What are you—Sarin's your son?"

Beifin nodded curtly to her, and now that she looked, Kajiya could see the resemblance. Beifin also had grey stripes, and warm green eyes. He was one of the oldest feas in the entire room.

"I'm afraid I've made a grave mistake," he

announced to the Grand Assembly, "in underestimating those vile creatures. Animo has been under direct attack from them for the past two months."

A gasp came from everywhere but the Animo delegation. Kajiya hung her head.

"I'm afraid that's not all," her throat closed slightly, but she forced herself to keep her head up. "I was foolish, we were all foolish. Sai organized an attack force, a pre-emptive strike. He didn't know who I was when I volunteered. I had hidden my mark."

The entire room stiffened.

"And he accepted a *woman's* help?" a condescending voice from the Royalin section called out, earning some well-deserved glares from the Palinda congregation.

"Yes. I was to be one of their healers," Kajiya responded. "Nearly one-hundred and fifty of us went in. Only I and one other came out."

Proten immediately turned to his son. "Resurge."

Resurge shook his head. "I had been injured. I couldn't go."

Proten breathed a sigh of relief, "Thank goodness. This is the first time I've ever been glad you got hurt."

Kajiya figured the murmuring Assembly had had enough time to digest her words. "However, I discovered something disconcerting in those caves."

She turned to Turten to look him in the eye. She had been waiting to say this for so long. To bring justice. The words were just as sweet as she had imagined.

"Turten plans to work together with the spiedes

to take over the surface, and turn all women, if not all the tribes, into slaves."

The silence in the wake of her words was absolute. It almost seemed like no one dared to breathe. Until at last, Turten broke out into laughter. Kajiya drew back a bit; not the reaction she had been expecting.

"Have you rockras in your brain, child?" Turten said, standing. "If you retract your statements I might forget you made them."

Kajiya only stood straighter, that was a threat, loud and clear. She smiled.

"I won't. You've endangered our people long enough, Turten. Besides," she said, turning to face the rest of the Assembly, "no matter what we do, we go to war! The spiedes plan to betray Turten, and attack the surface!

Beifin nodded. "My general and my son have confirmed her words in writing. Animo is with you, Magik Kajiya."

Kajiya could have jumped for joy. Now she just had to convince the rest of them!

A younger magik, a sand-coloured fea with golden stripes who was clearly from Palinda stood. Kajiya's heart leapt. He had to be Jiblin—Emera's husband!

"And how do *we* know you speak the truth? Why should we prepare for war?" he asked, the fringes on his pavoki-skin shirt rustling.

Kajiya reached her hand into her bag and pulled out the light-orb. "Palinda already is. We met with Emera."

He stiffened at once. "Are they safe? How do I know you didn't attack them and steal that?"

Kajiya didn't take his words harshly, but merely summoned the magic. Given what she was saying and the tension of the situation, his reaction was only justified.

The orb started to glow, and she opened her eyes. "You can ask anyone from Mirabilia, they wouldn't have a clue how to activate it. Emera taught me before we left Palinda."

Turten raised his snout. "It sounds like you've been doing a lot of travelling. Perhaps we should adjourn to let you get some rest. And actually *think—*"

"She *has* thought!" Ainee stepped forward, tail lashing. "And she's not the only one who's been hunted! We've been with her every step of the way. She's grown since you've seen her last."

"And I know her honesty!" Chase-Sarka called out, not bothering to disguise her voice, which prompted a few rather confused looks from the Assembly. "Because they accepted me even when I was not honest with them," Kajiya nodded at her, and Sarka let the illusion fade.

Another gasp spread throughout the crowd, and Kajiya gestured to the now-pink fea.

"This is Sarka, and she has something very, *very* important to say, so please, give her your full attention, and respect," she added forcefully.

Sarka stepped forward, pink tail swishing, "I too was captured by spiedes, not in the same manner that Kajiya was, but as a slave. Fortunately, I was made to be the slave of Sharack, a spiede who does *not* believe in slavery. Sharack believes that our two species can live in peace, and help each other."

Beifin nearly crumpled the parchment in his hand, bristling, but it didn't look like he was going to say anything, for a little while at least. Kajiya realized he was probably just respecting her words to respect Sarka.

"More than that," Sarka continued, seeming to grow bolder, "he is not the only one who believes this. And they want to overthrow their king and outlaw slavery."

Beifin stopped bristling, and Kajiya smiled.

"They have sent me as their representative and as a plea for help in this endeavor. They can't do it on their own."

Turten sneered. "And why should we believe a freak like you? And where'd *you* learn magic?"

Gaorun's fur bristled, and he stepped forward beside her. "Every word she says, no matter how far-fetched it sounds, we know it's true! If nothing else, her magic should *attest* to that! Her fur colour doesn't matter!"

Turten seemed to smirk a smirk of glee. "Really? Would *you*, a liar by trade, vouch for her truth?"

Gaorun clenched his fists. "That's not who I am."

Turten broke out into laughter. "I thought I hired you to *take care* of Kajiya during her banishment."

Kajiya's fur stood on end, no. It couldn't be. She looked back at him, ears low.

"Gaorun, that can't be…"

Gaorun gulped. "It's true. I was supposed to make sure that we camped at the base of that mountain the second day out. They came for me right after you left my camp on the day of your banishment. They were going to kill Onta right there if I didn't say I was going to help, and my father if I betrayed them."

Kajiya took a step back, mind racing. It couldn't be, but... Wait... They had only survived because Gaorun had warned them about the warriors coming to kill her.

Gaorun's face fell, and his ears with it. He took a deep breath, then turned to face Kajiya.

"I couldn't do what he said but..." He sighed through his nose. "I still lied. I was going to tell you! That day in the forest, when I got the firewood—I really was. After you saved Onta and," he shot a glare Turten's direction, "after I realized that in order to hurt my father, Turten would have to find him first. And *my dad's* far too good of a trapper to be found! At the very least, he would understand. I couldn't let him hurt you though—but...I choked. I lied. I never saw those warriors. I just knew they were coming. I just went with the first thing that came in my head, looked you in the eye and...lied."

"Can you really trust the word of someone who has admitted to lying?" Turten cried out, and the Assembly looked at each other nervously.

"Yes," Resurge's thick voice filled the room, and made Kajiya's heart soar as her brother placed one hand on Gaorun's shoulder, much to Gaorun's apparent shock.

Onta rubbed up against her master's legs, and she seemed to smile up at him. Ainee placed her hand on Gaorun's other shoulder, and Sarka intertwined her tail with his.

"It is only because of Gaorun's words that we *escaped* that day. He warned us, and has proven his honesty, his integrity many times since. I'm sorry that we made you shoulder this burden alone," Resurge added.

"You know you could have told us at any time," Ainee said gently.

Kajiya smiled as everything clicked. The amount of time they had to get over the mountain… It was far longer than they would have had if Gaorun had really run into the warriors while gathering firewood. She smiled, and stepped forward, head high.

"Turten, I hope you're aware, but you have sealed your fate," she turned to the rest of the Assembly with triumph shining in her eyes. "You all heard him! He may not have said so directly, but his intent is clear enough. When he banished me, he intended to kill me. But because of a great man," she said, casting a glance to Gaorun with a smile, "he failed."

Turten laughed. "Can you not see through the taic-fur he has pulled over your eyes? He lies even as he speaks."

Kajiya's fur prickled; Turten had regained his composure. That could not be a good sign. Kajiya gritted her teeth; anger would not help her here. Still, she could feel her blood turning to ice. But… Yes. She was sure. It was His ice. That thought alone quelled her wrath, but not her anger.

"Tell me," she addressed the Assembly, "does he have the countenance of one who lies?"

Turten raised his snout. "So he's an experienced player—a player of emotions. Who do you trust? Them or me? We *all* know what *you* did, *Kajiya.*"

Kajiya stiffened, and the Assembly's murmurs grew louder.

"You *attacked* an Assembly unprovoked!"

Turten rose from his seat, sneering. "She purposely broke one of her tribe's *own* laws!"

"Liar!" The word left Kajiya's lips before she could stop it, and she had no choice but to finish the thought. "There is no law in Mirabilia that says caves are off-limits. Warriors just aren't allowed to use them for tests of courage."

Her words echoed off the back walls of the hall. One by one, the Mirabilian delegation turned to Turten.

"She's right you know." The words were said at barely a whisper, but they may as well have been shouted.

"A slip of the tongue." Turten waved a hand casually.

One of the Royalin officials turned to Kajiya. "You deny that—but not attacking your own tribe?" he wondered aloud.

"I do not deny it." Kajiya's gaze didn't waver; she wouldn't let it, "because I cannot." She had accepted her actions, and their consequences, whatever they may be, she would accept those too. "It is the truth, but not a truth I am proud of. I have served, and will continue to serve my punishment, banishment from my own tribe—from my family, my childhood, and my people until such a time as they see fit to accept me as their own yet again. It would be folly for me to expect to be taken back as their leader once more, and that's okay. I came here to stop you—all of you—from making a grave mistake and passing *his* law." She looked directly at Turten.

"And what would you know of law-making? You said yourself that you are not fit to lead," Turten growled.

"I know that it is wrong for the weak to serve the strong! Those who are strong should serve the weak. Your law—it will not bring peace. It will bring dissent. It will bring disaster. Put yourselves in their position for a moment," she turned back to most of the Assembly, "if you were one of those *under* the law he wishes to make—is it fair? Can you trust those above you to show kindness, to deal with you fairly—or will they take advantage of their power, and make you work while they do *nothing*?" Kajiya let her words sink in. "Now, tell me—does it still seem wise?"

The Assembly was silent, but Kajiya could see smiles from the Palinda delegation, and heads shaking in response to her question.

"So we should let women be reckless with magic whenever they please? Go where they like— where they can get into danger? So they can cripple feas for *life* through their helplessness?" Turten's voice became bitter. "Then refuse to even give them the slightest *hint* of gratitude in return?"

Kajiya blinked. Turten had lost his tail saving a woman from a taic. Never in his recounting of his 'valiant efforts' could Kajiya recall him mentioning the woman saying 'thank you.' Perhaps—perhaps it was that bitterness, like an infection allowed to fester under the skin, that caused Turten to act the way he did.

Kajiya felt her father stiffen beside her—she hadn't been the only one to figure it out.

"Turten," Proten spoke, and Kajiya's father's voice turned stern and commanding with all the weight befitting a magik. "In light of what has transpired here, and the *enlightening* words you have just spoken, I, Proten, magik of Mirabilia, in the presence of these witnesses, hereby ask you to step down from your position as Mirabilia's Assembly head."

At once, nods and murmurs of agreement came from throughout the Grand Assembly, until the Mirabilian delegation stood.

"We support this motion," one of the feas in the front rows said, glaring backwards up to Turten.

Turten's face contorted with shock. Then rage.

"You. You fool. You could have ruled by my side once I killed the spiede's foolish 'king.' I always had a soft spot for you, Proten. If it hadn't been for you, I would have ordered *her* killed on the spot. But she had to be *your* daughter, didn't she?" A twisted, deranged smile spread over his face, and Kajiya felt her fur rise involuntarily.

Yet, there was a joy in her fear, and she managed to force her fur back down. Turten was showing his true colours now.

Those sitting closest to him inched away, and everyone acted as though they had just opened their eyes. Kajiya felt magic surround her. His magic. He was here. She had nothing to fear after all.

"Too bad, that without me," Turten sneered, "you won't stand a chance."

A scream rang out from outside, and the messenger from Mirabilia burst through the doors, eyes as wide as the white plates they had eaten off of that morning.

"S-spiedes!" he cried out breathlessly. "Spiedes are attacking the city."

Kajiya gasped, and shot Resurge a look, remembering the cave he had spotted on the map. She turned back to Grand Assembly.

"We don't have time for this now! The feas of

Royalin *need* us."

The final magik, a dark blue fea with darker stripes, stood. "This Assembly is adjourned until further notice, by order of Dorat."

Immediately, most of the Assembly got up and rushed for the exits. Beifin and Jiblin jumped down the stairs and out into the fray.

"Ronin!" Dorat called harshly to an ocean-blue fea beside him who had stood, but not yet moved.

"Yes, Father?" he replied.

Dorat shot Turten a yellow-eyed stare. "He may have been working with them, but his plan to *stop* them should still work. Do it."

Ronin shook his head. "I can't. He never told any of us how to work the canon. He wanted to do it himself."

Kajiya blinked at the Royalin's feas' words. Turten was planning to *stop* the spiedes? Since when? Had he realized the error of his ways? Kajiya looked at Turten, who was now being held by two of the Assembly's members. They were leading him towards an interior exit, no doubt to imprison him until the end of the attack. The hate and despise in his eyes shone brightly now, as though he could finally reveal it. *No,* Kajiya realized. *He hasn't changed at all. He must have figured out that the spiedes planned on betraying him. He just wanted to use the situation to his advantage,* she growled silently. If she had been living in another tribe, and heard that a fea almost single-handedly led the charge against the invading spiedes, she would have given that fea her respect. It would have been easy for him to pass his law, no matter how wrong it was, if he stopped the spiedes. Perhaps that had been his plan all along!

Kajiya whipped around to the door; regardless, there were feas out there who needed saving. Turten could wait.

Suddenly, she felt something grab her hand. She turned to see her father. He had wiped the tears from his eyes, and a look of determination had placed itself upon his face.

"Where are you going?"

"To help, Dad! I can't just sit back and watch these people get hurt!" she said, pulling her arm away, but her father's grip was tight.

"No. I won't allow it! Your magic has always been strong but—" he said, pulling her.

"I'm not relying on *my* magic!" Kajiya burst.

She knew now why His magic had come to her. It wasn't reassurance. It was preparation. His magic was even more powerful than the spiedes.

Proten drew back as a loud thump came from Resurge's pack as he dropped it; he held his broadsword in his hand. Sarka had likewise ditched Ainee's pack on the floor, and Gaorun took the moment to abandon his as well. Ainee, however, merely tightened her pack and Kajiya nodded to her; the purple fea would need her herbs to heal those hurt by the spiedes. The hall was almost empty by now.

"Kajiya's stronger than when she left," Resurge said as he stepped beside his father. "We can handle this."

Gaorun took out another net, and Onta held her tail high in anticipation, hissing gleefully.

"If anyone can take down a spiede, it's Kajiya," the green fea said, slinging the net over his shoulder.

Ainee nodded, and Kajiya breathed out. As

always, they stood beside each other.

"Dad, we can't do this alone. We have to fight them together," she twisted her hand around so that she held her father's. "Will you join us?"

Proten breathed in sharply, then dipped his head. "On my honour as a magik."

Kajiya tightened her grip, then released him so that she could ditch her own pack as well. It was nothing but dead weight now.

Another ear-piercing scream echoed through the halls, and Kajiya nodded to her friends. It was now or never. She burst through the double doors, and sure enough, there were spiedes of all shapes and sizes. Small lithe ones attacked without mercy, while the largest, nearly four times Kajiya's height, slammed against the buildings. Beifin and the majority of the Animo delegation were trying to use their magic to unbalance it, but it wasn't working.

Kajiya hesitated a moment as a sharp stabbing pain hit her neck. She forced herself not to touch the scar hidden by her fur as she bristled. Instead, she turned to Sarka as fast as she could.

"Sarka! You've lived with them! What are their weak points?" she blurted.

The pink fea seemed to come out of a stupor. "Where their legs attach to their body. They don't have any armor there."

Kajiya nodded, then held out a hand. This time though, she could feel the magic's strength. From her outstretched fingertips a light blue sparkle emanated, condensing itself into a small dark blue ball. Everyone looked to her with confusion on their faces, but Kajiya knew what she was doing. She had done it before. And if she could even get a moment to relay what Sarka had told her…

"Stun," she hissed, imploding the sphere and sending out a dark ripple of magic through the crowd.

Just like when she and Sarin were in the spiede's cave, only the spiedes were affected, and seized up, allowing the feas to overtake them for just a moment. Kajiya grimaced as she felt an immense drain in her energy; she knew the effect wouldn't last long. She summoned the magic to her throat. It was the only way she'd be heard.

Aim for where their legs connect to their bodies! she cried out with magic, projecting as far as she could. *They're weak there!*

A few of the fighting feas looked at her in shock, others started to immediately take her advice, and a few ignored her completely.

Kajiya breathed out, she was going to need a moment. There had to be at least twenty spiedes in just this section of town. And with the thick canopy blocking out the sun's rays… What were they going to do?

"Wait," she whispered to herself, eyes widening as she turned to Resurge. "The cave! We can drive them back to the cave."

Resurge said, "If we can drive them back there, we can keep them there. They can't enter the village any other way."

Kajiya nodded. "Well, what are you waiting for? Go! I'll catch up!"

A look of joy came onto Resurge's face as he charged at the nearest spiede with Gaorun and Sarka on his heels. Ainee veered off course as one of the Royalin warriors was tossed aside by a spiede—and she did something Kajiya had never seen her do before. She used magic that most males couldn't do. Ainee held out her hands and suspended the warrior in midair. Then she lowered him to the ground, where he regained his footing, gave her a nod of thanks and, without a second glance, charged at the spiede.

Kajiya's heart filled with dread; what if Ainee had used too much magic? The purple fea was breathing heavily, but seemed to regain her strength quickly as she dashed off to the nearest wounded, grabbing herbs out of her bag as she ran. Kajiya breathed a sigh of relief; Ainee would be fine.

She felt a hand on her shoulder. She looked up at her father.

"Shall we? Magik?" He smiled.

Kajiya smiled back and pushed herself off of the wall of the hall, cracking her knuckles as she did so.

"I believe so."

Kajiya's feet drummed out a solid pace, and her bell jangled with every movement. This fact she was grateful for; the more noise, the harder it would be for the spiedes to fight. Still, if they could get more light through the trees, it would be better. Or maybe…

Kajiya reached into her yellow shoulder bag, smiling as she realized that she had forgotten to take it off. Her hand tightly grasped the light-orb, and she summoned the magic, creating a great store of icy air around it so that she wouldn't have to focus on it too much. The orb shone brightly, and Kajiya shoved it towards one of the smaller spiedes. The creature may have had its eyes closed, but it still cringed away from the light. Kajiya advanced without hesitation, and summoned a fire to the other hand. A bright blue and white-pink flame exploded from it, and she threw it forward, hitting the spiede directly in the face.

It let out a loud screech similar to the one she had heard back in the Narine, and Kajiya got an idea. She changed the composition of the ice in her veins, and moved it out over top of the spiede. Fortunately, the air was humid, so it didn't take her long to get enough water to form a giant spike above it. Of course, water was just water. She inclined her claws, and the water turned to ice.

Before she could do anything, however, another screech came from the side. It was one of the larger spiedes, and it was coming right for her! She gasped, but lightning thundered from behind her, and hit the spiede's legs. It crumpled to the ground, roaring in pain.

Proten smiled at her, his hands still crackling with electricity. Kajiya smiled back, and brought the giant ice spike down parallel with the ground.

"Back! Back!" she cried, poking the spiede with the spike, enough so that it knew she meant business, but she had no intent to kill.

Some of the other feas looked at her strangely, and she turned to them, feeling her blood turn to solid ice.

"Drive them back where they came!" she yelled. *"Drive them back!"* she cried again, with both her voice and magic.

The spiedes all turned to her and the colour drained from her face. They had heard her. They leapt over whatever feas they were fighting to converge on her and Proten, but before they could reach them, Jiblin slid underneath and used his own magic to pull sharp rocks out of the ground, sending a wave of them towards one side of the advancing spiedes. Then, with a flick of his sand-coloured wrist, he curved the rocks so that the spiedes were forced to retreat to the side where Kajiya held her own spiede adversary.

"Ya looked like ya could use some help." He smirked, brushing dirt off of his pants.

One of the smaller spiedes from the other side went flying over their heads to land behind the spiedes they had already corralled. Beifin had donned a cape with a shoulder pad on the right side and held a long stone-tipped spear in both hands. He then let go with his right hand and splayed his fingers, creating a circle of wind that even the largest spiedes couldn't penetrate. A few of the smaller feas went flying, and he sent another gust of wind to put them with the ever-growing group.

"Heh," he said as he adjusted his cape and walked over to them. "Who knew a sky-clearing spell could be so useful?"

Kajiya nodded to him, and faced the spiedes again. More and more feas were getting the idea, and two lines were beginning to form as they pushed the spiedes out of the city and into the forest behind the Grand Assembly hall.

Kajiya quickly realized that her ice-spike wasn't going to cut it anymore. Resurge and the others had just managed to add their spiede to the large group. Gaorun was using his net as a makeshift whip, easily striking the spiede's mandibles from a safe distance while Resurge and Onta worked in coordination to strike on opposite sides of the spiede so that it couldn't go for just one of them. Sarka managed to flip around the spiede with precision and strike at their vulnerable joints while staying far out of reach of their legs.

But, as Kajiya looked over, an Animo fea's head was bleeding, and his tail was missing more than a little fur. Some of the Palinda feas whipped the spiedes with their tails while their arms hung limp. Kajiya took a closer look at her friends. Resurge was favouring his right side, and attacking often with his left. Gaorun was limping, and Onta's side was missing some fur.

Suddenly, Kajiya felt a blow to her chest and was thrown across the street, into a building's window. Kajiya felt the glass give way behind her, and heard it crack as the jutting windowsill stopped her motion by hitting her tail right where it connected to the spine. The ice spear she had created fell to the ground and disintegrated, and the spiede leapt for her.

Idiot! she chastised herself as she slid down the wall and rolled out of the way. While she had been worrying about everyone else, she had forgotten her own imminent danger.

The spiede hit the wall where she had been hard, and its head flew through the window, shattering the glass. Jiblin was there at once and sent another barrage of small stones at it until it was forced to draw back once more. Proten grabbed Kajiya's upper arm and pulled her to her feet.

"Don't lose your focus," he hissed, sending another wave of lightning branching towards the spiedes as they threatened to advance.

Kajiya nodded, breathing heavily. Her father was right. She couldn't lose focus. Not now.

She summoned the fire again, this time it was so bright the flames appeared white. Heat radiated from it, and Kajiya breathed in. She would have to be careful not to start a forest fire. Unless…

That was exactly what she needed to do. Not light the forest on fire, but spread fire throughout the forest! Even the spiedes knew the danger of fire.

When she had fallen back, the spiedes had attacked as one, and regained some ground. Kajiya raised her hand to the sky; ground she was going to get back. The fire stretched out from her hand horizontally and Kajiya passed the light orb off to Jiblin, who took it without question. She needed to give this all her attention. Nothing less would do.

The ice in her veins reached a state of crystallization that sharpened her mind. She turned a segment of that ice to her eyes and used a sight spell to travel down the line between the two warring parties, spreading the fire from where she stood meticulously. Finally, she finished creating a ring of white flames around the spiedes, all the way back to the cave's entrance. She inclined the claws of her hands, causing the border of flame to shrink. Other fires, some normal, others turning blue and purple, joined her own.

She knew they had passed the turning point of the battle. The spiedes would fight back, but their only real option now was to return to the cave. Alone, but with His magic, Kajiya knew she would have been a forced to be reckoned with. But with all the feas of Royalin—the assembly members using magic; the warriors with wit, courage and strength; and even some animals who had rightly perceived the spiedes to be a threat—Kajiya knew the spiedes had no real clue what they were dealing with. Everyone had put aside their differences to fight, to save Royalin, and their homes. Kajiya was even sure that she saw a blue-faced onti fighting alongside a deep green chirpl against one of the smaller spiedes.

As the first few spiedes backed into the cave, Kajiya realized something. If Turten had intended to betray them from the start so he could portray himself as some sort of hero, he would have in no way revealed what feas were capable of. At least one good thing had come from his lies.

As the feas advanced, a few retreated to the line of healers that had formed as the perimeter around the spiedes got smaller and smaller. Finally, the last of the spiedes had retreated into the shadows of the cave. The feas were silent, until at last, not even Kajiya's magic-filled ears could pick up any trace of their scuttling. She let the magic melt from her veins, and the fire flickered out of existence. The smaller flames soon followed, and a loud cheer went up from all present.

Kajiya, however, did not scream in joy. She could not join their cheer, because she knew what was coming. They would report to their king that they had been betrayed. That the feas were stronger than they had thought. The next wave would be intended to subdue the feas completely, if not utterly annihilate them.

Kajiya tried to flick her tail, and cringed as pain erupted at the base of her spine; she knelt to the ground. When she had hit the window earlier—what if it wasn't the *window* she had heard cracking, but her own tailbone? The coolness of her magic had completely numbed the wound before, but now, she felt it loud and clear.

"Ainee," she said as soon as she could regain her breath. "Get Ainee!" she hissed to her father, who was cradling his hand.

He nodded and ran off. Kajiya tried her best not to move. A broken tailbone was a very serious injury. If she so much as *twitched* wrong, she could paralyze her tail, or worse, her entire lower half.

Still, the familiar rustling of Ainee's green dress soothed like a splash of cool water on a hot day, and Kajiya placed one hand on the ground to wait.

Ainee skidded to a stop beside Kajiya, and placed her bag of herbs on the ground without so much as a word. With a quick burst of coldness, Kajiya felt Ainee hit the back of her neck with two fingers, and paralyze her bones from the neck down.

"What hurts the most?" she asked as she used magic to remove all her herbs from her bag,

"I think, I broke a tailbone," Kajiya managed to get out.

Ainee moved her hand down Kajiya's back, and the area began to feel warm. Ainee said nothing, but then moved up her spine, until she had one hand on Kajiya's back and one on her breastbone. She then moved Kajiya onto the ground, and twisted her head and arms so she might have some semblance of being comfortable.

"You're right," she said after moving Kajiya's legs so that she was completely sprawled out on the ground. "It's not a big break, but it's dangerously close to your spinal column."

Kajiya gulped. It sounded as serious as she thought it was. From where she lay on the ground, she could see the others coming towards her. Gaorun's limp was slightly less pronounced now, and Kajiya guessed that he had at least suppressed the pain by summoning magic, if not performed a healing spell of his own.

Healers, both trained and those who knew enough to deal with superficial wounds, were dispersing themselves among the crowd. A different healer was tending to Kajiya's father, and another to Jiblin, who had apparently stabbed himself in the foot with one of his own rocks.

Kajiya couldn't feel anything as Ainee worked, and a few of the higher trained healers came to help her. Kajiya didn't want to feel, she didn't want to think. They were safe for now. But how long was 'for now' going to last? She had to get together with the other magiks. Come up with a plan! Her blood chilled as she thought about the other tribes. Certainly Royalin would not be the only one targeted.

A fire lit in her tail and she screamed out in agony. The pain wiped all other thoughts from her mind, and she began to summon the magic to see if she could get rid of the heat.

Kajiya! Ainee's voice infiltrated her mind. *You can't summon magic. I know it hurts, but it's the only way. If you continue, you'll stop the bones from knitting properly!*

Kajiya gritted her teeth. She would have to endure it. After what seemed like years, the fire slowed from a blazing inferno, to something like the campfires that they had made so many times during their journeys, until finally, all that was left were embers.

Ainee and the other healers all let out a collective sigh of relief, and Kajiya could see Ainee give them a nod of thanks out of the corner of her eye.

"I can take it from here," she said, and the others all started off in other directions.

They walked tiredly, and Kajiya could tell that

they had all used a ton of magic on her. Wait… How many of them had attended to her? Surely there were feas with more serious injuries than hers! They needed to look after her people first.

Kajiya wanted to get up, but Ainee's bone-chilling spell still held her tightly. She could not move on her own.

She felt Ainee slather a poultice above the base of her tail, under her shirt. Finally, she felt the ice leave her bones, and she started to move.

"Slowly, slowly now," Ainee instructed, weariness permeating her voice.

Kajiya nodded slightly, and brought herself to a sitting position. The flesh around the former break was still sore, but it no longer erupted in pain.

Ainee sighed, wiping sweat from her forehead. "The area's still inflamed, but I'm sure you can live with that. You're very lucky, Kajiya. If it had gone just a little further…"

Kajiya nodded, and Proten turned to Ainee.

"But, she'll be fine, right?" he said with all the tact of a father.

Ainee nodded as Resurge reached out his good hand to help her up.

"Yes, she'll be fine, Magik Proten." She turned to Resurge, then let out a little gasp. "You're hurt!" She started to hold her unsteady hands to his bad side, but he grabbed her wrist first.

"And you're exhausted. I'm sure my body will do fine without magic for a while," he said as he started to lead her to a tree.

"At least get one of the other healers to see you," she protested, tail skimming the ground.

He shook his head. "You know, all this has

made me realize something…"

"Kajiya, then, is it?" Dorat's voice broke Kajiya's concentration, and her ears swivelled to him before she turned to face the Royalin magik.

"Yes," she said.

He held his hand out to her. "Then I am pleased to make your acquaintance. I apologize for being unable to welcome you personally to Royalin," he said, looking at her as he bridled.

Kajiya took his outstretched hand regardless; part of his dark blue tunic had been stained a vibrant green—spiede blood. In spite of his manner, he too had fought against the spiedes, and for his people when they needed him. Kajiya could ignore the attitude.

"And you're, Dorat, correct?" she confirmed.

He nodded, then turned to the other magiks, "And now, I believe it is time that we have an Assembly of our own. A private one," he said, eyeing Gaorun, who had snuck closer to the group.

Onta brushed up against her legs, and Kajiya scooped her up, attempting not to bend as she did so.

"Gaorun's a hunter," she said. "If we intend to stop these spiedes, we can't allow them to hunt us, we need to hunt *them*."

"A most ingenious idea." Kajiya's fur stood on end as a mid-sized spiede appeared on the crest of the hill that concealed the cave.

Chapter 11: Plan of Attack

At once, every fea bore their claws, and a few summoned fires, but a flash of pink that bounced up to the spiede without any hesitation caught Kajiya's eye.

"Sharack!" Sarka called out as she reached the spiede and *hugged* him.

Sharack returned the embrace with a leg, and Kajiya could see that he was far older than any of the spiedes who had appeared so far. He tussled Sarka's hair with a mandible, and Kajiya noticed with surprise that the small protrusion that spiedes used to inject their deadly venom into their prey was gone. Did this spiede not have them, or were they retractable? Sharack also had a different body shape than most of the spiedes, with an elongated head and abdomen that were much more flat than the other spiedes Kajiya had seen.

No, that wasn't true, she *had* seen spiedes like him before. Back in the spiede's cavern, they had tended to the giant fire that provided all the light they needed to live. And just like those spiedes, he had no eyes.

"It's good to hear you doing so well," he said, and Kajiya smiled.

Sharack's voice had deepened with his age, and wasn't quite as grating as the usual voices she heard from spiedes. It was a nice change.

Jiblin stepped forward at once. "Ah reckon' that's the spiede yar liasonin' for?"

Sarka nodded, then announced loudly, "Feas of all tribes! This is Sharack, part of the spiede rebellion. They wish nothing but to live in peace with us. This is something they cannot do without our help, and without overthrowing the king."

Some of the feas stepped back warily, and Kajiya gulped.

"Of course," Sharack said, stepping forward as he lifted Sarka onto his back. *"We would not ask for your help without giving any in return."*

There was movement over the hill as a group of about twenty younger spiedes appeared, almost all without eyes or already blind, lacking pupils.

"This is only one of our troops, and with so few of our people willing to stand up to our king, the rest have remained underground to fight that battle. This is all we could spare to help you," Sharack said as he began to walk down the hill.

Dorat stepped forward. "Thank you, but do not be offended if we do not accept—" he paused as a deep ocean-blue fea grabbed his hand.

Kajiya blinked as she recognized Ronin, Dorat's son. His grip looked firm.

"Dad, look around. We won't survive another attack like that one. We need their help," he said forcefully.

Dorat didn't say anything, but Jiblin stepped forward.

"We'd be *honoured* to have such noble creatures such as yarselves joinin' us," he said.

Kajiya glanced over to Beifin, but he didn't look as certain as Jiblin. He seemed to think for a moment, then stepped forward as well.

"You must forgive us for being unsure of your motives," he said as Sharack reached level ground with them. "But perhaps it would be best if you were to leave your troops on that hill—just until we get used to you," he added hastily.

Sharack nodded, and brought all four legs closer to himself, one at a time. Kajiya recognized the gesture; it was the same one a spiede messenger had used when she had watched the king hold an audience with it. It must have been a sign of respect.

"A wise decision. It will take my troop a while to get used to the surface as well." Sharack approached slowly.

Sarka jumped down from his back and made her way over to Kajiya, blushing a fair amount.

"I owe him a lot," she said simply.

Kajiya nodded, then turned to Jiblin. "Jiblin, can you and your feas create a meeting-tent here?"

Jiblin blinked his blue-green eyes at her. "Here? Now?"

Kajiya nodded. "If they come back, we won't have time to get back here. We have to be ready right away. Unless, of course, you want to have our mini-Assembly back in the hall? Or just out here in the open?"

Dorat turned to her. "Magik Kajiya is correct. An impromptu war tent would suit our needs best." He eyed the spiede. "Although you had better make it pretty roomy."

Jiblin nodded, then turned to some of the Palinda delegation. "Ya heard the man, don't pretend ya weren't listenin'! Let's get to work, boys!" he commanded.

While they set off, Resurge and Ainee returned. Ainee looked to be more energetic already, and Resurge appeared not to be in pain. Ainee walked over to Gaorun, readying her herbs, but he shook his head and pointed to Onta. Kajiya laughed gently. He always put the onti first. Ainee didn't even bother trying to argue, and instead set about healing the onti. Gaorun held her herbs for her, and stood by as a willing and able helper.

Resurge left them, and started to walk over to Kajiya, when Proten intercepted them.

"I still can't believe you're both alright," he said, embracing his son, then his daughter.

"Dad," Kajiya said, struggling against his tight grip.

"Kajiya," he said, drawing back, "you have no idea what it's like when they tell you one child is dead, and you can't find the other," he turned to Resurge. "You could have left a note or something!"

Kajiya felt a sudden wave of guilt wash over her. All this time, she had been worried about what she had put her father through, and it didn't even occur to her that he might *possibly* be worried about Resurge as well.

"We had a few things on our minds," Resurge said quietly.

Kajiya let her ears fall. "Dad, I-I'm sorry. I never meant for any of this to happen."

Her father took her hand. "It's okay. All is forgiven. I'm just so glad that you're alive. If it weren't for those, things," he said, casting a glance to Sharack, "I would declare this day a holiday and we would have a feast."

Kajiya let out a laugh, and her father grinned.

"Well, at the very least, we certainly would have had a feast," he said, "in your honour." He took Resurge by the shoulder and gave him a powerful shake. "In *both* your honours!"

Resurge shared Kajiya's look of awkwardness, embarrassment, and joy.

"If only your mother could see you now."

Kajiya looked to her father; there were tears in his eyes again.

"I can't tell you how proud I am of both of you," he continued.

"Dad," Kajiya said before he could start a speech, "what about Turten?"

Her father's gaze turned dark. "I cannot believe I ever trusted the man. Do not worry, I will deal with him."

"An' we're done! Come on in." Jiblin's light voice carried though the crowd, and the other magiks moved towards the tent.

Ronin fell in step beside his father, and Beifin eyed Sharack. Sarka was lightly touching her tail to one of the spiede's legs to guide him. Kajiya followed her as Proten started for the tent as well, but Resurge hung back.

"Are you coming?" she asked.

He shook his head. "This is a *magik's* meeting. It's not place for a warrior like me."

Kajiya rolled her eyes. "No, it's exactly the place for a warrior like you. Gaorun, Ainee!" she called. "Get over here!"

Proten turned to her. "Now, Kajiya, I know that you like having your friends around but—" "No, Dad," she said. "I wouldn't have survived these past few months without them. They know things that magiks would never think of."

She turned to them, "Ainee showed me that magic can't fix every problem. Gaorun taught me that sometimes I have to trust my instincts. Resurge showed me what 'honour' truly means. Even Onta taught me to find joy in the small things. And sometimes, you fight for those you love," she paused, then turned back to her father. "I wouldn't be fit to lead without them."

Proten blinked, and everyone grew still as they listened. Kajiya let her head sink into her shoulders. It was true.

"I—I am so proud of you." A tear streaked down Proten's fur. "My little girl finally grew up," he wiped the tears from his eyes. "Your council is welcome anywhere you are."

Kajiya looked up at him joyfully, tears beginning in her own eyes, but she rubbed them away. They had an Assembly to get to.

The tent had been constructed very well for the short amount of time the Palindian feas had spent on it. The Royalin feas had brought in large table with two detailed maps spread across it. Jiblin had set Kajiya's light-orb up at the top of the tent, and Kajiya increased the icy cloud of magic around it. She didn't want it dying during the meeting.

Sarka sat with Sharack on the far side of the tent, which had clearly been made larger to accommodate his vastness. The rest of the feas took their places standing around the table. Dorat shot Resurge and the others a look full of disapproval, but said nothing. Kajiya figured his silence would be the closest thing she would get to approval from the Royalin magik, and accepted it. She took the spot closest to Sarka and Sharack. Resurge took the other side of Sharack with Jiblin and Gaorun beside him. Ainee positioned herself between Proten and Kajiya, and the others took the table's other end.

Now that she looked, Kajiya could see that one map was of Royalin, and the other was of Mysterium.

Kajiya felt slightly uneasy. Now what?

"I hereby call this Assembly to order," Dorat began, but Beifin gave him a quick glare and interrupted.

"I'm afraid we don't have time for formalities, Dorat!" he chastised. "They could be upon us at any moment."

Jiblin nodded in agreement, and crossed his arms. "One thing is for certain, we can't let 'em attack the village again. Too many innocents 'round."

Proten nodded. "So why don't we take the fight to them? We can use that light-sphere to light the way."

Kajiya stood at once. "No! That's what Animo tried. You don't know how many are down there—"

"But they did not have us." Sharack's voice sounded confident. *"The king does not yet know of our rebellion, we could bring a group of feas, it would have to be small, down as 'slaves,' and then…"*

"Whamo!" Gaorun thumped the table with his fist, causing them all to jump and puff out. "Hit them where they're weakest!" he continued. "I like it. Let's see. There're how many of you?"

"Twenty-four."

"Alright, I say, forty warriors. That's just under two feas per spiede. The best, the elite. One of yours will need to carry their weapons though."

"Of course."

"Hold on a second," Ronin interrupted. "What about up here? We can't be defenceless! And they'll get creamed if we send *just* warriors."

Resurge nodded. "He's right. Even knowing their weaknesses, warriors alone can't take this on. Spiedes have no honour. Uh, no offense."

"None taken. The spiedes you will fight truly do have no honour. They have enslaved even their own kind," Sharack hissed.

"I should go with them," Sarka's voice trembled. "I know more about them than anyone else here. How to tell friend from foe. Stuff like that."

Beifin shook his head. "Which is exactly why we'll need you here. If they manage to break through, or a group get past the group going down to meet them, we'll need your expertise."

Sarka looked a little too relieved in Kajiya's eyes, but at the same time, she understood. The darkness of that cave frightened Kajiya as well. There was no way she would go down there if she didn't have to. She would if she needed to though.

"Tell me," Sharack said, raising his head. *"Is it night or day?"*

Kajiya looked up before realizing that she would have to rely on her own sense of time to answer.

"It is almost night," Dorat responded suspiciously. "Why?"

"Then we must choose our plan of action quickly. Our spies told us that this afternoon's attack was nothing more than a scouting party. The main force is set to come out tonight."

The entire company flinched, and Kajiya's tail flicked automatically, causing her bell to ring and her to cringe in pain. Ainee touched her back gently, and the throbbing subsided. Kajiya sent her a quiet nod of thanks before turning back to the other magiks.

"Perhaps," Kajiya said, "we're going about this all wrong."

Beifin raised an eyebrow. "Go on."

"Look, Sharack," the spiede raised his head at Kajiya's words, "you'll have the power to outlaw slavery as soon as you overthrow the king, right?"

He inclined his head. *"Correct."*

"And you'll also have the power to let the spiede troops know he's been overthrown, and call them back?"

Sharack nodded again. *"I believe so."*

"Then maybe," Kajiya continued, "we need to focus not on fighting, but on helping the spiede's revolution. They should take thirty warriors with them, two healers and eight other magicians. There's your forty." She nodded to Gaorun. "Up here, we should focus on keeping them in the cave until the king's been overthrown."

"She's right," Resurge said, "we'll spread ourselves too thin if we try to fight them all. But a single target is much easier to take down."

The other magiks dipped their heads, but Kajiya could hear Jiblin's tail whipping.

"Ah jus' wish I could check on Palinda, see how they're doing."

Beifin nodded in agreement. "My tribe will be ready for an attack, but I can't help but worry about them as well."

Kajiya's ears fell. It was only natural for them to worry about their tribes—her blood turned cold and she started to sweat.

"Mirabilia." She gulped. "Dad! How much do the people of Mirabilia know? The Narine—they could be in danger!"

Her father didn't look at her. "There's nothing we can do, Kajiya. Sometimes you just have to accept that."

No. *No!* He couldn't be telling her there was no way to get a message to them. No way for them to prepare themselves, no way for them to defend themselves… She looked around to Ainee, Gaorun and Resurge, but they offered no solutions, only shared her look of dread. They couldn't get a message to anyone in time. They couldn't. They couldn't…

Kajiya blinked. But *Rotari could.* More than that… She was a *blakeslee.* She could defend Mirabilia! And Kajiya knew that there had been more advanced magics that the stone creature had not shown her or Ainee, but kept to herself. After all, they had trained a couple of weeks; she had had four-hundred *years.* She could get to Mirabilia, warn *and* defend them! All Kajiya needed to do, was figure out a way to ask. She knew her magic voice wouldn't carry that far, but…

"Rotari," she gasped at last. "We need to contact Rotari. She could protect Mirabilia!"

Ainee's fur puffed out a bit, but she seemed to follow Kajiya's logic. Gaorun practically jumped over the table.

"My magic is yours if you need it," he said, taking Kajiya's hand.

Kajiya nodded as Ainee took the other hand.

"What are you going on about?" Proten asked as the rest of the magiks watched.

"No time, Dad! We'll explain later," Kajiya said as her blood froze with magic.

She felt the magic flow between the three of them, and then felt someone grab her shoulders. She started to stiffen, but soon felt Sarka's magic flowing into her as well. They had never told her about Rotari, which made Kajiya all the more grateful for the assistance. The ice that welled up within her now was His magic too. She concentrated it all. She had to make this work. How would she make it a two way communication? She had to trust.

Rotari! Kajiya cried out with magic, imagining it becoming a beam straight from her to the blakeslee.

K-Kajiya? the weak response came, barely audible, but Kajiya's heart leapt for joy nonetheless.

Rotari! I'm sorry we left like we did, we didn't know—

It's fine child. I can understand the damage I did.

You're forgiven. Kajiya said as quickly and genuinely as she could. *But please, I haven't contacted you just to talk. You've been watching?*

Rotari's voice grew warm. *Always.*

Then you know what I need you to do.

I'm afraid I haven't yet mastered the fine art of mind reading, Kajiya, the blakeslee replied dryly.

Kajiya nearly growled. *Mirabilia. I want—no, I* need *you to protect Mirabilia. They're in grave danger. None of them know about the spiedes. You can protect them.*

Why should I? Rotari's voice lost its warmth.

Because-because—because Resurge and I aren't the only family you have there!

It was true. Kajiya had noticed in her family tree that Rotari had had three direct nieces, all of whom married and had children. The book had stopped after that generation for the other families, but Kajiya was sure that it was because they were no longer directly related to her family. They probably had their own family trees elsewhere in the library.

Rotari sighed. *You're right. I suppose I can't*

let my heritage be wiped out, now can I?

Kajiya broke into a gleeful smile. *Thank you. Thank you!*

Ah, now don't go thanking me yet, Rotari's voice had a touch of her mentoring tone to it, *I think it's finally time I tested how 'indestructible' I really am.*

The ice melted from Kajiya's veins, and her knees weakened. The group fell as a unit to the floor.

"Kajiya," Ainee growled. "One of the first things, you need to do, as a magik," she gasped out between breaths, "is invent a way, to do, *that,* without using magic."

Kajiya, who had ended up barely holding herself on the ground, nodded. "Agreed."

"What did she say?" Ainee asked quietly.

Kajiya smiled. "She said yes. She said yes!"

"Will someone *please* tell me what on Mysterium just happened?" Proten snorted.

Ronin and Resurge moved to help the feas off the floor, and Jiblin brought over some chairs for them.

"Mirabilia's safe, Dad. I mean, not perfectly. But, Rotari will protect them," Kajiya said as Jiblin helped her into the chair.

"And who is Rotari?"

Resurge turned to his father after making sure Ainee was comfortable. "She's a blakeslee who's been alive for four-hundred years. She's also our great aunt."

"Fourteen 'greats' to be specific," Kajiya added.

Ainee turned to her in shock. "Since when?"

"Since last night when me and Resurge went to

the library. I found a family tree dating back to the Great War," Kajiya said quietly.

Proten put his face in his hand. "And you expect me to believe this?"

Kajiya smiled. "Well, it's the truth, whether you believe it or not."

The other magiks looked at her, and Sharack turned to Sarka.

"What is a 'blakeslee'?"

Sarka shrugged. "No idea."

"Alright, now that *that* is over, shall we turn back to the task at hand?" Dorat didn't even try to conceal the disdain in his voice.

"Then we're agreed on the 'send-a-group-down-to-ambush-the-king-while-we-fend-them-off-up-here' plan?" Beifin asked, turning his head to the other magiks.

Proten sighed, then stroked his chin. "It does seem a little simple. Lots of room for error."

Jiblin nodded in agreement. "If only we had more time…"

Gaorun got up from his chair, his strength apparently returning quickly. "How about this then?" He swept the maps flat on the table. "Kajiya and Ainee can use their magic to check on the battle anywhere. Resurge and I can stay here with them and plan counterattacks, as well as let you guys know if anything goes wrong."

"I'm staying too," Ronin interjected. "This is my tribe, and I will not see them overrun."

Gaorun nodded assent. "Sure. We'll need someone who knows the layout of the land. Kajiya can then use her thought-speech to communicate to you guys, and you can communicate to your troops."

Kajiya began to tune out as the boys started to plan strategies. Which warriors should go with the spiedes? From which tribe? Did they really want to send all twenty-four spiede rebels back into the caves? Where would be the best places for a sneak attack? Should they trust magic, or use the tribes' messengers to communicate?

Kajiya sighed, and leaned back in the chair, holding her pounding head. All the talk and magic had given her a splitting headache. Still, there was one thing she needed to do. She cast a quick glance to Ainee and Sarka and saw with relief that their ears were pointed towards the discussion at the table as it turned to healers.

"Please," she whispered so that she could barely even hear herself. "Protect my people. Protect my friends. And help us, in any way you see fit."

"Kajiya?" Ainee turned to her. "Did you say something?"

Kajiya shook her head. "Nothing anyone needs to know."

The purple fea nodded, then turned back.

Kajiya breathed in. Midyan's light was starting to filter through the trees outside. She stood.

"Enough talk," she said calmly, but with a fierce determination shining in her eyes. "It's time to put our plans into action."

Chapter 12: Revolution

Kajiya's heart pounded in her ears as she stood at the entrance of the cave. She had been able to change back into her normal half-tunic, and she stood ready, breathing deeply. Behind her, Dorat had managed to call together the majority of his warriors, and had stationed many more at the bridges between the islands. Thanks to many swift-footed messengers, all of Royalin was on the alert.

All the magiks stood beside her. Except for Dorat, none of them could help their tribe in any way. So each of them had sworn to do what they could in Royalin, in the hopes of directing more spiedes their way, and thus away from their own tribes. Had Kajiya and the others had more time to rest, they would have sent word to both Animo and Palinda with magic, but now, she could only watch. She was to stand and help the fighting until a significant amount of time had passed, then retreat with Gaorun, Resurge and Ronin and keep an eye on the forty 'slaves' that went with the spiede rebels.

Still, as she stared into the open mouth of the cave, it seemed to be opening wider. Almost as if it were trying to swallow her whole. There seemed to be giant circular eyes coming from each dark spot.

"Now remember," Beifin was finishing briefing the Animo warriors who had been chosen to go into the heart of Mysterium, "because you are going under the guise of slaves, you are not to carry any difficult-to-conceal weapon, and you must *trust* the spiedes taking you. You will have no light to see by. Cooperate, and you shall taste revenge for your fallen brothers soon enough!"

Kajiya grimaced; Beifin must have told them about what happened in Animo. A cheer went up from them, and then they were silent.

Everyone was standing, waiting. A few leaned on trees, or got some last-second healing done. Others sharpened their blades. Sarka and Sharack's spiedes waited over the hill, out of sight until they could join the battle and take their 'captives.'

The Animo warriors dashed off to go join those already with the spiedes from Palinda, Royalin and Mirabilia. Ronin had brought up the great fact that feas could not tell spiedes apart, and it had been decided that those going down would wait with the spiedes to avoid any mix-ups.

The forest grew quiet, and Kajiya gulped. Now, it was just a matter of time.

But she didn't have to wait long before the quiet skittering of four tiny feet echoed through the cave. Magnified. Until, at last, an army stepped into the light.

Fires lit up at once, and Kajiya took an involuntary step back; there had to be hundreds of them, if not a thousand! There were far more than she had even seen in one place.

Magic filled her being, and Kajiya summoned her own fire to the world. She would do her best, for her people, and for the spiedes who understood compassion.

There was no battle cry as the spiedes charged forward. There was no time for one. Just the dull roar of movement finally reaching its peak. Kajiya ran forward and the other feas followed her lead.

The first hit was far more painful than last

time, as the spiede aptly dodged her fireball, and pushed her back with a leg, a look of amusement on its face. Kajiya, however, summoned the ice once more and controlled the winds around her until her feet were on the ground. She longed to go and confront it again, but the battle was already full-blown. Every spiede had at least one fea attacking it, and every fea was battling at least one spiede. Kajiya lit a fire in her hand again, and kept an eye out for any spiedes trying to make it past the frontlines. A few of the smaller spiedes looked like they might be getting through, but a swift fireball in the face often gave the feas pursuing them the moment they needed to catch up.

After what seemed all too short a time, Kajiya saw the rebels and a group of feas climb into the cave. Gaorun and Resurge managed to retreat from the battle and run to her, with Ronin no more than a minute behind.

"This way," Ronin said without pausing as he passed them.

Kajiya nodded, and the quartet set out. Kajiya's fur rose for a moment, and she looked at Gaorun.

"Onta?"

"With Ainee. This is no place for her," he said as Ronin skidded over a tree root and vanished.

Kajiya looked over the root before she jumped. It concealed a small crevice in the ground that would make the perfect spiede-proof shelter. Already, six messengers waited with Ronin, ready to run out to the magiks and healers. Ainee sat on the ground, holding Onta in her lap.

Kajiya jumped over and landed hard on her feet, but hastily moved out of the way so that Resurge and Gaorun could follow.

Kajiya sat on the ground with Ainee as the purple fea passed Onta to Gaorun.

"Are you ready?" Kajiya asked once she was settled.

Ainee nodded, and they interlocked hands. "I think we should check on the other tribes first. They haven't been gone long enough to get into much trouble."

Kajiya tightened her grip, summoning the ice yet again. It flowed like a river between the two of them, and Kajiya could feel it chill her eyes.

Palinda first. She opened her eyes. Midyan was high over the Palinda camp, it and the four moons were partially obscured by dark rainclouds. Another giant bonfire had been set up, and it was clear to Kajiya that they hadn't changed camp since last she had seen them. What they had done, however, was make some improvements. The spiedes were having trouble getting over the stacks of aimaia surrounding the camp, and she could see the tame kivoltas nipping away at their legs.

She could also see that the feas were having trouble attacking. They couldn't seem to find the spiede's weak spots. A green fea had just been knocked over. Emera! Suddenly, a very small spiede rammed the larger ones legs out from under it. It spoke quickly to Emera, and she looked bewildered, then nodded as she got up. Together, she and the small spiede beat off the other one, and all over the camp, some spiedes were turning on their brethren. The rebels! They must have infiltrated the attack forces to help.

Coballen joined his sister as the clouds began to break, and rain started to fall. Some of his yellow fur had been stained green. Kajiya grimaced; his arm was limp and a deep gash ran from his shoulder to elbow. Blood flowed down his forearm, turning parts of his fur red and orange.

Kajiya shuddered, and shifted her sight over to Animo. There, the spiedes were having troubles scaling the exceedingly straight walls that surrounded the city. Sai and his warriors were pouring some sort of steaming liquid over the walls. Suddenly, a diminutive spiede appeared beside Sarin and his cauldron, and cowered. Sarin grabbed his spear, then stopped abruptly, a look of recognition in his eyes, and he held out his spear to stop Rosa from attacking the spiede. He pointed to the spiede, then put his wrists together and brought them apart before finally pointing to himself.

Kajiya nearly gasped as Sarin seemed to realize that the spiede couldn't see him. She recognized those gestures! And if she interrupted it correctly, this spiede was one of the spiede children who help him escape the first time. From the way it then spoke to Sarin and Sai nodded in approval, Kajiya realized that not only was Sarin using magic to speak to it, but it had become a rebel. It called out to the other rebels in the crowd, and Sai yelled at his warriors.

Kajiya let her sight shift to Mirabilia; as long as they kept fighting, Animo would be fine.

In Mirabilia, the scene was the most chaotic. Warriors struggled against the spiedes on the ground, but other spiedes were attempting to climb the trees, towards where the rest of Mirabilia was yelling and screaming.

A giant stone hand that appeared to be made of many different stones squashed the closest spiede, then plucked it off of the tree, leaving a giant green stain. The people looked in awe as Rotari materialized herself, stone by stone into the clearing. No doubt she had started as soon as Kajiya asked, but she was still missing an arm and part of a leg. Her limbs were appearing slowly, and some feas fell onto their backsides as they watched her. No doubt she was telling them what was going on. The rebels were beginning to turn on the other spiedes here as well, and Kajiya saw a large one amply squish a small one before giving a blind wink to the warrior who it had saved. The warrior almost fainted. Kajiya almost laughed.

All turned black as she let the magic melt and gave a squeeze to Ainee, who squeezed back.

"Let Jiblin know that Palinda is doing well, and the spiede rebels there are helping. Same with Animo and Mirabilia. We're holding our own for now, but I don't know how much longer we can last, even with the rebels' help," Kajiya said.

A pale sand-coloured Palindian fea, the only female messenger, nodded and rushed out of the crevice without hesitation, taking advantage of another exit that let out into the forest. Three more followed her example as each received news of the tribe they were to report to.

Resurge cracked his knuckles. "And our troops?"

Kajiya nodded, then closed her eyes again. Her hands were freezing, as no doubt Ainee's were, but they couldn't stop now.

The world went completely dark, and Kajiya played with the ice in her eyes, until at last, she had altered her vision so that she could see the warriors and the spiede rebels. They looked to still be on the tunnel down, but their surroundings were fuzzy so she couldn't be certain. The feas were edgy to say the least, and it was clear that the rebels weren't particularly comfortable either. Kajiya added some magic to her ears, and felt Ainee do the same as another group of spiedes approached them.

"Sharack!" one said as it passed. *"Getting the spoils already? You selfish fea-brain. Way to go. We've got back-up troops on the way to every one of their colonies, and there's more waiting. Of course, just because we're good doesn't mean that I don't expect to see you back up here on the surface!"*

Sharack chuckled. *"I doubt that. I hear that if you open your eyes up there, you'll go blind."*

The other spiede seemed to lose his good humour. *"We'll see about that. Just wait."*

And with that, the troop passed right by the rebels. Kajiya let the ice fade again, and let go of Ainee's hands.

"They're fine. No one suspects a thing. But the spiedes have reinforcements on the way."

Resurge nodded as the sand-coloured messenger returned. "How's it looking out there?" he asked.

"It's pretty bad, and getting worse," she said breathlessly. "They're ganging up on the right flank from what I can see."

Gaorun nodded thoughtfully. "Sounds like a classic baiting technique. Get more feas to the left flank."

Ronin looked at him confusedly as the messenger dashed off. "Why would you say that?"

Gaorun smiled. "Let's say for a moment that

you want the eggs from a chirpl nest? How are you going to get them? Distract it so that its attention is on something else, preferably something far away from the nest, or at least in the opposite direction."

Resurge nodded. "That's clearly what the spiedes are trying to do, they want to ambush the left flank."

Ronin nodded. "Your logic is sound but…"

Gaorun returned Ronin's anxious look. "All we can do is predict, and hope we're right."

Kajiya's tail-tip twitched; was that really all they could do? She bit her lip and grabbed Ainee's hand.

"I want to check on the other tribes again," she said; she couldn't stand the idea of sitting around and doing nothing.

Ainee nodded, and they set to work again.

This time, Kajiya started with Mirabilia, where the large spiede rebel and his comparatively tiny comrades were working well with Rotari to keep the spiedes out of the treetops. Apparently, the few minutes they had been alone were enough for Rotari to start organizing the warriors that remained, and Kajiya's heart soared. They were winning!

Full of hope, she went to Animo, but they were still at a stand-off. Some particularly crafty spiedes had scaled the wall by pretending to be rebels, then savagely turned on both feas *and* spiedes. Sarin had managed to fight one back down the wall, but it had grabbed his head-scarf as it slid down, threatening to take the brown fea with it. Kajiya's fur stood on end, as the brown fea braced against the wall's raised edge—but Sarin hadn't survived in the colosseum for no reason. He shoved the entire headscarf off of his head in one swift motion, and smiled as the spiede fell to the ground.

Kajiya nearly gasped aloud at the sight of his face. How many times had she wondered what sorts of scars he hid under there? And now, she was utterly revolted.

There was nothing but bare skin around his left ear, and it looked a sickly red-pink, as though it had been burned. Another scar ran down from that patch of baldness and clipped the top of his right eyebrow with the same pinkish-brown splotched skin. On his muzzle were at least three distinct scars. A large pink one ran down his nose to his mouth. Another ran from his cheek all the way down to the base of his neck, and the last one looked like some creature had taken a giant bite out of his face.

Kajiya regretted ever wondering what he looked like. She also regretted being so revolted by him; how many times would she have died without his help? How many times did she turn to his warm green eyes for comfort during the week between the attack on the spiedes and the memorial service? She forced herself to stare at him just a moment longer, until it wasn't revulsion in her heart, but pity, and compassion.

Finally, she could take it no more and let the magic lead her. Animo seemed to be doing just as well as it had before.

Her sight shifted to Palinda, and fear filled her. The fire from the bonfire had nearly been extinguished by the rain and some of the feas had been pushed into the newly formed mud by the spiedes. Others were forced to fight alone against two or more spiedes, and often lost their footing. The spiede reinforcements seem to have arrived devoid of helpful rebels, and with clouds blocking out the blue sun, hiding even the moons' light, they were gaining the upper hand. She looked over the camp, then had to look away. There had been two fea lying on the ground, eyes open and lifeless with blood running from their mouths as rain pelted their bodies. Tiu and Pato. Kajiya couldn't watch anymore.

She shifted her sight quickly down the tunnels. There, outside the entrance to the king's castle, was a giant brawl. Feas and spiede alike were fighting, and Kajiya's heart nearly stopped. They must have been discovered!

She snapped open her eyes as the magic faded, and her hands trembled. They had to do something. Things were getting worse by the minute!

"They been discovered underground, Palinda's getting rained out, and Mirabilia and Animo are just scraping by!" she burst.

All the messengers looked at each other worriedly, and the four who had gone out before all rushed for the exit at once.

Kajiya's fur rose as the boys began to talk with the messenger that just returned.

Didn't they care that people were *dying* out there?! Kajiya tightened her grip, of course they did. She knew that. But… She wasn't content to sit back and watch anymore. She had to protect her people.

Kajiya broke away from Ainee and grabbed her yellow shoulder bag, which the purple fea had brought down before the battle.

"I'm going in," she announced as she stood up.

Resurge turned to her at once. "No! Kajiya we can't risk you."

"You're not risking me. I'm already dead, remember?" she hissed. "I can't just sit by, Resurge! I have to do something."

Resurge reached out and was about to speak when Gaorun took his hand. Resurge looked at him, but the green fea shook his head as he returned Resurge's hand to the blue fea's side.

"Good luck, Kajiya. I'm proud to have called you my friend. We have to stay here." Gaorun's orange eyes were warm and moist.

Ainee stood, and took Kajiya's hand, squeezing it hard. "I'll keep an eye on the other tribes, and you."

"Thank you."

"And if you die," she added squeezing Kajiya's hand even tighter, "I'll personally come to the afterlife and kill you again!"

Kajiya winced as Ainee's claws dug into her fur, but then the purple fea's grip loosened.

"But seriously," she added with a hug. "Be careful, and if you can, take Sarka with you."

Kajiya returned the hug. "I will."

She looked to the others, then embraced Gaorun. There was a good chance that this would be her last time seeing him, ever. She felt her brother take her hand, and she embraced him as well. Onta jumped up onto Resurge's shoulder as they hugged, and licked her nose. Kajiya laughed, pulled the onti close and kissed her on the forehead before she could get away. The onti scrambled off of Resurge's shoulder, gave a small hiss and snorted, tail high.

Kajiya let out a single laugh, then breathed in, preparing to run out of the crevice.

"Wait!" Gaorun grabbed Kajiya's wrist as she

stepped forward.

Kajiya paused, feeling her shoulder twinge at the sudden stop, and her wrist protest at the fierceness of Gaorun's grip. She grimaced; she needed to go. People were getting hurt!

Gaorun reached into his pocket, fingering something. "I just realized. You won't make it."

Kajiya's world stood still as the green fea's words sunk in.

"Wha-what?! Why not?" she hissed in disbelief as Gaorun released her arm.

"Because even if you *ran* the whole way, it would take the whole day just to get there."

Kajiya's blood turned cold, and her shoulders slumped. "Then I can't…"

Ainee's hand found its way to the blue fea's shoulder to give it a reassuring squeeze.

"You can't do everything, Kajiya," she said, her voice quiet and soothing, with a hint of relief.

"But I-I—I can't just stay here!" Kajiya burst, tears threatening her eyes as she turned back to Ainee.

All of this… All she had learned, all she had done—what was the point if she couldn't help them?

"But," Gaorun's voice was quiet. "There might be a way."

Kajiya's eyes snapped back to him as he drew something out of his pocket and, taking her left hand, placed it in her palm while covering the object with his hands so that she could not see it. Kajiya's brow furrowed; the object had seemed pleasantly warm at first, but its warmth quickly faded until it felt like it was even more frozen than the ice Kajiya had created back on the training platform in Mirabilia so long ago. But unlike that ice, the coolness on her palm felt right… Like magic…

At last, after what seemed an eternity, but was probably only a second or two, Gaorun took his hands away.

"A rock?" Kajiya was more confused than ever.

Gaorun's face flushed. "Yes, and no."

Kajiya raised an eyebrow as she picked up the stone betwixt the foreclaw and thumbclaw of her right hand to examine it. The sun-baked dull grey-brown on one side coupled with the deep rich brown on the other revealed the stone's origin in Palinda territory, but other than that, it was a rock like any other.

"You remember that light-sphere Emera gave us?" Gaorun asked.

Kajiya nodded. "Yeah?"

"Well," Gaorun's orange eyes started intently into Kajiya's, "it got me to thinking. If some fea could create an orb of glass that can reconfigure *any* magic to do a purpose, and if one can just put a store of magic around it as you say one can, why can't it, or say, an 'ordinary' stone be used as a magic *storage* device?"

Kajiya blinked as his words fell into place. The stone's coldness. Could it be?

"How much did you put in this?" she asked breathlessly.

Kajiya heard Ainee gasp as Gaorun replied.

"Five days' worth. I've been putting in as much as I could while we walk—and let's just say that a complete magic drain at the end of the day makes it a lot easier to sleep." He smiled sheepishly.

"Gaorun!" Ainee hissed. "Do you know how dangerous that could—"

"Thank you." Kajiya clutched the bi-coloured stone close to her chest, and felt the powerful throb of the magic within it. "But I don't see—"

"Fly, Kajiya. Fly." Gaorun's voice was even softer.

Kajiya's eyes widened—yes, if she *flew* down the tunnels, she could move much, *much* faster. And if Gaorun's stone held *that* much magic, then she would be able to conserve her own strength for later.

She nodded, and her veins froze with His ice; perhaps there was a way. Perhaps this was the way. Had this been His plan all along?

Her throat was small, and the full gravity of the situation settled onto her shoulders. If she succeeded…

"I'll do my best. Thank you."

Kajiya cast one last glance at her friends, marking their faces in her memory and then ran out into the fray.

Magic filled her senses and reflexes, making her much more observant and fluid than normal. She was able to find her way through the fighting, and even the bell on her tail was silent. Of course, the small amount of magic she used to keep it still probably helped. Last time Kajiya had gone down into the caves, she had been a liar. She had gone as someone she wasn't. Now, she was going with no lies. No deceit; hers or anyone else's. She was crystal clear. And like the bell she wore, just as she could count on it to make a sound when she wanted it to, she was going to ensure her people could count on her when they *needed* to.

A flash of dull pink caught her eye as Sarka jumped from spiede leg to spiede leg, striking the soft flesh of their joints in ways that made them crumple to the ground.

"Sarka!" she called out.

The fea's pink ears swivelled towards her. A few jabs later, Sarka landed beside her, and swiped some green gunk off of her skirt.

"What's going on? I thought you were going to keep an eye on everything."

"Things changed," Kajiya said as she tightened her grip on the shoulder bag, still clutching Gaorun's stone in one hand. "I'll explain on the way. Come on."

The two feas were able to sneak into the cave without much notice, and Kajiya realized that the spiedes had focused so much on their own attack, that they had failed to even consider that they might be attacked back. Of course, the spiedes in the city would be enough to fight if need be, but they didn't encounter any resistance the first few steps into the cave.

Kajiya pulled out the light-orb from her bag, and created a field of exceedingly weak magic around it. They needed to be able to see the tunnel's walls to ensure they didn't crash. No further. Kajiya also kept a magic eye on it, knowing that if she were to so much as hear a spiede footstep she would need to extinguish it at once.

Then, heart pounding, she reached out with her magic to the stone, and nearly stopped in her tracks. It felt like the stone held all the magic in Mysterium, overflowing, and ready to be used. Its composition was strange, different from her own magic, less refined somehow, but when she reached out to it, it acted as if it were her own.

"Something wrong?" Sarka whispered, breaking Kajiya's concentration.

Kajiya shook her head, and took the

opportunity to explain what was going on with magic. Sarka nodded where it was appropriate, and took Kajiya's hand to give it a reassuring squeeze. Kajiya smiled weakly, and began the spell.

Slowly, both she and Sarka lifted off the ground, and Kajiya turned her attention ahead. She would use the stone's magic first, and then her own. She had no clue how long it would last.

At first, the stone's magic seemed endless, but after a few hours, as Kajiya could tell it was starting to dwindle and their silent flight slowed, a brand new magic entered the stone. Kajiya blinked in surprise; it was not His magic, so who could—Kajiya smiled thankfully at Sarka, who shrugged and smiled back. Sarka was feeding some of her own magic into the stone, but Kajiya could tell she would have to rely on her own sooner or later.

Fortunately, they found the bottom of the tunnel far faster than Kajiya had anticipated, and she slid the light orb back into her bag. Even if they were going to be flying above the city, they wouldn't want a spiede sentry to happen to see them. No, it would be up to Sarka now. Already, Kajiya's eyes were straining in the darkness, but she didn't dare summon her magic to lighten the area as Sarka took her hand. She needed all her magic to take down the spiede king, or at least help the feas fighting alongside the rebels for their lives. Hopefully the stone's store would be enough to get them there.

Sarka led her over the city, and they discovered with silent joy that the majority of the spiedes must have been conscripted; the streets were empty save for the occasional female spiede and child. And they didn't really care if someone else's slaves were flying above the streets. They were too worried about their mates.

Kajiya heard one of them crying about how her youngest son had volunteered to go to the surface. How she feared for his safety. Kajiya could only let the sound fade from her ears as she continued on. The sooner the spiede king was overthrown, and the rebels put in command, the safer it would be for *everyone*.

Kajiya felt a heaviness in her body—the stone was almost empty, and although she could see the palace, she knew she had to set down soon. She lowered both her and Sarka close to the ground, not quite touching though. She would fly for as long as the stone would allow—it was still far faster than running.

It didn't take long for them to find the palace, as they followed the sounds of warfare: the dull thunk and scraping of metal as it hit spiede armor; the screams of bravery and pain calling out in harmony; and the hissing of anger that filled the air.

As soon as they came into sight of the fighting warriors, the stone emptied of magic completely, and both Kajiya and Sarka were thrown forward. Kajiya felt her blood freeze with her own magic instinctively, but Sarka landed swiftly, and caught Kajiya before the blue fea could hit the ground. Kajiya gave a small sigh of relief, then a nod of thanks as she slid the stone into her shoulder-bag. Sarka nodded in response, and then the duo continued forward until they were safely hidden behind some rocks.

The fires lit by the attacking feas revealed that they had reached a standoff with the spiedes. Neither side was winning, or losing. They were just, fighting. For each blow given, two more were received. However, Kajiya saw a dark movement out of the corner of her eye. Sharack and two of his spiedes were scaling the wall of the palace completely unnoticed by the guards!

Kajiya nudged Sarka, and they started towards the palace again. While Kajiya longed to jump into the battle, it would be safer and probably more productive to help Sharack and his comrades take down the king. She and Sarka managed to get to the bridge of the palace completely unnoticed, and they ran as fast and as quietly as their feet could carry them. Once across, Sarka looked around, then turned to Kajiya with a look of dismay on her face.

"Now what?"

Kajiya signalled with a jerk of her head: "This way."

They stuck close to the golden walls, and Kajiya held her breath as they neared the door. Illuminated by candlelight, it looked different than when Kajiya had first seen it, but it was definitely the same door. The door to the king's throne room.

There was no way for them to know if Sharack and the other spiedes were in a position to help them. As it was, there were no maids scuttling about the hall; they couldn't waste the chance.

Kajiya pulled open the doors, and let a thick fire burst from her hands as she led the way into the throne room.

She had hoped to catch the spiede king unaware, and thus blind him, but as she looked to his giant red pillow, there was nothing there. She walked out into the middle of the room. If he wasn't here, then where was he?!

Suddenly, the door slammed shut behind Kajiya and Sarka, and both girls looked. The king had a blindfold across his eyes, and he seemed to smirk.

"Well, well. My pet has returned to me," he said, stepping forward.

Kajiya cringed and stepped back. "I was never your pet."

The spiede king sighed. *"Oh no? You certainly smell like her. Sound like her."*

Kajiya bristled.

Sarka bared her claws beside her and hissed, "Your days are numbered, king!"

The king raised his head. *"Oh my... Isn't that Sharack's slave I hear? I do hope he won't miss you. It'll be hard to explain to him why I had to kill you."*

"It won't be hard at all, my king."

At once, Kajiya looked up to see Sharack and the two others with him jump down from the ceiling.

Sharack did not even try to hide the anger in his voice as he spoke, *"Sarka was never my slave! She has been, and always will be a friend though, but then again, what do you know of friends?"*

The king hissed and drew back. *"What are you doing here? Shouldn't you be out fighting against our adversaries?!"*

"I am."

Kajiya stepped forward until she stood beside Sharack, and she forced herself to put one hand on his head, so that he would know she was there.

"You have no heart for your people," she said to the king, "and that's why I'm going to help them take you down. Sharack cares, not only about his own kind, but about us as well. I hear they're going to choose the next leader," she added to Sharack. "If it counts, you have my vote."

Sharack turned to her and nodded.

"What?! You cannot do this! I will not stand for it. Guard! Guards!" the king called, his voice becoming increasingly more frantic with each word.

"They won't come," Sarka said, crossing her arms and flicking her tail as she walked to stand beside Kajiya. "You sent them all to take over the surface."

Kajiya had never seen a spiede so pale, and the king crumpled into a ball as they walked forward. Kajiya whipped off his blindfold, and Sharack placed one thin pointed foot on the king's head, pushing it until it was on the ground.

"You have been overthrown." He turned to his companions. *"Take him away! And send word!"*

Kajiya breathed out as the former king was helped to his feet. Was it really over?

The former king didn't seem to think so. He head-butted the spiede closest to him, and both Kajiya and Sarka moved in at once, but the other spiede jumped on top of him before they could get there. However, the former king dropped to the ground and rolled, nearly squishing the smaller spiede, forcing Kajiya and Sarka to back off as they avoided his flailing legs.

The first spiede got back up and tackled the king, attempting to bite him with one of his deadly mandibles. The two spiedes reared on two legs as they went for each other's faces, but neither hit their mark. Before Kajiya could even react, the king gained the upper hand again, this time taking out one of the rebel's legs so that he fell onto its back, where he laid, stunned.

Sharack let out a battle cry and charged, running with such speed that Kajiya had to brace herself against the wind that followed him. She placed a hand to her head, then looked again, only to have her eyes widen in shock.

The king had hit Sharack without mercy, pinning his head to the ground, and the elderly spiede appeared not to be able to do a single thing about it.

"Sharack!" Sarka cried, surging forward.

The spiede king turned to the sound of the pink fea's footsteps, glaring through his eyelids with such malice that Sarka skidded to a stop with fear.

The king sneered, then with one swift motion, flipped Sharack onto his back, just as he had done to the other spiedes, and charged at Sarka.

Kajiya's eyes widened.

No. No! If he reached her… Kajiya's body reacted before she even knew what she was doing. It was stupid. It was reckless. It was right.

The blue fea's arms reverberated as she plowed into Sarka, magic filling every muscle. As Sarka fell, Kajiya felt the spiede king's mandibles close in on her chest.

So this was it. This is how she would die. She closed her eyes.

But the pain she anticipated never came. She cracked an eye open. Was she dead already? Certainly she could feel His magic surrounding her. She looked down, then let out a gasp of confusion.

The spiede king's mandibles were encased in ice, and as she looked into his face, he appeared to be in shock.

"Cold," he hissed, backing away slowly. *"So cold."*

Kajiya blinked. The magic… The magic that froze him may have been coming from her, but Kajiya knew it was not her doing. She stepped out from between the ice-coated pincers.

"Where I come from, my dad has a saying," she began, "'one mistake does not an unfit leader make.'" She felt Sarka stare at her. "*You* have made many mistakes. But your worst mistake? You never loved your subjects. You never cared if they got hurt, as long as they did your bidding. You are *not* fit to lead."

Kajiya took conscious rein of the ice both within and without her body, making it creep up the king's legs until only his mouth and eyes were ice-free. There was a sound from behind the former king as Sharack and the other spiedes flipped back over. Kajiya smiled; for once, she knew *exactly* what to do.

"Without love, you can never lead. Nor will we let you." She lit a bright white fire right in front of the former king's face, and he flinched, opening his eyes.

His screamed echoed, and he struggled to break free of his ice prison.

"Arg!" he hissed. *"My eyes! What have you done?! What have you done?!"*

Sharack seemed to smirk as he walked back over to Kajiya and turned to face the king. *"She made you what you always have been. Blind."*

Now, Kajiya realized, it was over. Really. Truly. Over.

Epilogue: Destined to Lead

A breath left Kajiya's lips as she sank into the bath water, back in her hut in Mirabilia. She had forgotten how good a warm bath could feel.

Still, memories of the last week plagued her mind. The Grand Rebellion, they were calling it. Kajiya thought of it more as the Grand Massacre. Hundreds had died on both sides of the fighting. While some of the spiedes were more than willing to help repair the damage they had caused, some feas weren't quite so willing to accept it. Dorat had refused to take any help from even the other tribes while they were there. However, all the magiks had agreed it would be best for them to get to their own tribes as soon as possible. Kajiya, for one, was excited to go home. And that she could honestly call it 'home' again.

The trip back had been quite awkward though, and Kajiya blew bubbles in the bathwater at the memory. Due to her little 'stunt' with Sarka, as her father had called it, Proten had refused to let either her or Resurge out of his sight for most of the trip. It got to the point where Kajiya and her brother would trade off spending time with their father so that the other could have some much needed 'alone' time.

Nevertheless, Kajiya was itching to find out how the other tribes were doing. They had stopped on the way home after splitting off from the Animo delegation to help Palinda get back on its feet. They were hit with the highest casualties, being the only tribe without trained warriors. While they were there, Coballen had begun to pressure Jiblin to take the warrior's role in the tribe more seriously, and while it was clear that Emera agreed with her brother, the magik's wife refused to speak on the subject publicly. She insisted that Kajiya keep the light-orb though, and even gave one to Sarka, who had been appointed by the Grand Assembly to be the representative of the *feas* to the spiedes. Kajiya had almost burst out laughing when she had found out, although Sarka didn't seem to think it was so funny.

After the slaves were freed, it touched Kajiya's heart to see Sarka reunited with her brother, Orn. Kajiya could see still the tears on Sarka's face as she greeted her brother, hugging his midnight purple fur until it looked like his face was going to turn blue. Sarka had brushed back the overgrown lavender bangs from Orn's face, and he had wiped the tears from hers, and they embraced again. Sharack had asked for the spiedes to bring any former fea slave with odd colouring to him—there were no signs of Sarka's parents yet, but Kajiya hoped it was merely a matter of time.

Kajiya sighed, and lifted herself out of the bath; so much had changed in such a short time, and she was having difficulty adjusting. She dusted off the half-tunic that lay folded beside her on one of the hut's shelves. It would be the first time since she had returned home that she would wear it; her father had insisted that she give full tunics a chance, in spite of her protests. Finally, she had both it and her favorite pants on. She even had a new white taic-fur loin-cloth with Mirabilia's tribal symbol on it. It was exactly like her old one, except not dirty or ripped or ragged. Still, it looked and felt familiar to her despite of its newness, and she was more than proud to wear it around her waist. She slipped on the avian skins she wore to protect the soles of her feet, and finally placed her bell back where it belonged, on her tail.

There was a knock on the door. "Are you done in there, Kajiya?"

Kajiya gave her head one last shake to dispel the water from her wet fur, and flicked her tail. The bell rang out clearly.

"I think so," she said with a smile.

The wooden door of the hut creaked open, and Ainee walked in with a towel. She was wearing a long sleeved dress that bared one shoulder. She shook her head and rolled her pink eyes.

"You look like a mess, Kajiya," she said as she began to towel off the blue fea's hair.

"Well, you certainly look ravishing. Going out with Resurge later?"

Ainee flicked Kajiya's leg with her tail. "For your information, yes I am. After the ceremony, of course."

Kajiya attempted to nod, but found her hair and ears held tight by Ainee's dark green towel. After a moment, the purple fea whipped the towel away, and put a hand to her chin, then shook her head.

"Oh, this won't do at all." She snapped her fingers, and Kajiya felt her fur puff out, then lie flat, completely dry and smooth.

"You've been talking to Rotari again, haven't you?" Kajiya said.

Ainee grinned. "Well, she *is* my patient. And isn't the point of therapy to talk?"

Kajiya rolled her eyes as she stood. "She's supposed to talk to *you* though. You know, work through her emotional issues."

"And she's progressing nicely. Of course, the

fact that your father put her in charge of the magic school is helping. Sometimes people need to look after others before they can attend to their own needs," Ainee said. "Now, are you *sure* you don't want to do anything with your hair? It's kind of a big day."

Kajiya held up her hands defensively. "I'll be fine. Now come on, we don't want to be late."

"And who's the one who decided to take an hour-long bath?" Ainee said pointedly as Kajiya went through the doorway.

Kajiya stuck out her tongue playfully as they exited of the hut and walked along the platform to the village centre. After a couple weeks of repairs and Rotari's help, it was almost back to being exactly the way Kajiya remembered it. Wooden planks suspended high above the jungle, vine railings lined the platform's edges, and paths led to huts of all shapes and sizes, often built around a single supporting tree.

"So, how *are* you doing with your patients?" Kajiya asked as they started through the marketplace, with all of its brilliant reds and greens, and a single dark smudge caught her eye.

The healer's tent had been expanded since the spiede attack. After all, if a friendly spiede got hurt in the village, they needed the space to take care of it.

"I'm doing well," Ainee said. "But I must say, I didn't expect being a full healer to be so difficult."

"Oh?" Kajiya asked.

Ainee had recently been given the opportunity by Proten to take the exam necessary to gain full healer status. The purple fea had passed with flying colours, and was one of the most sought-after healers in all of Mirabilia, being the *only* female to ever pass the test.

"My case load doubled overnight, and everyone keeps coming to me for every little thing!" she sighed. "You'd be surprised at the amount of work I had to do just to get today off. I can't wait until the other female healers are ready to start testing."

Kajiya nodded; before they had left Royalin, part of Turten's punishment for his crimes against feas and spiedes, was to witness the passing of a new law, one that countered his own. A law that would allow woman to learn all healing magic, but still warned them to check with more experienced healers before trying anything too difficult.

Other than that, Turten was to spend the rest of his life in a Royalin prison, being allowed out only to do public service work—picking up garbage off the streets, feeding the homeless, helping carry things for the 'high class' Royalin women, etc. Even then, he was not allowed to speak, and always under the careful watch of three highly trained guards—a warrior, a magician, and a spiede.

Sharack had proposed that each society, the feas and the spiedes, deal with their criminals separately, but work together if it was deemed fit. Thus, a fea warrior and magician joined the spiede guards underground guarding the dethroned king, just as a spiede joined the feas above to guard Turten.

While in the prison, Turten was allowed visitors, but Kajiya seriously doubted that he would get any. She couldn't imagine anyone wanting to visit the fea who had nearly enslaved them. Although, the Assembly did consent to allow him the privilege of taking out a book or two from the library each week, as long as he was on his best behaviour.

Kajiya's face fell at the thought of Turten. It

had taken her so long to bring him down, and it was over in minutes. Still, where he was, he would never be able to hurt another being again. That thought gave her at least a little joy. Who knew, maybe one day he might realize the error of his ways and apologize. Or even start to perform his public service acts in earnest, and thus attempt to atone for his wrongdoings.

"Gaorun! Over here!" Ainee called, waving with one oversized sleeve as she shattered Kajiya's musings.

The green fea held up his hand and ran over to them, but Onta reached them first, jumping up onto Kajiya's shoulder and nuzzling her face before Kajiya could do anything about it.

"Onta!" she cried, pushing the onti's purple snout away.

Gaorun laughed as he plucked the onti from Kajiya's shoulder, and Onta promptly ran up on his head and made a nest there. They all laughed for a moment.

"How are the anfa running?" Kajiya asked once the moment had passed.

Gaorun walked slowly with them, trying very hard not drop Onta off of his head. "Reasonably well for this time of year. I must admit, it's a bit of a dry fair after travelling so much. I can't say I wouldn't mind a bite or two of pavoki."

Kajiya tapped him lightly on the shoulder with her fist. "Well, you're the one who said that the trapping lifestyle was best for you. You know my dad will give you practically any position you want."

Gaorun shrugged, and finally reached up to grab Onta from his head. "Well, yes. But, it wouldn't be right. Besides, this way I'm always available whenever you feel like having an adventure." He grinned, then added hastily, "Just, maybe not for a while yet?"

Kajiya laughed, then shook her head. "Oh no! I won't be ready for another adventure for at *least* a month or two."

Gaorun breathed a sigh of relief. "Good. We could all use the rest."

"There they are!" Resurge's voice floated over to Kajiya's ears and she turned to look for him.

The platform was getting more crowded by the moment, but her heart leapt as she saw her brother standing beside Sarin. She held up her hand as they came over. Resurge held his head high, decked out in his brand-new warrior cape. Proten had finally appointed a general, and Resurge had joined the Mirabilia warriors under him. The distinction came with a new wardrobe—well, the top half anyway. The cape was a strange metallic silver colour that shimmered in the sunlight, with one shoulder pad over the left shoulder.

"You look great, Resurge," Ainee said as he came closer, flushing as he bowed to her.

He took her hand and kissed it. "Only a lowly stone in comparison to a gem such as you."

Ainee giggled, and Kajiya forced herself to look away. Sure, she had seen it coming forever, but it was still *really* weird to think that her best friend was dating her brother.

Thankfully, Sarin chose that moment to poke her with a book. She turned to him, confused for a moment before she realized that it was very book she had lent him. She broke out into a small smile as she took it.

"Well? Did you like it?" she asked eagerly.

Sarin nodded, his new grey head-wrap flowing smoothly with his movements. *At the least, I now understand where you get your ideas for naming taics. But we can talk later. You must be excited.*

Kajiya giggled sheepishly, clutching the book closer to herself. "How could I not be? I'm glad you could make it for the ceremony."

Sarin's eyes smiled back.

"There she is!" Sarka's eager voice cut through the din of the platform, and she acrobatically jumped through the crowd to Kajiya, taking her hands. "Come on—your dad's been waiting. We're almost ready to begin!" Her purple eyes shone with excitement.

Kajiya laughed. "I guess we all better get up there then."

Ainee raised an eyebrow and started to stalk off toward the stage that had been set up in front of the assembly hall. Resurge held his arm out to her courteously, and Ainee took it happily. Sarka pulled Kajiya forward, and Kajiya just managed to reach back to grab Sarin's wrist as well. Beifin, Proten and the other magiks were already on the platform with Sharack. As Kajiya had predicted, the gentle giant had won the vote, and was now the spiede's 'Elect.' Proten stood at a podium, and off to the side of the platform, a string ensemble played a light lively tune.

Proten smiled at his daughter and her friends as they walked onto the stage and began to take their seats. Sarin went over to the far end of the stage to sit beside his father, while Sarka went to the middle to sit beside Sharack. Kajiya took her seat, the one closest to the middle on the right side of the stage, with Resurge beside her, Ainee beside him, and then Gaorun and

Onta at the end.

Proten turned to her, and she nodded. She was ready. She hoped.

As her father turned to speak, she was suddenly filled with nervousness; the entire tribe would be here today. It was important that she made a good impression to undo the bad one that she had left with.

"Well, now that we're all here," Proten said, and the band stopped playing so that the feas would turn their attention to him. "What say we get started?"

A loud cheer erupted from the gathered feas, with the occasional shriek from one of the few spiedes present in the crowd.

"Today, is a big day for not only Mirabilia, but for all the tribes, feas and spiedes," Proten began, speaking with all the attention-demanding ease of a professional. "Today, I am pleased to announce that the other magiks and I have come to an agreement with Elect Sharack," he held up a piece of paper, "and the spiede-fea treaty shall ensure that under no circumstances, are either of our races to be enslaved, eaten, or discriminated against. We are looking forward to a long, peaceful coexistence," he finished, looking back at Sharack.

Sharack nodded in agreement. *"As are we."*

The entire crowd lit up with smiles and breaths of relief. Some of the feas began to speak with their spiede neighbours a little more easily. Kajiya smiled; this is just what they had hoped for. It would take a long time for living among the spiedes to feel right, or anything close to normal, but it was definitely going in the right direction. The fact that the spiedes' tunnels shaved days off of traveling to Animo and Royalin was a big plus, and the underground market was open to feas from all the tribes, and spiedes from all walks of life. They had been down for the grand opening just the other day. Kajiya suspected that there would be disputes as Sharack hadn't figured out how to work law enforcement in the new 'democracy' yet. Sarka had assured Kajiya that he would though, and the pink fea's enthusiasm comforted Kajiya, even if it didn't ease her worries.

"But," Proten continued, breaking into Kajiya's thoughts, "there is one other order of business to attend to before our celebration, and it brings me great joy to be the master of ceremonies for this. Kajiya, please stand."

Kajiya gulped; here it was. The one thing she had wanted ever since her banishment from Mirabilia, and she could barely even force her legs to work. Still, she could feel the warm gazes of her friends, and when she summoned a trickle of ice to her blood, it was His ice. She could do this.

She stepped forward until she stood facing her father. He smiled at her, and spoke loud enough for everyone to hear.

"Do you, Kajiya, swear to protect your people as their leader, and always act in accordance to what is best for them, and never out of selfish desire?"

"I do," she said, her voice strangely clear.

Her father smiled all the wider. "Then it is with great pride that I renounced your banishment, and reinstate you as the future magik of Mirabilia."

Kajiya breathed out. A great, horrible weight had been lifted from her shoulders to be replaced by a wonderful weight of responsibility. She didn't care how many people were watching as she hugged her father tightly, and she was sure her giant blue ears caught a few sniffles amidst the applause.

When she finally released him, Proten turned to the crowd and said, "Alright then, now that the formalities are out of the way, who's ready for a celebration?"

A loud whoop went up from the crowd, and the band started to play again. Resurge stood and held a hand out to Ainee, who took it gratefully. Then, they started to dance, although, as far as Kajiya could tell, to some tune that was going on deep inside their heads, and not the song that was actually playing. They were dancing far too slow for that.

Sarka, on the other hand, grabbed *Onta* and started dancing with her while Gaorun chased the two of them around. Even the spiedes were dancing. Or, at least trying to. Kajiya couldn't really tell.

Sarin started towards her, but Proten held out his hand first and Sarin quickly veered back to his own father.

"May I have this dance?" he said.

Kajiya laughed, blushing, but accepted her father's hand anyway.

"Have you had enough time to think about what we talked about?" he asked quietly once they were moving.

Kajiya nodded. "I have. And," she said as she twirled under his outstretched hand, "I think I will."

She broke away from her father to survey the dancing feas, spiedes, and Mirabilia. Her people, and her tribe.

"It'll be nice to spend some time under you." Kajiya smiled, looking away. "Even if it *is* learning about all the boring stuff you have to do," she teased, blushing.

Proten shot her a quiet glare, and she skirted around him to go talk with Sarin, who had started towards her again.

"But," Kajiya said, white teeth showing as she grinned at her father over her shoulder, "I'm sure I'll grow to like it. After all, I am destined to lead."

THE END.

Destined to Lead:

Book 1 : Damage

Book 2 : Healing

Book 3 : Redemption

Afterword

Wow. Just. Wow. Of all the things I didn't see coming, this, this is one of them. Hey guys and gals, Laura Thornton A.K.A. the author here. I'm writing this to you from the past. November 22, 2014 to be precise. That's because today I wrote an insane amount of words, 14528(not including this section) and finished this book. Finished, this *trilogy*. And I still can't believe it. It still doesn't seem right. Who knows, maybe I'll be better with it after a few rewrites. Don't worry though, by the time you read this, the only thing I'll have done to this section right here is a good ol' spellcheck. Well, I hope you've all been enjoying Kajiya's adventures as much as I have. She's helped me through a lot in my life, and it's been nice to come to her time and time again. Oh, and occasionally torture her when no one's looking and send her to the human world. It's fun to watch her reactions. But really, when you write something like this, it becomes a part of you. And all of these guys have. I must admit that I'm kinda sad that some characters I made didn't get into the story, like Dorat's wife-slash-Ronin's mother Lera. Err... Okay, maybe she was the only one who didn't get in. *But!* I loved Sarka so much because she gave me a chance to use a design I created all the way back when I was writing *Damage*, a design I loved, but had no use for.
But before I go on, there are a few more people who need thanking:
Magdalena Richardson, who introduced me to NaNoWriMo on day one of 2012, and without whom *Damage* would not have been written;
Aryn Singer, who inspired Kajiya's world;

Duncan Cellend and Braeden Riggins, without whom I would have never developed Kajiya's world so in-depth and thought through all of my plot holes; Danielle Tosey, who gave me Sarka on a silver plate, named and everything(I apologize for butchering her); Rachael Dredge, who allowed me to use her character, Triekestria, as a messenger in Chapter 12, thus helping me flesh out the world just a little more; and finally, my mother, who I have forced to read through each book about twenty times looking for typos. Like I said, I still can't believe that it's over. Oh well, I guess it's back to university homework and real life for me. But as for you all, who says you can't relive the adventure? All it takes is a quick flick of the wrist, and *bang!* You get to start all over. Thanks for reading,

Laura Thornton

P.S. In case you're wondering, 'the being' that Kajiya can't seem to stop thinking about? Well, let me put it this way: the God of the universe is God of my stories too.

P.P.S. And don't forget to check out the Facebook page for access to exclusive concept art and other fun facts about the world of Mysterium!

www.facebook.com/destinedtoleadbyLauraThornton

About the Author:

Laura Thornton is an avid teenage writer who enjoys role-playing in her spare time, or playing with her two cats, Anabell and Amber. She grew up in beautiful British Columbia, where she attended high school, and met many of her inspirations. She has completed her second year of university towards a degree in Creative Writing, one which she hopes to complete in the next year.

She wrote her first book when she was twelve; it had a total of fifty pages, and a lot of errors. Nevertheless, it hooked her onto writing, and she hasn't looked back since.

She also developed an immense love for role-playing, and even created her own role-playing site. She enjoys it as it is not only recreational, but good practice for her writing skills.

When she's not role-playing or writing, she's often drawing or watching anime to help her practice her Japanese skills. She can also be found studying the Bible and its teachings, for she places her faith in God, and wants to know Him better each day.

Made in the USA
Charleston, SC
31 May 2015